HOME TO THE HIGH FELLS

HOME TO THE
HIGH FELLS

Elizabeth Gill

This first world edition published in Great Britain 2006 by
SEVERN HOUSE PUBLISHERS LTD of
9–15 High Street, Sutton, Surrey SM1 1DF.
This first world edition published in the USA 2006 by
SEVERN HOUSE PUBLISHERS INC of
595 Madison Avenue, New York, N.Y. 10022.

British Library Cataloguing in Publication Data

Gill, Elizabeth, 1950-
  Home to the fells
  1.   Class consciousness - Great Britain - Fiction
  2.   Love stories
  I.   Title
  823.9'14 [F]

  ISBN-10: 0-7278-6328-2

Typeset by Palimpsest Book Production Ltd.,
Polmont, Stirlingshire, Scotland.
Printed and bound in Great Britain by
MPG Books Ltd., Bodmin, Cornwall.

To the memory of my Uncle George, one of the many wonderful men of my childhood, who inspired the story.

One

It always snows in February in Durham. The people there have a tendency to think that if they've got nicely through the New Year and had a mild January they're home and dry, about to hit spring without any problem, and then down it comes, usually about Valentine's Day. The old farmers call it lambing storms because it always seems to coincide with that most difficult time so that the lambs don't get dried off properly. Sometimes they have to be dug out of snow drifts.

The snowdrops are already providing enough white under the trees and the daffodils have been unwise enough to come several inches through the ground and then the north wind sends the snow horizontally across the high fells. And it's magic.

The stone-wall tops are like iced buns, the house roofs give Hansel and Gretel a run for their money, the bairns sledge down the Store Bank and snowmen appear in all the gardens. There are days off school if the snow becomes three or four inches deep and people try not to get to work so that they can sit over the fire and eat buttered toast and watch films on television in the afternoons, John Wayne saving the world from Red Indians or Germans. In the winter afternoons the darkness comes down fast and there is plenty of excuse to shut out the cold night and the draughts which try to creep in past the wooden windows.

It is a scarred land. Little pit villages grew there quickly in the mid-eighteen hundreds and although a great deal of money was made out of coal there are few signs of it here but it is beautiful too. On the very edge of the Durham coalfield, just before you plunge into the glories of the Durham dales, there is a little town which came into being in 1840

1

and there men mined coal from small pits just beyond the village.

Rosalind West's family had been there from the beginning. They were not prosperous like the big coal-owners over on the coast but they made a living from it. By 1958 the coal was mostly gone or too costly to get out of the ground and her father was too old to move and start again even if he had thought of such a thing, which he never did.

Leonard West would not even spend a night away from the place he loved so much, her mother had to go on holiday (when she went, which wasn't often) with her Auntie Eileen. Rosalind didn't feel like that, she had been here for the whole twenty-four years of her life and she was desperate to get away.

One morning early in the year Rosalind looked out of the big bay window of her parents' sitting room and gazed across the garden. The bungalow was set high up on the very edge of the village. It had been a field before her father bought it and built on it and it had big gardens around it and a view way across the fields from the front bedrooms and the sitting room.

To the right were more fields, to the bottom the football field, to the left the house where the local doctors lived and their surgery and more houses and the Mechanics' Institute and then the sprawling of the small pit town where people like her father had made their living. It was no longer the thriving town it had been at the beginning of the century.

The tennis courts at the bottom of Ironworks Road below the Store Bank were neglected and knee high with grass. Few miners were to be seen coming home from work at teatime any more.

Three council estates had been built for the men coming back after the end of the Second World War and there was new housing but mostly people moved away to work or travelled. The steelworks was still going and employed sixty men and the house where the owner lived was just beyond Rosalind's own, she could see from the window his children making a huge snowball on the lawn and the evergreen trees at the bottom of his garden were clothed in snow.

On Saturday nights there was little entertainment beyond dances in the Institute, the boys fighting outside, the girls

2

egging them on with screams and laughter, broken bottles and sometimes the police. It gave the older people something to grumble about, the way that the music had gone on and on much too loudly and how the young people of today would never have survived a war as their generation had. Nobody was grateful for the freedom which had been achieved. Nobody cared any more.

The crazy-paving patio where her mother sat and sewed in the summer while her father gardened was also covered in several inches of snow and from there the garden fell away sharply. At the bottom, where the beech trees made a perfect windbreak across the lawns, little drifts had played into spirals.

Beyond that she could see down the valley to the big sheds of the steelworks, the council estate beyond the football field, the outskirts of the village marked by a few trees and then the fields going on and on. On a good day, it was said, you could see to Yorkshire but she was irritated with it. She wanted to go much further than Yorkshire.

She was bored here. She felt it to be a small life. Her parents seemed to have settled for it and were content with their small circle of friends. Her mother ran a sewing circle, her father drove a few miles most evenings to a pub in the country and had a couple of pints and came home. She could see herself, if she stayed here, marrying somebody very like her father and living the same kind of existence and there was a world beyond it which she was quite desperate to be a part of.

As she sat on her mother's well-upholstered flowered sofa her father came through from the back of the house. He was a tall, lean man, given of late to wearing cardigans, which made him look longer and thinner than he was. She had always adored him. Recently he had aged a great deal and she knew that they had financial problems. The lines of worry were etched on his face.

The Prime Minister, Harold Macmillan, would soon tell people they had never had it so good but it wasn't true around here, there had been a lot better times for her family and for many others before the pits were worked up. Fifty years ago had been the heyday in Durham. Now pits were closing and people found that they must move away from the communities they had lived in all their lives, some from their families and go to new places in search of work. Many of them went south and that was exactly what she wanted to do.

Her father smiled patiently at her as she waved the letter. That single sheet of paper spelled her freedom.

'It's a letter from the motor company in London. I got the job.'

'I knew you would,' he said and she could see him holding the expression on his face so that she would not see the disappointment. He wanted her to be happy but he didn't want her to leave. He wanted them to stay there and for life to go on but as it had gone on when she was a little girl and had gone to the small private school three miles into the dale, when he had had plenty of work and they had been relatively prosperous and he had not been fifty and realized that he would never gain the success which she felt sure he had wanted so keenly when he had been younger.

'I'm so excited.'

'Your mother doesn't want you to go,' he said.

'And you?'

'Can't wait to get rid of you.'

She had to stop herself from getting up and flinging herself at him. When she had been a small child he would throw her up to the ceiling and catch her when she came down. He had been busy then. Now he kept himself busy, in the garden, at the house. He went to work less and less.

'She wants me to marry Edward Holmes,' Ros said.

'He is the bank manager's son,' her father pointed out. He never made fun of his wife but her social ambitions were trying for him. 'He is also about to become a dentist.'

'He's very nice,' Ros said.

'That's what you have said about every eligible young man for miles,' her mother said from the doorway.

Ros looked apologetically at her and waved the letter. 'It's a good job with the Doxbridge Motor Company.'

'London is no place for decent girls to be alone,' her mother said. 'Where would you live?'

'I could stay in a B and B until I find a room.'

The excitement of having a place of her own, however small, and a job in a big city carried her through her mother's disapproval and her father's disappointment.

'And it's good money,' she said.

4

'That sort of money won't keep you well in London,' her mother said as though she knew. 'And there are teddy boys.' She shuddered. 'People are attacked and the walls are all written on and there are riots. Why you can't find a nice man, get married, settle down and have a family like other girls do I can't imagine. You've had half a dozen offers.'

She hadn't. There had been three and she had felt not a spark of excitement over any of them but she knew that her parents' fear was that she would stay in London. She was their only child and effectively they would lose her. She wished in one way that she could be satisfied with what they wanted for her but she knew that she couldn't be, that if she stayed here she would grow to resent them and the rest of her life.

'London is dirty and noisy and nobody knows anybody's name. Southerners don't even speak to their neighbours,' her mother said. 'You'll wish you hadn't gone five minutes after you get there. You'll be all by yourself in some nasty little room and you'll be living off tea and bread buns. They'll work you to death for a pittance and you'll be treated like a skivvy.'

Her father saw her off at the station some weeks later. Her mother would not come and had stood tearfully by the door of the house as they drove away. Leaving was hard. At that point she would have given anything to go back and when she had to get on to the train she faltered. Her father got on with her and stowed her luggage and then he kissed her and got off the train, waving her out of sight but ten minutes later she was already glad she had left and by the time she reached King's Cross some three hours later she wanted never to go back home. London beckoned and all the excitement.

On the first day of her new job she felt sick with apprehension. All she knew was that she was to be secretary to their chief designer. The interview had taken place in a hotel. She had not been to the large and splendid offices of the Doxbridge Motor Company in south London. It was modern, all glass and bricks, and everything about it spelled money and success.

She was walked down the corridor to meet her new boss by the chairman's secretary, a young woman of about her own age called Bernice Fortune, to whom she had spoken over the telephone and who was putting her up in her bay-windowed terraced house just until Rosalind found somewhere to live. She said she didn't think Rosalind ought to stay in a bed and breakfast by herself and although Rosalind could hear echoes of her mother she liked Bernice and it was very pleasant not to be by herself when she didn't know anybody.

Bernice lived alone and Rosalind thought it must be wonderful to have a house which was yours and Bernice had a top job with the company and was inclined to sing its praises and Rosalind was very proud to know her and to see how other young women could succeed in the city.

Rosalind could not help admiring her fashionable look, formal for work, a two-piece suit with cream, brown and green squares, the top sleeveless because the building was so warm, falling to hip length, a V-necked top, wide-pleated skirt and cream shoes.

They walked into the office and she was announced to her new boss and then she was left alone with him and it was impossible not to stare. She knew him. She hadn't seen him in at least ten years. He must be twenty-five or six and the last time she had seen him he was just a scruffy boy standing on a street corner with his mates, smoking and jeering at the local girls. She could not believe she had come all this way to work for a man she had known when they both lived in a tiny mining village on the Durham moors.

He had changed. He was taller than she remembered, slender, and had about him a confidence that had not been present before. He was dark as some northern men were dark. Was it Scottish influence? He had black hair and black eyes, pale skin and was only just recognizable, so prosperous-looking. He wore expensive perfectly fitting dark clothes and had well-kept hands, something no village boy had ever had, long fingers, neat nails.

He also had this huge office with a smaller one for his secretary beyond. He had done what her mother would be pleased with but her mother would not have liked her anywhere near him, he had been the vulgar, common boy, well beneath her in the strict class system of a northern mining town.

His mother had been a tiny busy chapel woman. His father had owned a small bus company but had originally been a pitman and they had lived in a terraced house next to the garage. She remembered vaguely that he had been the exception, a grammar-school boy, cleverer than the rest. The

6

transformation was not quite complete. He greeted her with a still discernible northern accent, something she did not retain, due to elocution lessons.

'Why, it's Rosalind West,' he said with a smile and she knew that he was not surprised to see her, he had been expecting her. She wasn't quite happy with the idea. 'Hello. Do come in.'

She couldn't remember his name. On the door it had said nothing but 'J. Neville'. John? James?

'Jack,' he said to her polite pause.

'Yes, of course.'

'Let me show you around,' he said.

It was strange to see him perfectly at home here, and obviously very well respected, so important apparently that there was nothing but his name on the door. The huge windows in the office looked out across the wide London street and there was what looked to her like half an acre of floor, easy chairs for visitors, an enormous desk and all very modern, clean lines and as though he had deliberately not filled the space there, as though he needed the emptiness in which to work. The furniture looked expensive too and it was the first time she had thought of an office as somewhere which would impress people, a showplace rather than just a workplace.

Jack Neville's office was an indicator of how well the company was doing and it was obviously doing very well and he was organized, efficient, maybe even more than that and considering she would be working for him it was rather frightening. She had worked for various people before but in cosy, cluttered, modest places, the local solicitor's to begin with, then a carpet factory in Durham and finally local government where she had swiftly become bored.

He chatted about home which put her at ease but the shock of finding him there tainted her getaway somehow, as though he was about to report back, judge her by some village standard, or worse still think that because she was from his past life she would not do, but he conveyed none of this and she thought, no, he was shrewd, he would know exactly who she was and what her qualifications were so he had been armed from the beginning, had even perhaps chosen her on purpose.

She was very good at her job. She tried to look as confident as he appeared but it wasn't easy. He introduced her to

7

people and Rosalind smiled and tried to say all the right things. The adventure was beginning.

That night she went home with Bernice well pleased with her new job.

'And what did you think of our chief designer?' Bernice said with a sideways look.

'He's northern.'

'And that's a mark against him? He's going a long way and some lucky girl is going with him. He smells of potential money, don't you think?'

'I didn't come all the way to London to get involved with a boy who lived in the same village,' Rosalind said and then regretted it. It wasn't a good idea to talk about her boss that way, especially as 'a boy' since Jack was obviously young but with plenty of talent, but Bernice only laughed and said that she had a point and with looks like hers Bernice didn't doubt she could have anybody she wanted.

She regretted being nasty about him the next morning too when he said to her that if she wanted somebody to go and look at flats with he would be happy to go with her, which she thought was unnecessarily kind of him. Bernice was busy, she was getting married soon and there were lots of arrangements to make and although she had said she would go with Rosalind it was nice to think she would have somebody else to ask. She was looking forward to having some place of her own, however small. Her independence had become so important to her. She couldn't wait.

Two

Jack stood in the chairman's office with his hands in his pockets and there was satisfaction in that, when he thought about it. His mother had spent most of his childhood telling him to take his hands out of his pockets. Jack felt triumph.

In a way maybe he had known even then that his hands

did have something to hide and in another way he wished now that he could and it was a futile gesture because what his hands had done Sir Trevor held in manicured fingers. They didn't look like they should have been cared for, Trevor's hands and nails, they were working man's hands, short and stubby, and he was to the world Sir Trevor Bailey, known to those beneath him in his company, the Doxbridge Motor Company, as Bayonet because of the aggressive way he went about the production of cars, the way that he had done what the newspapers called 'taking the motor industry by storm'.

Bayonet had brought them all to where they were today, the most successful car-production company in the country, possibly in the world. If it had been that long time ago when knights and soldiers and the like laid down their lives for their liege lords, Jack thought, he would have done that for Sir Trevor because of the way that Trevor held the papers which were detailed sketches, intricate drawings, minute detail.

Yet when Jack had created them he had been unaware of the effort – he had been able to see what was required at the back of his mind, beyond his consciousness, beyond anything, and he was waiting now for Trevor's verdict on the work which had had his attention for many months, and he was beginning to realize by the way Trevor held them, as though they were sapphires, the holy grail, the end of the holy grail, whatever it was you got at the end of it, that he was pleased with the work Jack had done. Trevor wasn't smiling but Jack was used to that. He wasn't saying anything yet either so Jack wandered across to the window to distract himself.

Outside it was raining. When it rained in London it seemed to him that the pavements held the water. It was not like at home on the Durham moors where the fells and the fields absorbed the rain, needed it, here it was an inconvenience, all umbrellas and complaints and shiny streets. He liked the rain.

You could work better when it rained, the cars and lights all reflected in the shop windows, running colours and you could sit there with the heating on and know you were missing nothing by being inside and the work took on its own shape beneath your fingers.

This was the end of two years' work and the beginning of what? It was the strange emptiness after the long struggle towards the idea he had been tearing from his mind but he

9

could see by Sir Trevor's steady gaze that it was just the start, as Trevor rustled the papers back together and Jack turned around.

'Sir?'

As a child, as a student he had called many men 'sir' but he had never called anyone 'sir' like he did with Trevor. 'Sir' was part of Trevor's name, it attached itself to him as no other man Jack had ever met. Trevor Bailey was God to him.

'You go ahead and do it, Jack.'

'What about the money?'

'I'll sort that out.'

They were the sweetest words in Jack's world and he knew that Trevor made no idle boast. He had opened doors that other men feared, he had seen the stars that other men cowered beneath with their eyes closed. Two years ago Trevor had come to him with an ambition.

'I want a car that every man can aspire to, a car that will seat four people in comfort, take their luggage, that they won't be ashamed of outside their houses, I want it built so that they call all afford it, small, neat, reliable, a proper car. We need something which uses less petrol but which has more dignity than what is on offer to the public at present, something small, and soon, Jack, I want it soon.'

It had not for those minutes before Trevor spoke to him seemed possible to Jack. He had agreed to it of course, he had gone home and imagined it and gathered in his mind a design team and then he had woken up in the middle of the night and seen the impossibility of it and been afraid. He saw himself going to Trevor and admitting failure, or worse still submitting sketches and seeing the disappointment in the man's face.

Jack tortured himself with images of failure through those long months while he worked and sweated and tried not to be short-tempered with the others and himself and discarded a hundred ideas and then a hundred more and the days and weeks and months ticked past and he imagined Trevor calling him into the office and saying that he had changed his mind, that it was obviously an impossibility, that he had decided somebody else could do it and much better.

In his more optimistic moments Jack knew this wasn't true, both Trevor and he believed that nobody else had the ability to do it but in the night, in the rain, on late Sunday afternoons on foggy October days when the light had gone he knew that it couldn't be done or that somebody would suddenly come along and announce as good or a better idea and his work would be lost, pointless.

Now he felt nothing. He listened to the other man's soft words while his mind stayed numb and then he went back to his office, to his for once cleared desk. Nigel, his friend and fellow designer, put his head around the door.

'Well?' he said impatiently.

'The old man liked it.'

Nigel let go of his breath and came into the room.

'You could have said,' he objected.

'He actually liked it, Nige.'

'Of course he bloody liked it, it's a work of genius.'

'You thought he would?' Nigel looked across the room at him. They had been friends for three years, since Jack had joined the company. Nigel came from Gloucestershire and had the kind of accent which would have got his balls chopped off in Newcastle and Jack cared about him.

'Everybody but you thought he would.'

Jack allowed himself a smile. Relief was easing his mind. He felt a lightness.

'He's going to finance it. What if it fails?'

'Oh, for God's sake!' Nigel came further into the room. 'Has the old man ever financed anything which failed?'

'I expect so.'

'He hasn't!'

The lightness was turning into glee. Jack wanted to dance around the room, laugh, instead of which he stood by the desk with his teeth clenched and his mouth tight and considered what might have been, what might not have been, the extent at which he could have failed and he shuddered. His work was all he had, it was his whole life, his past, present and future and the present was good, he had survived and would survive only because of it. He wanted to go home and never to go home, to be able to stop working for a while and enjoy his triumph and yet to sit down at his desk and begin again with enthusiasm.

He wanted everything and nothing, and for a while when Nigel had gone back to his office Jack sat alone at his desk and listened to the rain stotting off the pavements and then he knew what he wanted, he wanted to be able to tell his father what he had done. He couldn't tell anybody yet, the car had to be built and tested and nobody must know but he wanted his father to know and to be proud of his achievements.

His dad had always been proud of him, glad for what he had achieved, grammar school, technical college in London, the jobs, firstly at Coventry and then in London and always better and always offered to him. He hadn't had to chase a job in his life, they came to him. Sir Trevor had interviewed him personally when he joined the firm, offered him a very good salary, his own design team and a car.

'I don't drive.'

Sir Trevor had stared. 'Can't?'

'No, don't.'

'Any particular reason?'

'I'm not very good at it.'

He had made Sir Trevor laugh but it was true. Once a car was designed, once the ideas were in place, he lost interest completely. Up to that point, while the developing was going on, while the car was being built and all the way through the tests to prove and improve, he thought of nothing but it day and night and afterwards it was unimportant to him, nor would he give it a moment's thought because that moment would be wasted on something which was already completed. He wanted to go on to the next idea and the next. There was a long way to go with this idea yet and he was glad of it.

Only the present and the future mattered in this game and it belonged to him, he knew it did. It was the only thing which stemmed the horrifying boredom that was a spent idea, a car known too well could bring from him nothing but disgust. He could do better, he could go on.

Nigel came back into the office at six. A lesser man would have suggested a huge celebration but Nigel knew him too well for that.

'A drink?' he offered.

Jack agreed, promising himself that he would come back to the office later, like a lover he could not bear to be away for too long and had even set up an office at home so that there would be no gap between work and home, so that nothing would interfere or intrude. If he did not go back to work he could go home to work. Jack put his head round the door of Rosalind's office.

'Want to come for a drink?' he offered.

He tried to make it sound casual. She had been there for almost a month. She mustn't know how long he had pondered over the possibility of having her there. How surprised he had been to receive the application, how pleased at her standard of qualifications, how glad to look up from work and see her head bent over the typewriter. He even liked to hear her say his name, 'Mr Neville', when she was talking about him but they used their first names in the office. Jack had never liked his name until she said it.

In a way he did regret having taken her on because she disturbed his concentration. He had known that she would and had ignored his instincts but he had argued with himself over it and lost because she was very well qualified and had excellent references and he hoped he was not the kind of man who would not take someone on because they were known to him. He liked her better than he would have wanted to but he liked having her there too in the office next to his, understanding what he was doing, helping, shielding him from other people because through the glass door he could often hear her voice cool like ice cream and she would let no one through when he was busy.

Her biggest talent was that she knew the difference between when he was working at the top of his head and when he was working and didn't want to be disturbed and it was a line so fine that he didn't know it himself most of the time but he had the feeling that she would not even have let Sir Trevor past her if she had chosen. She could be very quelling, her voice cold and sharp if necessary, Nigel was frightened of her, he had said so privately to Jack.

'She scares the shit out of me,' he said over a drink one night in a bar. 'I like nice girls like Anna who are content to see you a couple of nights a week and agree with your political opinions.'

That made Jack laugh. Rosalind didn't frighten him but that was because she was somehow completely on his side and when he understood that he ceased to be uncomfortable around her and was glad he had chosen her and she liked being there, he could tell she did, was proud of his status. He wasn't sure whether she liked him and although that shouldn't have mattered the truth was that it did.

They stood by the bar. It was nothing, Jack thought, like the pubs at home, which were usually small dark places where only men went to play darts and dominoes and drink pint after pint of brown ale, unless they were country pubs with big open rooms where the farmers, businessmen and solicitors took their wives. This was a long bar, very well lit, very fashionable. The girls wore brief tight skirts, had long flying hair and black stockings.

Jack wished he could stand nearer to Rosalind and somehow claim her because even in a place like this with a lot of beautiful girls she stood out. She had worn a suit for the office, quite formal, even though he hadn't asked her to, a mix of green and blue, trimmed with fawn velvet at the collar and pockets, a slim skirt and neat jacket with double buttons, ten of them, and very high heels.

The jacket was short to her waist and showed off the smallness of it and she wore matching handbag and gloves in brown and her hair was neat and straight and shiny, dark and she had exquisite blue eyes, cornflower blue with long luxurious lashes. She was so beautiful he had to make himself not stare at her. He wanted to keep her all to himself, stay at the office for the rest of their lives.

A tall fair-haired man was standing nearby.

'Hello, Nigel,' he said.

Nigel turned, rather consciously, Jack thought.

'Freddie!' he said.

It was Rosalind's reaction to the man that Jack noticed most of all and then he realized that what he felt was jealousy and it surprised him. He watched her now watching the tall fair man and it was a strange experience, to realize that he was in love with her while she was admiring someone else and didn't notice him. She was so beautiful and the other young man obviously thought so too because he stared at her. Jack instantly hated him. Why had this happened now? he thought. The timing was all wrong.

He was shaken too, he had not known his feelings for her were so strong. Had he deliberately asked her to come and work for him because his inclination for her was already in place?

'This is Freddie Harlington, Jack. Freddie is a rally driver,' Nigel said.

Jack knew that. Freddie Harlington was famous. He came from a prosperous landed family who had an estate in Northumberland and his driving was legendary in car circles. He had won the RAC rally the previous year and come third in the Monte Carlo rally and he drove for Doxbridge Motors. They had met before. Jack had just forgotten. He began to detect a conspiracy, a set-up.

'I understand that you're designing a new car,' Freddie said when Jack declined to comment.

Jack didn't even look at Nigel. He held Freddie Harlington's blue eyes with his own until the other man hesitated, faltered and said into the space, 'I need something I can drive around corners.'

'What do you do now?'

'Aim and hope for the best. You know how you guide a billiard ball towards the pocket? I'd like a car like that, something contained but powerful enough, something that moves through the air neatly, rounded, the right size so that you know where it's going before it goes.'

'Like an aeroplane,' Nigel suggested.

'Something like that, with the air around it doing its best to help and you knowing how you can use all these things so that it moves as a part of you or you as a part of it. Is that what I mean? And much, much more, so that you can control it like it's a jacket that you're wearing.' His blue eyes were warm and light and smiling, more open than Jack would ever have dared as though the world was not a hostile place, as though there were things to own which mattered and nights where the moon never set and the blackness never arrived.

Jack was irritated by him, suspected Nigel of setting this up, hated talking about work and would have given a great deal to have gone off with Rosalind and danced close to her.

'There is no such car,' he said.

'There could be, you could design such a car, I know you could.'

Jack shot Nigel a swift sideways look.

'I didn't say anything,' Nigel said.

15

'You've got a gob the size of Australia,' Jack accused him.

'We could have lunch at my club,' Freddie suggested.

'Your club?' Jack almost laughed.

'Tomorrow?'

Jack looked swiftly at Rosalind before he walked out. He wished he could have asked her to go with him but he had better instincts than most men and he knew that she had already become trapped within the spell of the aristocratic young man who had everything, Jack could feel it coming off him, public school, flawless accent, good looks, and he was no doubt charming and intelligent and he was glamorous – what a God-awful word. He was a driver, speed, excitement, so much to lose, so much to gain. The last thing Jack saw as he slammed out was the way that she looked up into Freddie Harlington's eyes.

The following day Nigel came into his office. Jack thought he had timed it deliberately for when Rosalind had left for lunch. She and Jack had barely spoken and he wished he did not want to ask her about the other man. Had they left together? Had he walked her home? More, perhaps. Jack didn't want to think about the more and then he told himself that he had been through this before, that he had fancied other women but he mostly talked himself out of it. The trouble was that either he would be bored and wish he hadn't bothered or he would want to get involved and that was not a good idea. Emotional involvement ruined his work. If he fell in love it could be disastrous to the little car. It sounded daft, he knew, but it was so.

It was either work or women but he had a difficult time convincing himself because Rosalind West was very special and he had tortured himself with the idea that Freddie Harlington was the kind of bastard who would charm a girl into bed very fast. Then what? He was inclined to ask Nigel for details of last night but he didn't.

'I didn't say anything, not anything that mattered, just that there was a possibility.'

Jack didn't answer him, he had been at work an hour before Nigel arrived which was four hours since and talk was the last thing he wanted.

'You could have lunch with him, it wouldn't kill you,' Nigel said into the silence.

'I'm busy.'

'He's the son of an earl.'

Jack glared at Nigel. 'I don't care if he's the son of God, nobody discusses those plans until Sir Trevor says so and that includes you.'

Nigel didn't hold Jack's gaze for more than a second or two before he left the office.

Jack sighed. Suddenly he was tired. He hadn't slept well, he had been up at half-past five and the sodding rain never stopped. He worked until half-past twelve and then heard the office door and not until he looked up did Freddie Harlington move further in.

'I didn't mean to disturb you,' he said.

Jack looked at him. He was wearing a suit, very expensive, silver grey. He looked wonderful in it, as though he had been born to wear suits.

'What do you want?' Jack said.

'Oh, nothing,' Freddie said, smiling. He was a big smiler, Jack decided.

'You assumed we were having lunch,' Jack said.

'I didn't assume anything.' Freddie looked straight at him. 'I thought we might. Don't you eat lunch?'

'Sometimes.'

'But not with members of the aristocracy, eh?' He sat down on the edge of the desk as though he owned it. Jack despised people who did that. 'What are you, a socialist?'

'Get off my desk,' Jack said.

Freddie Harlington's blue eyes cooled to freezing but he moved.

'I'm a designer and it isn't your pedigree that bothers me,' Jack said.

'What, then?'

'That Nigel should discuss this with you.'

'I can be very persuasive but as a matter of fact he didn't say anything but that I should speak to you. We don't have to talk about it. We have things in common. I love cars.'

'Did somebody say I loved them?' Jack said.

They went to Freddie's club and had all kinds of wonderful things to eat though Jack had thought he was not hungry. He had not eaten since the lunchtime before, he hadn't realized

and then it was a sandwich because he had so many inter-
ruptions. The weather was cold and the food was hot and tasty
and good and the wine seemed excellent, rather autumnal, of
blackberries.

They had trout with almonds, steak with cream sauce, richer
food than Jack was used to, and this place was like something from another age, a Georgian building in north London,
moments from a busy street but once you were inside it was
all big fireplaces, lavish curtains, leather chairs, great big
flower arrangements, white cloths, silver cutlery, crystal
glasses.

Freddie sat back in his chair and considered the dark red
liquid in his glass and Jack thought he had been right, this
bastard was a charmer. Even he was susceptible to it. He tried
to dislike the man sitting opposite to him but found it impossible. Freddie was that most rare of people, he was enter-
taining. For once Jack wasn't bored.

'I had a wine this summer that was so soft you could have
sat in it, so bright and so warm that you could see the rasp-
berries. You know what fruit's like when it's taken straight
from the bush on a dry day and you can smell it – like that.'

'Where was this?'

'Bordeaux. My mother lives there. She has a house, a small
farm, a cow to each field, vegetables fresh from the garden
each day, the river quiet in the evenings and the village silent
in the afternoons. Where are you from?'

'A little pit village in Durham.'

'Do you miss it?'

'Sometimes.'

'That's what home is for, to miss. Are your parents still
living there?'

It was the garage he missed. His earliest recollections were
of the engines, bonnets up on cars, his father in overalls, the
smell of oil and petrol, the revving up and the dying down,
the turning over, the car seats smelling of leather, the shape
and shine of the doors and the wings and the bodies of cars
and then the buses which his father had liked so much with
their big ugly lovely bodies, each one like a pet or a child.

They were counted out in the mornings like chickens and
counted back at night. They were lovingly washed, their insides
diligently cleaned, their engines attended to and oil and water

seen to every day and his father was so proud of his name on the back – John Neville.

The bus drivers were known as 'Nev's lads' and the garage was 'Nev's'. Jack was proud to see his father's name all over the roads in north-west Durham and up on the front of the garage. The need for cars and warm oily engines had begun when Jack could hardly see the engine until his father lifted him up. He had liked the camaraderie, the men who drifted in and out of the garage, the tea breaks with plain biscuits and tea from the big brown teapot and he liked being with his father in this man's world.

'Do you have brothers and sisters?' Freddie asked.

'No, do you?'

'Four sisters, all older. There was another boy but he died. If he hadn't things would have been different.'

'Why is that?'

'My father needed an heir so he bred from my mother until she produced one and when it died until she produced another and then he wanted another – an heir and a spare, you know. I think that was why she left him.'

'Are they divorced?'

'Long since. They've both married again. My sisters are married too and I shall be obliged to marry and produce an heir, in time.'

'Nobody's obliged to do anything any more, that's what my dad says we fought the war for.'

'When you have property it's different.'

'That's daft,' Jack said.

Freddie looked down into his wine and Jack regarded him beyond the two glasses he had drunk, which was two glasses more than normal at lunchtime. He was, what did they call it, the quintessential Englishman, tanned, blond, blue-eyed, tall, slender, thin-faced, rather hungry looking.

'I'm from the north, you know,' Freddie offered as though that would make things better.

'But you live in London?'

'My sister Claudia has a house in Piccadilly. I stay there usually.'

'It's got more than one bedroom, eh?'

Freddie's eyes warmed.

'Yes, it's . . . eighteenth century, and has gardens and a

courtyard and state rooms . . . it's our family house, as a matter of fact.'

'Well, that's handy,' Jack said. 'Somewhere to rest your head when you're in the capital. You have a big place in Northumberland?'

Freddie looked across the table at him and sighed. 'Ten thousand acres.'

'That's fairly big,' Jack said.

'There was a castle before the house, some of it dates from the eleventh century.'

'It belonged to your family?'

'Oh, yes.' Freddie's eyes glinted with amusement. 'We've been hunting foxes, seducing maids and doing down the local population for countless generations.'

'I'll bet,' Jack said but he couldn't resist a grin.

'We owned lead and coal mines until the Jacobite revolution. Backed the wrong horse and lost most of it and then married well and regained everything. Things aren't so good now.'

Freddie eyed his empty glass. Jack didn't like to point out to him that a house with ten thousand acres, a suit from Savile Row, a shirt no doubt from Jermyn Street and lunch at a private very distinguished club hardly constituted penury. Was that what had impressed Rosalind, all that wealth over so many years, all that background?

'So, you like her?' Jack couldn't help asking.

'Who?'

'Don't be soft,' Jack advised him.

Freddie laughed. Then he looked down into his glass again and said quietly, 'Yes, I like her. I'm going to ask her to dinner. I take it you don't mind?'

'It's nothing to do with me,' Jack said.

Freddie looked at him across the table. 'Do you go home for Christmas?' he said.

Jack could not help reflecting that this question gave Freddie away. No real northern lad would stay away for Christmas if he could help it or unless he could be guaranteed to wake up with Rosalind West on Christmas morning. It was not discussed. His mother assumed he would be there for Christmas and he was quite looking forward to it, a real break and no thought of work for a day or two.

'Yes, I go back to Durham.'

Freddie sat there for a few moments turning the wine glass around and around in his fingers and Jack thought of what it would be like in Northumberland. Did they have a formal meal with lots of silver, crystal wine glasses, special plates, an enormous tree in the entrance hall, posh people to stay and lots of parties, midnight service in Hexham Abbey and gentle walks through the gardens on Christmas Day, shooting parties and fox-hunting with everybody in those bloody daft coats, champagne and pheasant, somebody playing a grand piano in the music room and dancing until the early day?

Freddie shot him a straight look across the white tablecloth. 'May I come with you?' he said.

The moment she saw Freddie Harlington, Rosalind was lost forever. She didn't know who he was. All she knew was that he was everything she had ever wanted, everything she would ever want, and it was not something sophisticated as she had thought it would be, it was the full onslaught of total physical attraction. How incredibly shallow.

She had been aware of Jack Neville ever since she met him. Jack was obviously clever but to her he was the boy who would always be socially beneath her, the boy from home whose mother was undoubtedly very proud of him. Her mother would have been horrified if she had gone all the way to London only to become involved with a man she lived half a mile from at home.

Jack was difficult to work for, exacting, and he had the kind of ability which she had not seen in anyone before. He was a perfectionist. Not for Jack the letter with a typing error or a phone message where you hadn't quite heard the caller's name. Everything had to be right.

At first she found it irritating but within days of starting work at the motor company she realized how important Jack was, for all his youth. The design team were almost reverentially polite and at least as far as she was concerned Jack was calm and hard working and he expected the same of everyone else. He could also be very quelling but he didn't do it with her.

She didn't think he was in love with her, as so many silly young men had been. She thought with Jack it was almost a

21

family thing. He went with her to look at bedsits and called around at Bernice's so that Bernice was giving to teasing Ros about him. He didn't like any of the places where she went to try and rent a room but she stopped him from saying too much.

'It's what I can afford,' she said, when they finally found a small flat that she thought would do.

Jack looked around it in exasperation. 'It's horrible,' he said. 'Let me talk to—'

'No. I won't have you interfering. I told you.' She looked severely at him as he stood there looking very out of place in the dark little room with the sad gas fire and the view across the yard and other people's fire escapes.

It was three long flights of stairs up but carpeted and reasonably well-cared for. Also it was bigger than many she had seen, with a bedroom you could actually get a double bed in, a horrid little bathroom which was so dirty she longed to clean it, a kitchen narrow like a galley and a sitting room from which you could see various housetops.

'It's damp and—'

'It is not.'

'They should pay you more.'

'I'm perfectly adequately paid,' she said, feeling uncomfortable at the subject, 'and it isn't damp. That's your overworked imagination.'

Jack had smiled at that. That was what he liked about her, she thought with some pride, she kept his feet firmly on the floor, she kept his moods from overwhelming him. She no longer made mistakes and they had gained a respect for one another which she was extremely proud of.

Also she knew that if she had any problems she could take them to him and he would try to sort them out. They were friends, partly because they had known one another when they were children, and he had looked around a dozen horrid little flats with her and rejected them.

'It'll do, for now,' she said.

Freddie Harlington was something else altogether. The night she met him she had gone back to the little flat and not been able to sleep and the following evening when she got back there he was standing leaning against the wall of the old red-brick Victorian house where she lived, as though he had been there for a long time, and she was astonished, flattered and felt as though she would burst with joy. He was what she had come to London for, even though she had not known it at the time.

'What are you – what are you doing here?' she said.

'You know what I'm doing here, Ros,' he said, smiling as though they were old friends. 'I want to see you.'

'I didn't think you . . . I didn't think . . . '

'Yes, you did,' he said. 'I've been waiting for you.'

'Jack kept me late at work—'

'No, not like that.'

'Not like that?' She looked into his dark eyes and couldn't remember what she had been trying to say.

He put his slender hands at either side of her face, smiled into her eyes and kissed her and it was the best kiss ever, she felt sure of it. She was terribly inclined to prolong it, to put her arms around his neck and never leave him.

'Come dancing with me,' he said.

'I have to change. I—'

'I wouldn't change a thing about you. You're perfect,' he said but he went inside with her and sat on the lumpy sofa while she dashed into the bedroom and took off the suit and put on a dress, bright red cotton with white polka dots and a V-neck, and changed her shoes for a pair of red pointed-toe shoes with high stiletto heels which matched and redid her make-up.

It was the best night of her life, her first date with him. He was a good dancer too, perhaps dancing was like driving, very coordinated, and she loved rock and roll, she loved the dancing and the music and the other people who were there but it was so much better than any date she had had before and she had not known she could feel so much for one person. She didn't need alcohol, she felt as though she had had several glasses of wine.

They stayed out very late and walked home even though it rained and he kissed her just outside her door, like men had in all her best dreams. He was in all her best dreams. She couldn't believe it.

Three

Jack and Freddie went back to Durham by train. Freddie would have driven. Jack's nerves wouldn't stand much of that, he knew, having driven with Freddie several times by then. Freddie had no fear, he also had the kind of eyesight which made everybody else's normal sight seem almost blind and instincts and reactions like a jungle animal and the Great North Road was too straight for somebody of Freddie's dimensions to resist. They practised a Durham accent all the way back so that Freddie would not risk being beaten up on his first night in the village.

He could do a Bellingham accent and a Newcastle one but he had to flatten all the singsong from his voice to reach the vowels of the Durham fells.

'You're a foreigner, man. Forget your "a"s, make them disappear. How many pints can you down?'

'I'm on good ground here, like, Jack, I can sink ten.'

'Nice,' Jack said. 'I'll say you've been abroad a lot.'

When they got to Durham station the small city was lit like a bloody Christmas tree. Light spilled from the little houses and you could see as you came into the station the big shadows of the cathedral and the castle because the railway was high above the town so you always knew you were home, the buildings were so impressive.

Jack's dad had come to pick them up and was driving his pride and joy, an Austin Shiline, big and silver. Freddie admired it and Jack knew that Freddie couldn't have said anything which would please his father more. He just hoped his dad wouldn't offer Freddie a chance to drive it but he insisted that Freddie should sit in the front beside his father, the better to appreciate its qualities.

Jack could feel rather than see Freddie peering from the car windows as they made their way through the small pit villages, the pubs and the houses lit, and when they came out of Esh Winning which was the last village before you hit the fell there was nothing but bracken and gorse, crouching low and dense, and a full moon in a clear, empty sky.

Jack always wanted to cry when he got that far and when he was away in London it was one of the things he missed most. The car wound its way out of the valley and on to the top and there was nothing for miles and miles but the fell, no trees, no animals except sheep. In daylight there were the farms to be seen in the valley and some, where braver folk had lived on the tops, the buildings all grey stone, many of them little more than shells, without roofs, with the remains of fireplaces, some of them with what had been barns and byres on the end for shelter because when the wind screamed across here there was nothing to stop it, icy, cutting and merciless.

To take a living from such a place was a triumph indeed, to pull a living from the land where there was nothing was hard but it was all some men could face. There was evidence of their proud failures, of broken-down buildings and empty farmhouses, and some of them which Jack had known when he was a child where the yards and barns were deserted, the walls broken down and the fields empty but he thought in all the best ways it was still more of what really mattered than for people to make money where life was easy and soft.

Nothing was soft here, it was all in your face and bitter and there was nothing to stop the winds and the snow and the hail and the rain and the screaming elements across this wild and strange place. People had died here in snowstorms or had survived with their bodies and wits and nothing more and their houses were monuments to their endurance and their bravery and he was always proud to be a part of it, that his parents had chosen to take a hard living from a hard land in the belief that God expected it of them.

The car pulled into the little town which was home and it had never seemed smaller or poorer, past the little pit rows on the edge of the town, left at the Catholic church on the corner and then down the long sweeping bank with terraced houses on one side and council houses on the other which had been built after the war, for the soldiers coming home, and the cattle-market offices and the auctioneer's premises and behind it all the unmade back lanes where the women hung their washing when the Mondays were fine and the little bairns played in the yards and in the muck beyond. Many of them still had outside lavatories and coalhouses and the coal was delivered in great heaps.

When he came back like this Jack couldn't understand why he had left. With all its poverty and prejudices it was still the best place in the world. So was everybody's home, he thought.

At the bottom of the bank stood two pubs, the Cattle Mart on the left with the cattle market itself beyond where the farmers gathered every Thursday to buy and sell cattle and sheep and the Market on the right, a small, low-set pub with orange lights.

There was the parish church down a long narrow lane and the vicarage off to the left and over the railway crossings on the right was his dad's business, the bus company and their house. It had not occurred to Jack before that their house was nothing special either, he had always been so fond of it, it was just the last house before you got to the garage, one of two.

The other one was Betty and Bert's house, good friends such as neighbours were here in the north. His mam was always saying that she would never be able to move because she couldn't leave Betty and Bert, who had lived next door for as long as Jack could remember.

Jack was warm with shame and worse that he should feel so but he could see from the first that Freddie was happy here. His dad stopped the car out the front of the house and his mother put down the net curtain she had been gazing out of the bay window from and came outside. Jack wondered how difficult it would be, he had never brought anybody back before.

Freddie had the best social manners of anybody Jack had ever seen and he realized then that he had been stupid not to know it. He got out of the car and cuddled Jack's mother, not something visitors normally did on meeting her, but Jack could hear by her voice that she was pleased and Freddie's voice had landed somewhere between embarrassingly upper class and local so that the sounds were all soft and pleasing.

They went into what had never before been a tiny house and there his mother had made a meal for them. The smells met them as they stepped into the hall, pork sharp and salted crackling, apple sweet with sugar and butter, carrots in a syrup and gravy which would roll gently off a spoon. There was brown ale to drink.

His mother had put the visitor into their small third bedroom and Jack ventured in there, not knowing what to say at such modest lodgings, to find Freddie hanging out of the window.

'Look at the stars!' he said.

Jack went over to him.

'I swear there are more stars here than in London,' Freddie said.

'It's just that they don't have competition from the lights and there's no noise, nothing happening,' Jack said.

Freddie was almost falling out of the window. 'Everything important is happening,' he said in the enthusiastic way which Jack was beginning to like. 'Smell it, it smells wonderful,' and he shoved Jack at the open window.

'I can smell snow.'

'Really? Do you know, I think you're right. I hope it does, then we won't be able to go back to London.'

'Why don't you go to Northumberland for Christmas?'

Freddie didn't answer immediately, just gazed out at the night.

'My stepmother is there.'

'You don't like her?'

'She's a complete bitch and besides . . . '

'And besides?'

He drew back slightly from the window and his voice took on a hard edge which Jack had not heard before. 'They expect me to marry. I thought I told you. They keep dredging up suitable women.'

'What about Rosalind?' It hurt Jack to say the words. They had not talked about her, as though Freddie was shielding her from him but he was aware that they were seeing one another almost every night.

'I've just met her,' Freddie said but he sounded uncomfortable.

'But you must like her a lot, you see her all the time, don't you?'

'I just can't.'

'Why not?'

Freddie hung out the window for a few more moments

taking great breaths of air and then he said glibly, 'Because I have to marry money. We have none left and the estate is dropping apart.'

'But if you love her—?'

'Oh dear,' Freddie said, leaning back inside and closing the window, 'you are so naive. It's not just that.'

'What, then?'

'Her parents live in a bungalow.'

Jack was sure he was meant to laugh but it wasn't funny. Ros was in love with this man, he felt sure. She came into work singing, her eyes shone, she was distracted for the first time, she even sometimes made mistakes which he tried not to mention. And what right had Freddie Harlington to engage the affections of somebody so special when he had no serious intent?

'Is she coming back here for Christmas?'

'I really have no idea,' Freddie said.

'You didn't tell her you were coming here?' Jack guessed.

Freddie leaned against the window and looked across the room as though into the distance. 'Have you any idea what my home is like?'

'I've never seen it.'

'There's the village which has belonged to my family for so many generations that nobody knows how long we've lived there. The local people tell tales about it. All the people in the village are related to me and the village has my name. The drive is two miles long and winding and there is the house which isn't old, it's eighteenth century, and the castle which has been there since at least eleven hundred and before that my family lived in that place as far as I know. I belong there. I was born there and I'll be buried in the family vault. My name is there not just in stone but in the very air.

'You drive up the road and turn left and pull into the court-yard and there it is . . . and it's falling apart. I'll inherit it all since I'm the only boy and I've been brought up knowing that I would do that. I can't afford to marry a girl who lives in a bungalow.' Freddie stopped there for a few seconds and then said, quickly, 'For God's sake, I'm going to be the ninth Earl Harlington. Do you see?'

Jack did. At least he thought he did. He was even pleased to some extent, at least it meant he might have some kind of a chance with Rosalind. Freddie seemed already to have forgotten and was leaning out of the window again.

'I hope it snows,' he said.

'When it snows here you can be shut in for a fortnight. It's called a hap-up.'

'That would be good. Then we wouldn't be able to go back. Your parents are so hospitable, so kind.'

'I don't know what the bed's like.'

Freddie went across and tried it. 'Feathers,' he said. 'Bliss. Perhaps they could adopt me.'

'My mother's halfway there already. Pork dinners at this time of night. I don't know.'

There are special, magical times in your life that you remember. All right, so a lot of times are awful and Christmas in particular does a better line in awfulness than any other but when Christmas is good, like the first Christmas you can recall when there were so many toys under the tree that they looked like a small mountain, when you stood outside and leaped about in the snow beneath the porch light and the Salvation Army band played 'In the Bleak Mid-Winter' which was your favourite and made you want to cry, the Christmas when you got a big box of Meccano and the one where you got a train set with three working locomotives and miles of track which your father and Uncle George and you spent all day setting up and playing with and the one where it snowed so much that you couldn't get to school and missed all the exams.

This Christmas did itself out for magic. It snowed in the first place, decorative kind of stuff, just enough so that it outdid the Christmas cards but not enough for inconvenience, sufficient for the bairns to sledge down the Store Bank and hinder what traffic was bold enough to come up it, past the slag works and the houses and the railway crossings. Snowmen appeared like polite intruders on front lawns and on the tops of hills, graced with woolly scarves and hats and coal noses and buttons.

On Christmas Eve, Freddie and Jack went round the pubs. Freddie could not only sink several pints he could play darts brilliantly and nothing could have endeared him faster to the pitmen and the steelworkers who made up most of the clientele. They wanted to know what business he was in.

'Cars,' Freddie said.

'Like our Nev?'

'Aye, like Nev.'

'The Nevilles have always been car men.'

'Jack's not,' one jeered, 'never was. Doesn't like driving, would have nowt to do with them buses. Wasn't happy till he went down to London.'

Freddie grinned, privately but Jack could see.

'Howay out the road, man, Freddie,' he said, sending a dart past Freddie's nose.

'Howay yourself, man,' Freddie said in his best and increasingly good Durham accent and they laughed.

The beer went down well, pints of it. You couldn't have asked for a half here like you did in London, it would have been shameful and nobody under the age of sixty would have had whisky. Some of the men could put away fifteen. Jack could only manage eight and even Freddie stuck at ten and that was after a great big tea and at the pub there were pork pies and pickled eggs and crisps.

On Christmas Day Jack's mother produced a huge dinner. Betty and Bert from next door were invited with Auntie Sadie and Uncle George and various other relatives and there was a turkey smothered in good farm butter and stuffed with sage and onion, which would only just fit into the Rayburn and had to be lifted out from time to time to check whether it was ready by one of the men because it was so heavy that Jack's mother couldn't lift it, and there were the obligatory Yorkshire puddings and half a dozen vegetables, yellow turnips covered in white pepper, Brussels sprouts, small and sweet from Bert's garden, carrots, cauliflower in white sauce, mashed potato and roast potatoes which were from the allotment and had to be King Edward's, and cranberry sauce and bread sauce and afterwards there was Christmas pudding and rum sauce. They had brown ale to drink and Jack's mother had sherry.

Jack and Freddie took Ben, the Labrador, for a long walk across the fell in the darkening afternoon and threw snowballs at each other. Finally they stopped for a cigarette, leaned on a gate. Freddie surveyed the small white fields and stone walls which were used as dividing lines and they listened to the silence.

'People here don't know what you do, do they?' Freddie said.

'I just work in an office as far as they are concerned. It wouldn't be anything important to them. Anyroad, you didn't tell them what you do.'

'It isn't a job to people who do proper work, it's a pastime like darts and dominoes.'

'Neither is mine to a man who spends eight hours a day hewing coal or sweating over hot castings.'

'But you're not ashamed of it?'

'No, I love it more than anything.' Jack stared across the familiar fields to the nearest farm where grey smoke rose in the still afternoon sky. 'That was why I wanted to invent a special car.'

'A car that can be rallied?'

'I don't know, just something that will matter and last and be important.'

'A small ambition,' Freddie mocked.

Jack smiled. 'What's the point in ambition if it has to be small?'

'Now there speaks the London lad. You don't belong here.'

'I never did. I always realized I wouldn't stay. I wish in a way though that I had wanted to, it would have been so easy to be a garage man like my dad.'

'He wouldn't want you to.'

'Not as I am but if I'd been like him—'

'Do men want their sons to be like them?'

'Didn't yours?'

The minute Jack had said it he wished he hadn't because Freddie said, 'Yes, he did. And I'm not. He's a proper Northumbrian. He looks like one, he couldn't have been born anywhere else. Not like me. I look like I'd been born in bloody Gloucester on a cricket field' – that made Jack laugh – 'and he's a countryman. I hate all that hunting and shooting stuff—'

'I'll bet you're a good shot, though.'

'That makes it worse. He was all set to admire me when he found out how good I was. I don't like killing things deliberately, especially something you can't eat. It's asinine. Did your dad expect you to be like him?'

'If he did he was too clever to show it. I wonder if he wanted to get out of here like I did but he couldn't. He doesn't talk about it, he doesn't say that he might and I haven't thought he's envied me anything.'

'He has nothing to envy you and you have a lot to envy him.'

Jack laughed at the idea. 'You think so?' he said.

Freddie turned around and leaned his back on the gate as though the view no longer satisfied him.

'He has your mother for one thing, a good wife who's kind and warm and a hell of a cook and he has the work that he loves and he has a view from his house better than anything I've ever seen and he has good friends and good health and a reasonable income and a son who hasn't disgraced his name. What more can a man ask? What more can he gain that would benefit him? You and I don't have any of that.'

'We might.'

Freddie shook his head as he finished his cigarette and threw the butt into a snowdrift. 'We might not an' all,' he said.

Rosalind had stayed in London. Before Christmas, long before, she had dreamed that Freddie would say to her, 'What about coming back to Northumberland with me for Christmas?' but he didn't. Other people went home. Freddie only went when he couldn't help it, she knew. She had imagined dancing, glitter, parties. In the end he had told her that he was going home to Durham with Jack. She was astonished, hurt.

'Aren't you coming?' Freddie said. 'Your family lives there. We could spend some time together.'

And that was when she realized that she had not asked Freddie to her parents' house. She did not want them to see him and she certainly did not want to be there. Her parents went to dreadful parties where they talked about golf and gardening and there were various boring relatives. She couldn't imagine Freddie in such a place or, for that matter, with Jack's parents.

'Jack's people are . . . they're very ordinary people.' They lived in a ghastly little house on the main street. Jack's mother was a Methodist, his father drank. Her only comfort was that Freddie would hate every minute of being there.

She couldn't say to him I want to spend time with you here and because she couldn't have what she wanted, she thought, she reacted like a little girl and refused to go anywhere.

It rained in London almost the whole of Christmas. She felt guilty about not going home, she knew her parents were very keen to see her but the dullness of it would be so awful and her family and Jack's family had no friends in common so she was horrified at the idea of being invited to the awful little house in the main street and having to see Freddie there where he would no doubt not fit in and her parents would wonder what was going on and she would not be able to invite Jack to her house because her mother thought he was common and Freddie would think it strange and it was not something she chose to explain so she made excuses, that she thought she was getting the flu and it was too far and she did not have enough time off work to make the journey home.

She was invited to several parties and to spend the day with friends and if it had not been for Freddie's absence she would have enjoyed it. She had never thought she was particularly attractive but everywhere she went young men asked her out. She didn't go. They seemed dull beside him. She longed for him, ached for his touch.

He had been very careful with her up to now, more so than many men had been in an evening. They would try to put their hands all over you and she had not permitted anybody to touch her but in six months he had yet to offer more than a goodnight kiss and she lay in bed and imagined what it would be like when he did.

Freddie had been out of the country for a good deal of that time. He had been involved in the various things connected with work in the autumn and had not been able to avoid several days in the country with his father so she had not seen him often, yet when he was away he always got in touch and when he came back he came straight to her.

They were not often alone, she did not like to take him back to the squalid little cold flat and when he was in London he lived with his sister Claudia, so they could not go there either. Also she had discovered that she did not like his friends. The girls had swiftly discerned that she was not their social equal and hardly spoke to her. They wore twinsets and pearls and tweed skirts. They talked about people she didn't know and never included her in any of their schemes.

The men he knew ignored her and they talked about hunting and shooting and fishing and all the country pursuits she knew nothing of. He did not seem to notice that when they were with friends she very often didn't speak at all. He would keep an arm around her and he thought that was enough, she could see. She took to spending more and more on clothes so that she would not disgrace him but her style was different, more fashionable. These girls had their own traditional fashion and they were so sure of who they were.

Their parents had houses in London and very often chalets in Switzerland and they had travelled all over the world and many of them had parents who holidayed in Monte Carlo or had houses there. They had country houses, sometimes country estates in Yorkshire or Lincolnshire. It was another world to her and a long way from the neat bungalow with the beech hedge on the perimeter of a tiny pit village in Durham.

She missed him. He was away only a week but the time dragged and when he came back she was already at work. Freddie called in briefly and as he did so the sun came out across the wet London rooftops. There were other people in the office so he said only, 'Tonight after work?' and she nodded and he left.

The day went on and on, more and more slowly, but finally it dragged itself towards half-past five and when she left there he was, in against the building for shelter against the softly falling snow, like any ordinary young man waiting for his girl. She put her hand through his arm and they walked until they found a pub which they knew had a big fire and they sat beside it and drank beer and Rosalind was very happy again.

'How was the north?'

'Cold and wet.'

'And did you get the information you wanted from Jack?'

He looked at her.

'That is why you went.'

'The car is almost finished and I will get to test it soon.'

'What makes you think it's what you need?'

'Nigel says Jack has invented something completely new and if I can get it it will make my career.'

'And what does Jack say?'

'Jack's a canny northern lad, he doesn't say much but we are now friends and I think I will get to try the car before anybody else.'

They had one drink and then he suggested they should go back to his sister's house. 'She's away,' was all he said.

Rosalind should have refused, she thought, but since he had

not suggested it all these months and they couldn't sit in pubs together forever they went.

It was a big building in the heart of the city and the house, two storeys up, had a balcony which must have looked wonderful in summer. It had French windows which opened out to look across the rooftops and inside it was politely scruffy with polished wooden floors, huge rugs and a number of pieces of furniture which were old and undoubtedly valuable.

It was silent there. They sat on the sofa by the gas fire and drank coffee and then Freddie did what she knew he had intended all along, he took hold of her and kissed her properly for the first time and it was much better than she had imagined it would be, close in his arms.

She had thought before then during all that six months that he cared for her and this was the demonstration. He told her that he had missed her and that he loved her. Men had told her that before, mostly to see where it would get them, but Freddie didn't go any further until she encouraged him to. That was strange. She had not ever encouraged any man to touch her.

She knew that she shouldn't. It had been bred into her, that it was men who wanted to go on and women must try to stop them, but she didn't know how to because he was the very opposite of all her mother had told her. He had no devious ways, no complicated ideas. He was slightly clumsy as though he didn't know anything about women's clothing, and he hesitated.

Any woman could have stopped him at any time. The honesty of it astonished Rosalind. Men were the enemy, but he was warm like beer which had been left out of the shade, kind and funny and unsure. Besides that he was so physically beautiful, no scars, no blemishes, a slight tan still from when he had been to France and the weather had been good.

His body was pale gold, his hair was almost silver in the firelight and there was no mystery, nothing held back, no deviousness of any kind. He loved her and he wanted her. They didn't go to bed because the bedroom would be freezing with its high ceiling and full-length windows. They lay on the big rug in front of the fire and learned how to touch one another.

It was the relief from the aching of her body which mattered most to her, the sheer relief of his hands on her and the excitement of his bare skin. It was all a bit messy and the sensation of having him in her hurt rather and was uncomfortable but the sense of occasion carried her through, the idea that he belonged to her and she to him.

They did go to bed afterwards, huddled together like puppies in an enormous four-poster which was as broad as it was long. Rosalind lay awake, glorying in the idea of love, listening to the cars making their way through the slush outside.

'I never imagined it could be as good as this,' she said, smiling at him across the big white feather pillows.

'Didn't you? I knew it would be with you,' he said. 'I love you, Ros. I shall never love anyone again as I love you.'

She didn't go to work the next day, they didn't get out of bed except to go to the bathroom and to make scrambled eggs. They slept and talked and made love and lay close together.

Rosalind rang the first day and said that she was ill. She had the courage to telephone Jack personally and he accepted it. She suspected he didn't believe her, when he hesitated and then told her not to come back until she felt much better, everything was fine at work. They knew one another so well by now that she could almost see his dark mocking eyes. She was at once ashamed that she hadn't told him the truth but as her boss she knew he couldn't hear it and she couldn't say it and as her friend he chose not to interfere in her life. She was so grateful that she babbled her excuses.

She didn't go to work the day after either. Nobody came to the house, nobody broke the intimacy and she grew to love the way the shadows fell and the various sounds outside during the different hours of the day. It was another world, theirs and private, nothing to do with anybody else. She wanted to stay there with him forever.

Jack put down the telephone receiver in his office and stared at it, hearing the lie over and over. First he told himself he was disappointed that she needed to lie to him and then he told himself he was being stupid, what else could she say? People should be allowed days like these, a little time to themselves. That was his gift to her, it was all he could do. He had a feeling it would end badly and in that case she would need this time to look back on. He only wished they had the kind of friendship where she didn't need to lie to him and he could have told her what he thought but then he was unfairly influenced by his own feelings for her. He had never felt quite so left out, never felt quite so alone.

Ros blew a month's wages on a dress the first time that Freddie wanted to take her to a big party. It was a short evening dress in pink with V-shaped neckline, flared sleeves with scalloped edges, a bell-shaped skirt, a silver-grey sash at the waist. She bought silver shoes with pointed toes and stiletto heels. She ran around in her lunch hours for several days before coming up with this ensemble and when she finally bought them both she came back to work rather late, hoping to sneak in, but Jack had heard her and came in from his office saying hopefully, 'You didn't bring me a sandwich, did you? I'm starving.'

She turned guiltily, blushed crimson. Jack's gaze fell on the expensive box.

'Something nice?' he said.

'Freddie's taking me to a dinner. I can go out and—'

'No, no, hell, I'll go myself. Are you going to try it on? I'll be back in a minute.'

'I shouldn't. We've got a lot to do.'

'Oh, go on.' And that was when she realized how their relationship had changed in the short time she had been there. He didn't treat her like his secretary any more and that was why she liked being there. They left the door between the offices open most of the time and he was always calling her in for help or showing her a new idea and very often in the afternoons they would sit across the desk from one another and throw ideas around and she loved being part of it, nobody had ever done such a thing before.

There was a sandwich place just around the corner and he was back just in time to see her trying to observe her reflection in the tiny mirror which she kept in her handbag. Jack halted in the doorway. When he didn't say anything she turned around self-consciously.

'You – you don't like it?' she ventured.

'You look absolutely stunning.'

Ros, very pleased, laughed. She liked that straightforward northern way.

'And I brought you a sandwich, since you so obviously blew your wages on that little lot.'

'Thanks,' she said, giving a happy little twirl.

He went back into his office and she went to the cloak-room and got changed but when she came back he was sitting on her desk eating his sandwich and he said to her, 'I've already told Sir Trevor that you have to have a wage increase.'

'What? Just because—'

'It isn't just because. You stay here late, you have good ideas, I couldn't manage without you, so I told him.' Jack finished his sandwich and threw the wrapper into the waste bin. 'A big wage increase.'

He went back into his office. Ros was too surprised to say anything but pleased. Things are going so well, she thought.

She was nervous about the party but even more so when she got there. Freddie was greeted with enthusiasm on all sides and introduced her but her instincts had been right from previous occasions when he took her out, she was so very obviously what they called NQU – not quite one of us. He had told her before that she was paranoid but now she watched and listened carefully and she thought they would never accept her. Nobody spoke directly to her.

He kept an arm around her as though for protection and she tried to smile and not to look about her too much and to follow the conversation but it was all about people she didn't know and various events like horse racing and concerts and parties which she knew nothing of.

Nobody talked about work which was the main part of her life and nobody asked about anything which she found strange and they did not talk about Freddie's rally driving which was after all the most important part of his life. She was dismayed to find that she was bored.

Later, having escaped to the ladies' room, she overheard two girls talking about her. They called her 'Freddie's little tart' and wondered what he could have been thinking of to bring her here.

'And that accent. Ee by gum with overtones,' one of them said and they giggled.

She knew that he had been reluctant to introduce her to his friends but had gradually done it. Now she knew why. He seemed not to notice her discomfort or did not choose to acknowledge it but persevered, taking her with him for week-ends in the country to vast houses where she invariably got lost and he was obliged to creep down draughty corridors so that they could sleep together. It should have been fun but the older people would invariably ask her who she was, who her parents were and then immediately she told them would lose interest. Trying to engage them in conversation was met with a blank stare while the men looked her up and down but didn't address her directly.

She found herself buying more and more clothes to try and keep up so it was just as well Sir Trevor had seen fit to increase her salary. Even so she found that she did not have enough to live on. She could barely afford to eat. Jack, in unspoken understanding, had taken to going out every day for sand-wiches and not letting her pay for them. And often he would say to her casually, 'You going out tonight?' and when she was not they would work until seven and then he would take her out to eat.

'Not happy?' he enquired one evening when they were sitting in their favourite dark little restaurant and she suddenly had no appetite for the meal he had just bought her.

Jack knew a lot about food, she thought, and of late she was enjoying the dinners and the time she spent with him much more than anything Freddie took her to. They were rarely alone any more so that in a way she felt as though part of the intimacy had gone.

'I shouldn't let you buy me dinner.'

'You worked an extra hour and a half for it,' he pointed out.

It was a good dinner, they always were. He liked wine, rice dishes like risotto or paella, roast chicken with herbs and tomatoes, beef with olives. She knew also that if she didn't go with him he wouldn't eat, he would spend all evening in the office because he forgot the time when he was on his own. Often when she and Freddie were at another dreadful party she would think of Jack working and the rest of the building dark and silent.

She liked to talk about work and they would discuss their parents and the village they had both left and the people they knew and when she had news from home she always told him and he was always interested. In a way Jack stemmed the homesickness for her.

Four

Four months later the new car had taken shape, the big mechanical parts were ready and the pretend wooden body. Jack and Sir Trevor test-drove it and after that gave themselves a year to get it into production. The problems were, or seemed to Jack, to be phenomenal. He had told himself that they would be but when it came to trying to put them right the pressure was almost too much to bear. If this failed he would go down with it and never be heard of again and there was a good chance that it would.

The first car was built in one day, coming down the production line, the first of four, two men allocated to put it together and then the testing began and so did the problems. All through the summer and into the autumn everything went wrong. Jack got to the point where he thought he couldn't stand any more. He wanted to run away, he wanted to bolt himself into his office, he wanted to drink too much and since he couldn't do any of these things he went through the problems day after day. He didn't eat or sleep and all the time he tortured himself with visions of Sir Trevor saying to him, 'Well, it was a nice idea, Jack, but . . . '

The water poured in at floor level, despite extensive tests which Jack thought had solved the problem. There was metal fatigue, the very idea made him shudder, the noise was terrible and so was the vibration. The brakes locked going downhill, the clutch slipped, the steering was unreliable. Day after day it went on until finally, one Sunday several months later, Jack couldn't get out of bed. He tried to make himself but he couldn't. He lay there like a landed fish and stared up at the white ceiling.

Jack had had several choices about where to live, outside of London altogether, Islington which was full of slums, a new place like Stevenage or a Georgian town house here in Canonbury which had been dropping apart and infested with God knew what. He had taken to this house, he didn't know why, and when the bugs had gone and the house had been renovated he fell in love with it and stayed. His friends thought he was mad but when you worked in the city it was easier to live among the dirt and the dust and he liked the atmosphere.

Nigel and Anna had married and bought a similar house but it was in West Horsley, Surrey. He didn't want that.

There was a banging on the door. It was half-past two in the afternoon and he had promised himself a good deal of work that day. The banging didn't stop and so eventually Jack pulled on the clothes he had taken off the night before and went downstairs and shuffled to the door. When he opened it Freddie and Rosalind stood there.

He didn't want to see them. It was quite obvious to him that they were screwing the living daylights out of each other while all he did was work but he left the door open and wandered back inside. They hadn't ever been to his house before and he saw them taking it in. Rosalind followed him into the kitchen. Jack put the kettle under the tap to fill and then put it on to boil. She was gazing around. He let her. Then she looked at him.

'You look awful.'

'Are you my mother?'

'No, really, Jack—'

'You didn't come here to see how I was, Freddie wants the car.'

At that moment Freddie came into the kitchen. 'This is strange. Your house is empty. There's nothing in it, just white walls and bare floors. And you look like hell, seriously you do. You look like something out of *David Copperfield*, a blacking factory or something.'

'Believe me,' Jack said.

'Is it ready?'

'No, it bloody isn't.'

'What's gone wrong with it now?'

'Everything.'

'Everything has already gone wrong with it. What else could happen? It must be costing a fortune.'

Jack glared at him. 'Job's friends were bringers of sweetness and light compared to you,' he said.

They sat in the living room and drank coffee.

'You don't have any ornaments or anything,' Rosalind said, gazing around her.

'I don't like clutter.'

'I've seen fuller deserts.' She got up and went to the window.

'Do you want to see the car?' Jack offered.

'About six months since,' Freddie said.

'All right.'

For once Jack let himself be driven by Freddie. He sat in the back with his eyes closed most of the time, partly because he was tired but mostly because he feared death. When they reached the factory nobody said that Jack had promised to be there eight hours earlier.

Jack was so sick of the cars, particularly this one, the first. He had insisted on it being white, that was his colour. Now he thought he would never want to see another white car again. Freddie walked around it and Jack tried to look at it as though he had not seen it before and couldn't because he had never not seen it before, it had been inside his head, possibly for years.

Freddie's face filled with disappointment. He tried to erase it but Jack could see that he couldn't. He had waited for so long to view this car and now that he had he obviously wished that he hadn't. Jack remembered that he did not make friends for this reason and he wished very much that Freddie had not cultivated him purposely because this was the pay-off.

This little car was the biggest dream that Jack had ever had and he knew that it had begun in his mind as nothing more than a rectangular box and for all that had happened that was what it remained. The wheels were small, the space was nearly all used for passengers, four of them and their luggage.

Not an inch was wasted, it was as small as it could be. His vision was that he would enable everybody who wanted a car to have one and he wanted to be generous and give them a car that they and nobody else would ever forget. The solution, the future of automotive engineering, was here.

Freddie didn't say anything for so long that Jack wanted to run away but he didn't because everything that Freddie could have thought or said he had already told himself and there had been so many problems that he had dealt with, everything except that Freddie did the one thing that Jack couldn't stand. After a lifetime he turned, eyes dismissive and scornful.

'I couldn't drive that, it's like an orange box on wheels. Everybody would laugh.'

'They'll be laughing on the other side of their faces before I'm finished,' Jack said.

'You don't really expect the public to buy it.'

'Freddie . . . ' Rosalind said.

Jack had not expected her to come to his defence. He had reached the conclusion long since that she no longer liked him except at work and he had been spending little time in the office during the past few months, he had been busy here and she put up with him because of what Freddie wanted because she loved him. Freddie looked at her as she said his name.

'You haven't driven it yet,' she said.

'I'm not going to either,' he said and he looked at Jack. 'To think I made a friend of you,' and he walked out.

Jack rubbed a hand across his eyes, he was suddenly so very tired. When he could bear to look out at the world again she was still there.

'Go with him.'

'No.'

'If it fails, and it looks now as though it will, I'll be back at my dad's garage in no time and the fallout will be incredible. You won't want to be around.'

'It's not going to fail.'

Why were the words such balm? Nobody else had said that and he had not realized the immense pressure of no kindness and no comfort. Sir Trevor would back him to his last penny, to his last breath, but he had said nothing.

'I keep telling myself it will be all right.'

'Sir Trevor believes in it.'

'He just won't back out on me.'

'Let's get a cab, I'll take you home.'

'I have work to do.'

'Not today,' she said.

He tried to argue with her but somehow he couldn't. They were soon back at the house and she made tea and then she disappeared for a while and he fell asleep on the sofa and he could hear pigeons cooing on the roof. When he awoke she prepared a meal for him and opened some wine. They ate, at least he did, she just kept him company, and they finished the wine and then Jack went to sleep and when he awoke it was late, it was dark, the winter's day had not lasted long and he was lying on the sofa with his head in her lap. Bliss. He was embarrassed.

'Sorry,' he said, removing himself to the other end of the sofa. 'Don't fight with him because of the car.'

'It isn't over the car,' she said.

'What is it, then?'

'It's him,' she said.

'He couldn't help not liking the look of the car, I didn't like the look of it myself when I first saw it. He's been wanting to see it for ages and it was bound to be a disappointment.'

'That's not the point.'

'What, then?'

'He could have said it differently. He didn't have to do his superior act.'

She got up and went to the big window which was one of two close together and she watched the winter wind tear through the empty trees.

'He's never taken me home or come home with me. All we ever do is . . . go dancing, go to bed, you know. We don't move on, we're just . . . '

'He loves you.'

'I know. That's what makes it so . . . we're in limbo. He's my whole life, I love him, I want us to be married. I thought maybe this Christmas he would finally give me a ring but I don't think he will. Do you think he's ashamed of me?'

'How on earth could he be?'

'Because I have no money and no class.'

'That's not true. As for money I don't think he has any either.'

'That's different. He has an estate and thousands of acres. He has an old name. He can ride a horse and shoot and he can row—'

'Very useful.'

She laughed. 'I know it sounds silly. I wish I didn't love him. I wish I'd never met him.'

The last thing Jack needed was a weeping woman. He had kept away from women for a long time because he did not want to be distracted from the most important thing in his life and now that this girl stood there, crying and trying not to in the middle of his bare living room, it all seemed incredibly stupid, the car, the ideas, the work, the isolation, the obsession.

She didn't cry much and that was worse somehow, as though she had long since learned not to because there was no comfort. He thought of her in her awful little flat. He had been there once since she had moved in and was appalled at how basic it was, how soulless.

She had nothing but a bed and a rug and a chair, a sofa with uneven legs and lumpy cushions and a little rickety table which was trying to be a desk. The windows looked out over grimy back streets and were filthy. It was all she could afford, he knew. She spent all her money on clothes to keep up with Freddie's friends.

A less brave girl would have gone back to Durham a long time ago and married some nice lad and had a couple of bairns and probably been a lot happier than she was now, hanging around the edges of a circle she could not be part of. He was angry with Freddie for having bedded her in the first place. Where they came from when you laid a woman you mostly married her, either because you had to or because you were supposed to, you didn't go on bedding her relentlessly while she struggled to keep up socially.

There were plenty of men she could have married at home and some of them were successful – doctors, solicitors, businessmen. She could have done that without breaking into a sweat, she was so pretty and she was kind, she had showed that today. She didn't really like him much, it was just loyalty that kept her there, the old loyalty, the best kind.

She had just about stopped crying which was just as well because somebody was banging on the door and when he opened it Freddie stood there, looking ashamed.

'I'm sorry.'

Jack left the door open and went back into the living room.

'It just wasn't what I expected.' Freddie stopped when he saw Rosalind. 'Ros? What have you done to make her cry?'

'I'm not crying,' she declared.

Freddie put an arm around her. 'I thought it would be interesting and stylish.'

'That wasn't the point, it was meant to be functional.'

'I don't like to say this, Jack, but I think you're making a mistake. I don't think people will buy such a car, it's a completely new idea and people don't like new, they're afraid of it. As for rallying – I wouldn't touch it with a bargepole.'

'You're doing it again,' Rosalind said, twisting away from him.

'Doing what?'

'Being bloody offensive!'

'It isn't meant to be offensive.'

'Well, it is.'

'In six months' time you'll be begging me to let you drive it,' Jack prophesied.

'Like hell. You're going to lose your shirt over it,' Freddie said and he walked Rosalind out of the house.

Five

Jennifer Erlhart was beginning to hate England and London in particular. It wasn't just London she had a prejudice against. She also hated Paris which was like London except that the food was even worse and Venice which was freezing at this time of the year. It was freezing at home, at her real home in New Hampshire too, but it was a different kind of thing, the people were equipped for bad weather, expected it, went skiing.

Not that she cared for skiing, she was not the outdoor type, but she loved the wonderful predictability of the seasons, the colours in the fall, the snow in winter, the way that the spring was warm and that summer never failed to be hot at least in part. She hated Europe, that was what it was. But there was a particular reason for it and that was that her father had brought her to Europe to find a husband, somebody suitable. Suitable meant somebody with a title. Nothing less would do for the daughter of John Bernard Erlhart, self-made man, multi-millionaire. Nothing was enough for her father, only her marriage to a man of title and property.

She hated him and she hated herself for being afraid of him and her mother for not stopping him from bringing her here on such an errand. They were based in London and had made various trips to other cities but now they were back at their hotel in London and she hated how pompous it was, how the staff were made to bow and scrape because she was rich and how her father expected it, enjoyed his status.

He had put her on a diet before she came here and she was expected to stick to it. When she could she sneaked out and ate at teashops, which were the only things she had so far enjoyed in England because she was allowed so little food, when everybody around her was always eating, that she could think of nothing else.

Her father had seen that she was introduced to all the best people and there had been a number of young men whom he deemed suitable to be her mate but all of them had somehow fallen short. They were so obviously poor and grasping, they disliked how plump she was, they were boring, they talked of matters he knew nothing of. They certainly talked of people she knew nothing of and none of them had held her interest until a certain evening when she had seen across the room a tall, fair young man. He was in company and he was laughing.

'That,' her father said into her ear, 'is Earl Harlington's son, Frederick. What do you think?'

'He's very handsome.'

He was but so had several other men been and she had been very disappointed when she met them. They didn't have any of her interests, they didn't want to know anything about her, all they cared about was her money and their shining greedy eyes told her so.

She didn't manage an introduction to Freddie Harlington but her father somehow spoke to his father and manoeuvred an invitation to stay at their country estate in Northumberland. Jennifer had not heard of Northumberland and had been convinced that after Yorkshire there was Scotland. She looked it up on the map and it was almost into Scotland. If it's freezing here just think what it will be like so far north, she thought and shivered.

She found a book in the nearest bookshop and read about the north and it seemed so wild and woolly, she thought with a giggle, like the old west had been, so empty, with lots of moorland and ruined castles. How very romantic. She didn't want to go.

All she wanted to do was go home to New England and be an old maid and paint. She wanted to learn to paint properly. Her father had never allowed her to do this though at school it had been her biggest joy. She wished she could spend every afternoon for the rest of her life sitting by a big window as she had at school, gazing from it and dreaming and painting, making sketches of the house where she had been so happy in New Hampshire when she was a child.

She remembered the hills, the calm water of the lake before the wooden house and the comfort which her great-aunt had offered, basic things like good log fires in the winter and bathing and boating in the summer, good food and friends who dropped by, people who read books and cared about music. She didn't imagine she was going to find any of that in the borders between Scotland and England and she didn't think for a second that the young man would be interested in her. When she said this to her father he scoffed.

'He has to be interested. He's broke,' he said.

Her father's Rolls-Royce complete with chauffeur took them to the north and it was a longer journey than she had thought it might be and somehow that was good. She shed the south as she had shed New York where she had been brought up and had always hated because her every hour was filled with the activities which her father deemed necessary for her education.

After she was ten she was educated privately at home and that did not include painting and drawing. She learned cordon-bleu cookery – she hated it – and how a lady ran a house, and embroidery which she also hated, and darning and knitting – when was she ever going to need such things? She was not often allowed to read novels unless they were considered improving.

48

She had no friends because her father did not consider anyone good enough. She had a tutor, an old man who spoke several languages and expected her to do the same and he knew a great deal about chemistry and physics and maths, all things she had no talent for. She was miserable. She was taught to dance but never went to a party and she was bought a great many clothes and sat about in the window of the house in her finery.

Her mother believed that if you had family you didn't need friends but her cousins, her father's sister's children, were slender, beautiful, blonde girls who thought her fat and ugly. The Ugly Sister, she thought. Well almost.

There were often family parties but they were dull, the men going off to smoke and drink by themselves, the women gossiping about other women, and the children would go off and play in the garden and they were all older than her and did not ask her to join in. At such times she did what Jane Eyre had done and hid behind curtains with a book, taking an apple with her. These were her happiest times.

The countryside around her changed as the Rolls-Royce ate up the miles. Daffodils bloomed in the south but here she could see in the various gardens she passed that they were nothing beyond long green stalks amongst the grass.

There were hills which grew higher and several dark towns with narrow streets and ill-clad children and when she reached Northumberland she thought it was as much like *Wuthering Heights* as the Yorkshire she had seen. Finally she had found somewhere she thought she was going to like. There were long stretches of nothing but the sky and the moors and neat little towns, big farms and ruins which looked to her as though they had been castles or some form of defence many years ago.

She said nothing to her parents, she did not want to show her enthusiasm because she had discovered that every time she had done so before somehow it was taken away from her.

The house was in the middle of nowhere, with a pretty village, and then the big car purred in at the gates and a little further along she had her first glimpse of the Harlingtons' Northumberland home and it was set amidst a hundred green fields and had big gardens around it and it looked like the sun was permanently shining on its stone.

The car made its way up the circular drive to the door and Jennifer fell in love for the first time, with a house.

That Easter Freddie began to suspect that something important was happening at home and that this time it was serious. For one thing his mother came back and since she hated his stepmother and disliked his father there must have been a good reason and both parents were insisting that he should go home for Easter. His mother came to stay in London and she turned up at the house unexpectedly when Rosalind was there.

His mother, Robyn, who was tall, blonde, slender, elegant and beautiful, wore a very expensive suit (she had married for the title first time and money the second, so she said) and was charming to Rosalind, so charming that Freddie felt ill, smiling and asking about her work. Usually he was happy with Rosalind, she was so pretty and wore nice clothes, but beside his mother she looked gauche and ill at ease. He was glad when she left soon.

'What a lovely girl,' his mother said brightly. 'Darling, are you coming home for Easter? You know your father wants you to.'

'Yes, of course.'

'I knew you would. There are things we must talk about and you know we have invited the Erlharts to stay. You must remember me talking to you about Jennifer. She's been staying in London.'

'I don't.'

'I long to see White Maddens again,' his mother said.

Freddie knew what she meant, he longed to see it too but without his stepmother. The trouble was that his father, William, adored Sybil and Sybil clearly loved him so it should have been all right but it wasn't. She didn't like his children, Freddie thought. He blamed her because he had been sent to boarding school when it ought to have been obvious to him that boys always went. It was just that he had the uneasy feeling they had been sent away so that his father and his father's new wife could be alone.

As an adult Freddie knew that this was not unreasonable, as a child it seemed that he was in the way. After their parents had parted, when he was two, Claudia had looked after him but she was away, firstly at school and then at finishing school and then she married and it seemed to Freddie that he spent his entire holidays on trains between Northumberland and Gloucestershire and then on boats and trains between France and Gloucestershire and Northumberland and his mother was busy with her new husband and as a child he was always in the way.

His mother adored Alain, the businessman she had married, but he was not interested in children, had none of his own, liked sports, was rarely at home and never, that Freddie could remember, ever spoke to them other than pleasantries. He always looked so relieved when they went home so that he could get on with his life and have Freddie's mother all to himself. Freddie was so jealous.

On the other hand the children had a fine time in Northumberland. They had ponies, lots of toys, acres and acres to run about in. Now there was no money, not the kind that was needed to keep the estate going. It could not be sold though the treasures from it could be. His father was loath to part with anything which had been in the family for hundreds of years and much of it had and besides, Freddie knew that the keeping together of the place was part of his duty for future generations.

He and his mother went there together. He drove but for once in his life he didn't concentrate on his driving. It was the first time in years he could remember having had his mother to himself like that and it was a strange sensation as though a small boy had taken control of the car. His mother was either fearless or didn't care because she was the first passenger Freddie had ever had who didn't complain about his driving.

That was when he remembered his mother teaching him to drive in France. When he had gone there during the summer holidays she had let him take her car along the drive and back and since it was a couple of miles in total he had learned to drive. He remembered her showing him the gears and the controls, and sitting with him, quite unconcerned when he drove her car into a wall.

His mother, he knew, was the epitome of good breeding. He did not think she had ever lost her temper or raised her voice. That was one reason, Claudia said, why she did not

51

understand her parents parting, there had been no fighting. He knew now that the fighting had gone on inside his mother's head and inside her womb and between her legs and that the fight had been lost. Women perhaps always would fight against the very essence of their existence, to be more than mothers, to be more than objects, to be used less and respected more, to be beyond their cycles and inside their brains.

His mother was too beautiful for men ever to have imagined that she was intelligent and she had not come from the kind of society which would educate her or give her the independence which would have enriched her life. She had had to use that beauty to gain her position and wealth and when he looked into his own eyes through the driving mirror he saw his mother. Freddie had long denied to himself that beauty but it was too obvious. Women had looked across rooms at him for years and seen themselves naked beneath him and he hated it.

She smiled at him as they turned the corner, the final bend in the road and he thought of being a child and of coming home and of how this had always mattered to him; the excitement rose in him as it did without fail when he reached this place. He slowed the car to better appreciate what was to come, as he did when about to enter Rosalind's body, slow, very slow because at any moment the sweetest thing in the world would happen.

He would be safe there, sure, he would pretend to himself that he need never come out again, that there was no world beyond it, no emptiness in the night without it. Best of all he liked to turn over in his sleep and feel her there and now the final corner was past and there before him the dearest place of his life. His home.

Easter in Northumberland was the time when the snowdrops were no longer providing white carpets under the trees between the house and the castle, where the winter-flowering rhododendrons with big pink or red flowers had given way to thousands of daffodils. He couldn't wait to see it even though the house would be freezing.

You came in off the main road to Jedburgh and Edinburgh and then along tiny roads, very often not bigger than a car's width and sometimes with no signposts so that anybody unfamiliar would have been lost in minutes. All around were big

Northumbrian farms, here and there on the skyline a ruined castle. Thick-fleeced sheep graced the fields and the land rose in big waves from time to time as though to remind you that you were not far from the border. Edinburgh was fifty miles away. There were a lot of country houses in this area, some of them elegant farms with ivy growing over the front of the house, sometimes you could see the house from the road and sometimes they were set back, square-built, splendid.

The road came into the village that bore his name and then beyond the houses which at one time had belonged to the estate – some of them still did, all built in honeyed stone – you turned into the private drive and there were farms and cottages which were part of the estate and the road twisted and turned for a couple of miles. There was a big lake to one side where he had the feeling his grandfather had gone fishing and then the house came into view. He thought it was the most wonderful house in the world.

The local people told tales about it. All the people in the village nearby were related to him and to one another. His grandfather had been curtsied to and acknowledged with caps off but times had changed. In the village now it was a different thing. People smiled and in the shops they acknowledged him by doing what Jack would have called 'pulling his leg', a gentle respect which showed him to be their own.

He urged the car up the road and then turned in among the buildings at the back of the house where the cars lived and there were stables and pigsties and all kinds of outbuildings. There was a circular drive at the front of the house where he had no doubt hundreds of carriages had turned in their time when there were parties but nobody went in that way.

A hundred thousand memories nudged him and when he got out of the car it was the smell of home, horses and hay, buttercups and grass. His practised eye already told him that things were getting worse financially, he had noticed how shabby and neglected everything looked. The land was bare in places and the grass was long. Broken-down machinery hid around the sides of the buildings and cottages which had fallen into disrepair over the years were in ruins.

Sybil came outside as though she had been watching and waiting. She wore a pretty floral dress such as his mother would have died rather than be seen in but then Sybil could scarcely afford new clothes. His mother was wearing a linen suit and though she was no longer mistress here she looked it. His father came out too and called him 'my boy', as though he couldn't remember Freddie's name, as though he had a dozen sons, as though they had met yesterday, as though they liked one another.

Freddie had tried to forgive his father for being nothing more than a man but it was difficult. They had not even a likeness in common. Freddie's sisters looked like their father and Claudia had often complained because Freddie was like their mother and they had their father's big nose which ruined them for beauty but he remembered them wearing shorts and wading in streams and they all had long slender brown legs because their parents were both tall.

Since having Rosalind, Freddie knew that once people had bedded together they had a bond which could not be broken and his parents hated one another with such purity that they could not touch. Even their words tried to get away, they turned slightly away from one another so that any breeze there was would carry off the lightest words, the most innocuous of greetings.

His father couldn't make conversation, noises came out but nothing was said. Freddie thought he had long since become inured to seeing Sybil act the hostess to his mother. They both knew that it didn't work but his mother was gracious and Sybil did her best. They did what Sybil called 'taking tea'. It was a family joke that Sybil didn't just drink tea, she took it, and with other people, what's more. It wasn't funny, he knew, but anything against Sybil, in the old days, had been funny because as children they were powerless and he was especially because he had been such a little boy when his parents' marriage ended.

Sybil had made the mistake of trying to mother him and he had retaliated with the worst that he could manage, calling her names, biting her, and he knew that she could not understand that such a beautiful small boy could hate her with such venom. He felt guilty because of it and that guilt did not marry well with the way that he felt about this house.

He could not enter it without wanting to throw her down the front steps outside and it was not her fault, he knew. But his father loved her as he had never loved his mother, had

had an affair with her while he was still married and Freddie had when young erroneously thought Sybil had caused the break-up between his parents, whereas she was a result rather than a cause and he could not forgive any of them for that so he took tea with Sybil and, rather like his father, made polite noises and as soon as he could he escaped to the gardens but not before his father had said, 'We have guests coming to dinner.'

'I heard.'

His mother said nothing more to this so that Freddie realized the arrangement had been made between them. He walked a long way from the house and wished himself back in London, imagined himself in bed with Rosalind, in her arms, safe from the world.

The gardens were considered by some people to be the best part of White Maddens, big parklands at the front and terraced gardens, further over a rhododendron garden which had been his grandmother's favourite, red, white and pink, a yew garden, a magnolia terrace, a winter garden, a meadow garden and best of all the garden which had been made after the stone for the house had been quarried.

One of his favourite memories of the house was of walking there in a heavy rainstorm in June and the flowers had been gashes of colour amidst the water and the gravel paths had run almost white and the croquet lawn was like a pool and the stones of the quarry garden were dark and dramatic with its huge ferns, ivies, trees and shrubs, some of them growing out of or on top of the rocks, making it darker and even more dramatic.

It was all very neglected now because it needed a team of gardeners and his father could no longer afford to pay people with skill and dedication. He hated seeing it now and contrasting it with how it had looked in his early childhood.

He opened the big wooden door and soon the quarry garden ended and the light flooded in and he could see the castle, part of it built in the days when a defensible tower was the best option in these lawless lands.

Later more comfortable quarters were added on, and it had its own chapel. Most of the building was still there and he and the girls had played endless games of hide and seek around the grounds beyond the chapel when they were young and various family marriages had taken place there.

He walked slowly back to the house, thinking of how when he was a little boy he had been astonished to think that such a place was his inheritance, that he was lucky, honoured. He had not had enough imagination to see that the whole thing would become the most tremendous burden because they were poor.

The people arrived. Freddie wished there had been a draw-bridge and a moat like in the old days so that he could keep people out, high walls with long grassy meadows beyond so that they could have been shot from narrow windows before they reached the house, bolts on his door, those big wooden sleepers which people had once used to barricade themselves in.

As it was he had to dress for dinner like some bloody waiter. He tried not to look at himself, straight into his own eyes in the mirror, but he caught a glimpse of what he looked like before he went downstairs, and shivered.

They were impressive stairs, sweeping right round as though the architect had nothing but his work and was determined to put every last drop of himself into it, and as he walked down them the people arrived, slightly early. How vulgar. His father had impressed upon him that he must be downstairs before they came but he didn't quite manage it. He heard the shrill blast of American voices echoing in the vast stone hall and as he came down the stairs they looked up.

There were three of them, a man, short and stocky, a woman, shorter and stockier, and a girl, the same size as her mother. She watched him as he walked down the last few steps and it was then that he was reminded uncomfortably of what he was doing here. It was a mart, a market, a sale. He and the house were being put up onto the slave block and stripped for the highest bidder; and this girl with her keen gaze, she was a possible buyer.

The last few steps moved before his eyes, his breath gone. If there had been a spell to evoke he would have been back in London, safe in Rosalind's arms, eyes closed, pillows and the bed all around, the London rain drumming so neatly and so kindly against the window, Rosalind's hair to hide him, her body to shield him.

He knew now why he had wanted her, why he had held her so closely to him in those last few months, why he had kept her apart from this, she was his tree house, his cave, his garden shed, his allotment. She was his country retreat, his pub, she was the last pint, the final cigarette, the whore's bedroom. She was the working-man's club, the cricket pitch, the Garrick, the newspaper, the cigars, the silence. She was the sanctuary knocker on the door of the cathedral, sweet dungeon, the silent desert, the football terrace. She could hide him.

The girl's brown eyes were heavy on him though she smiled and spoke politely. She had no claim to beauty and she looked scared, as though she too would have run away if she could have. Freddie tried to look objectively at her and his first emotion was pity. Red hair was usually so attractive but hers was orange as though it had been dyed, though the freckles which covered her face assured him that everything about her was natural.

Her skin was as white as flour, she regarded him helplessly as he walked slowly down the stairs towards her. She wore the most hideous dress he thought he had ever seen, white satin, displaying her fat shoulders and arms, and the pearls around her neck, all of equal size, were ostentatiously large as though her family had not been rich for long and needed to display their wealth to the world and about their person which anybody else would know was the worst way possible of doing so.

She had small pudgy hands which peeped out from the ample folds of the four yards or so of cloth which made up the skirt and her hands and arms were covered in long white evening gloves. When he reached her she looked startled and blushed until her cheeks were magenta.

Her mother did not say much but then she didn't get the chance. Mr Erlhart asked questions all the way through the meal, about the castle, about the family, and he offered a lot of information all pertaining to his wealth: about the houses he owned, the businesses he owned, how he liked various parts of England and where they had been to before they came here. Even when he didn't speak it seemed to Freddie that the echo of his booming voice went on and on.

Appetite gone, voice lost, Freddie sat at the table with them and took retreat in a glass of cold white wine. He wanted to swim in it, dive in and disappear. The dining room, they didn't eat in there unless they had a lot of company, looked even bigger with only half a dozen people in it and though the fireplace was enormous the room was also and he pitied the American women, who obviously knew nothing of country houses and had come to dinner with their plump shoulders bared.

The walls of the room, like all the other reception rooms, were bare too. All the valuable paintings had been sold to repair the roof, to keep the dry rot and the damp at bay. Many of the rooms were shut up, locked, more and more it seemed each time he came back and as far as he could judge only this room and the small drawing room were in use downstairs for social occasions

Course after course arrived at the table as though it was a banquet. He thought of those few times when his stepfather had not been at home in France, and neither for some reason had the girls been there, and he and his mother would sit in the garden by the river and there would be the very ordinary red wine which was the local stuff and cheese and bread and salad. It was all he would ever want and because it was all he could ever want it had gone by with the swiftness of a fleet horse. He wished that he could have put it into a locket like the Victorians did with the hair of a loved one, women with a silver locket hanging between their breasts, warm and cuddled there.

The food came and went and there was talk somewhere above and around and from time to time he would smile at something the girl said and she would laugh as though something witty had been uttered. Afterwards everybody went outside as though there would be fireworks and later still his father called him into the study, which lay to one side of the huge pillared hall which was the centre of the house, a two-storey affair with Greek pillars and a stone floor, the staircase to the upper storey going up to one side and the front entrance beyond it. It was a cruelty to be there in the winter, it was so cold, though there were two fireplaces in the front entrance which the dogs usually gathered round.

The study was a much smaller room than any of the others so the fire and the central heating made a difference here.

Freddie remembered being called in there as a small child, usually for something he had done wrong and almost always something against Sybil.

He had known even as a child that his father loved Sybil more than anybody in the world and he could not understand that and was jealous of it, on behalf of himself and his sisters and his mother who at that time he had thought banished to France from the place she loved the most.

He had never understood that his father and mother had thought their own personal satisfaction or lust was more important to them than their families and Freddie knew with a horrible realization that your family was more important than anything on earth and that that was what they were doing here now. Ironically, now for the first time, he knew what it was like to love someone as much as his father loved Sybil.

William fidgeted and moved about the room and talked about money and the need for it, about the house and its upkeep, about want and the past and the future and about duty.

Freddie thought his father had had the same talk from his own father. Could it possibly be that he was remembering it? At last he paused but stood with his back to Freddie as though the words were so important that he could not face him.

He stood beside the window looking out across the vast sweep of lawns beyond and then the lake further over and the stream at the bottom and Freddie thought of how they had played there as children, building dams and trying to catch non-existent fish, splashing and wading and lying on the bank of the stream in the sunlight which had seemed endless in childhood.

It had never occurred to him then that he would have to make impossible choices, he had thought that the estate which he alone would inherit would always be as dear to him as it was then. It was his destiny and he had always known it. White Maddens.

'I don't know what to say to you,' his father managed at last.

Hello, how are you, would have been a good start, Freddie thought. He never asked anything about the rallying, had never, as far as Freddie could remember, mentioned it. At one time it had seemed to him that he could make his father proud of him by achieving what seemed to him so much but in his father's world it was inherent things which mattered, who your grandfather had been, stupid things like which side you were on in the Civil War and who various members of your family were married to and whether you had a good seat when you rode a horse and your tailoring.

It was laughable really. You couldn't achieve any of it, especially by such obviously stupid things as driving. That was just something for you to do. The important things were who you married and how soon you could produce a son and also things like whether the roof leaked, because it cost a fortune to repair, and the state of the cottages and the cleaning of pictures and staff and money.

Money was the most important thing of all though people like his father had a terrible tendency to pretend it wasn't. He had the awful feeling his father was rather ashamed of what he did, as though work of any kind was completely beneath them, especially the kind of thing he did where he would have to mix with people from different classes.

His father, Freddie thought fondly, would never have noticed Jack Neville, he never did notice people who were beneath him in class. He had never remembered any of the servants' names in the old days when there were still a lot about. Now all they had were two women who came in to do the housework, a part-time cook, two part-time gardeners and a general man who kept becoming so overwhelmed with the amount of work there was to do that he was always threatening to leave.

His father talked about the family and how important it was and Freddie remembered his mother leaving and how he had cried for her when he was so little in the night. From the open windows he could smell the roses which his great-grandmother had so much loved and which were gone wild long since.

Finally William turned around and that was the first time Freddie could remember an open honesty in his face.

'I have worked hard to persuade the Erlharts to come here. I trust that you will say and do all the right things. I wouldn't want them to be disappointed in us. You have a huge responsibility and I know that you will meet it with every degree of . . . ' He seemed to forget what he was trying to say there and after that seemed to remember that he didn't usually speak at all and took to clearing his throat and fidgeting as though he was bored and didn't want to be there. 'You must have seen how bad things are. We need an enormous influx of cash. Keep it in mind, won't you?'

Later still his mother came to him in his bedroom. She watched him throw his jacket onto the bed and haul off his black tie. She watched as he turned angrily to her.

'I know what you're going to say,' she said.

'No, no, go ahead, lecture me on my duty. I love it. My father has already attempted to talk to me, which is more than he's done since I shot his best spaniel by mistake up on the moor when I was fifteen, but don't let that stop you.'

The thing which he admired about his mother was that she acknowledged he had any kind of a life, that she even addressed some of the issues which mattered to him. She did it now.

'I know you think you're in love with . . . '

'Rosalind. She's called Rosalind. Couldn't you even remember that?'

His mother was angry too, he had known it, all that evening because she must be a party to this, because she was helpless.

'What do you like best about her, her poverty, her background, her accent?'

'Stop it.'

'Did you deliberately choose her so that you could not even bring her home? You know dozens of girls, all of whom would be more acceptable, so what do you do? You bed a little office worker. You are sleeping with her, I can see by her eyes. She has that horrible shiny look that women have when they're . . . '

'When they're being fucked well and regularly? Say it.'

His mother was silent.

'She's not a little office worker, she's perfectly respectable.'

'Darling—'

'Don't "Darling" me. I love her.'

His mother sighed and looked down. She was so beautiful, he thought, in her black evening dress, almost without ornament. She didn't need it, even at more than sixty.

'You're being deliberately obtuse. You knew very well that you couldn't marry her. She doesn't know that, does she?'

'I don't know.'

'Of course you do. She's read too many fairy tales. She thinks you are the prince come to rescue her from her dull life.'

'I was the one who needed rescuing.'

'I see. So you will marry her?'

He didn't say anything. And then, 'Do you really want me to marry this dreadful American girl?'

'She's not dreadful. She's lovely.'

'You mean she's rich.'

'She likes you.'

'How on earth can you tell that? She's probably just like the rest of us and is doing what her parents think best. She doesn't look happy and for such a fat little git she ate nothing at dinner.'

His mother looked as though she was going to hit him. He knew that look. Her eyes brightened with temper. She didn't, of course, she wouldn't have done such a thing. Instead she said tightly, 'Well then, go ahead and marry your office worker and when you tire of her and her pedestrian mind and her even worse family you will be pleased with yourself and then you will remember how you let everyone down because you had forgotten who you are,' and she walked out and slammed the door. That came of practice. The doors were heavy oak but she did it well.

Jennifer was uncomfortably cold, even with a fire in her bedroom. Freddie's stepmother had been in her room, asking her if she was comfortable and she could hardly say that she was frozen. The room was enormous, the sheets were darned, the coverlet was so old it looked like it might drop to pieces at any minute and the bed was a four-poster and big enough for half a dozen people, even her size, to sleep in. She dreaded the idea of trying to sleep. Surely the place was haunted.

She pushed back the old curtains to see from the window and it was a lovely night with a big moon across the gardens. Someone opened the door behind her and she was glad that she had not undressed. It was her father. He stood, letting in the draft for a moment or two and then came in. He never knocked. She wished he would. It implied disrespect but then he had never respected her, she thought.

'So,' he said, closing the door, 'what do you think about the viscount, Frederick, hm?' He spoke lightly as though he was being amusing.

'He's very nice,' she said vaguely.

'Nice? Jennifer, this is the guy who will become an English lord, an earl, and he's yours if you want him. The poor bastard's broke. The place is like a mausoleum. Do you want him?'

He had done this to her in her childhood with toys, horses, dogs, anything. Freddie Harlington was just a plaything, he implied, not important and he could be bought, just like anything could be. Only she had the feeling that Freddie couldn't, that he was like a shadow in a sense, you couldn't hold him. She had been surprised to see how he looked up close. She had seen him at a distance in London and thought he was fabulous but now the idea of being married to him was so scary that she couldn't think.

'I don't know,' she said.

Her father snorted. 'Is there something wrong with him? He has everything except money. He's not too bright, of course, the English aristocracy don't go in for brains—'

'He's quite famous,' she said.

'Oh yes?'

'Yes, he . . . races cars or something like that.'

'Don't you want an English lord? I've gone to a lot of trouble to set this up, Jennifer.'

'Yes, I know.'

'And you needn't worry that he thinks he's going to marry you and then run things the way he likes because I'm going to make sure that he toes the line every step of the way. I've got him over a barrel. I'm going to make sure the contract ensures that I say where the money goes and if he puts a foot out of line I'll make him wish he hadn't.'

Jennifer was already feeling sorry for Freddie Harlington. He quite obviously didn't want to be there and he would hardly want to marry her, they didn't know each other and she was not exactly beautiful.

'I'd like to spend some time with him.'

'How much time?'

'If I'm going to be with him the rest of my life it would be nice to think we had anything at all in common,' she said.

Her father laughed. 'How could you possibly have anything in common? He needs your money and it'll be nice for us to have a title and for our grandchildren to be English aristocrats. I like that. Your mother and I will be able to come and stay here a lot.'

The very idea made Jennifer shudder.

'We could even buy a house nearby. Not as big as this of course but there'll be something to suit us so that I can keep an eye on everything. Well, I'm going to go and let you get some sleep but remember, just say the word and he's yours,' and her father went out laughing and closed the door.

Freddie couldn't sleep. He hadn't told Rosalind that he was going home for Easter and she hadn't asked but she had talked brightly about what she would do over the weekend. He wanted to rush back to London and into bed with her, he felt as though he was imprisoned here. In the dawn he finally fell asleep and when he awoke the day was bright and he knew it for late morning. He ventured downstairs and there was the girl, Jennifer, alone in the breakfast room, cramming toast into her mouth. Her chin was shiny with butter. She smiled dimly at him.

'Can I pass you some toast?'

'No, thanks,' he said, pouring coffee from the sideboard and sitting down opposite. She watched him. 'Where are you from?' he asked.

'New Hampshire. We live in New York now but . . . when I was a little girl we had a house on a lake there, my grand-parents had it. I used to spend a lot of time with them. I miss it.'

'Have you been in England long?'

'It feels like a long time,' she admitted.

After that there was silence and he felt sorry for her. He wished he didn't but somehow it was impossible.

'Are you homesick?'

'For my grandparents and my great-aunt and the house by the lake? Oh yes, I think I'm always homesick for that. They died and my father didn't like the place. He sold it. We never went back.'

'What are you doing today?'

'I think my parents are going to take the car and drag me around the countryside.' She looked faintly apologetic. 'I'm sure it's very beautiful but . . . '

'Do you play tennis?'

'I don't get time.'

They played. She was very out of condition, the sweat ran

down her but she didn't give up. He even let her score a few points and he thought that for somebody who knew nothing about the game she did quite well.

'You have a good eye,' he told her when they sank down onto the grass in the sunshine.

'I do?' She looked sceptically at him and laughed.

'With a bit of practice you could be a decent player.'

'Why, thank you.'

Freddie rather liked the sarcasm. When he offered to take her out for lunch she looked at him.

'You're very kind but I don't think you want to and I do so hate to be a bore.'

'You're not,' he said and meant it.

Freddie took her out in his new car which he was very fond of. It had been given to him as a prize when he won a race abroad. It was a Mercedes 300 S roadster and had been much admired. Jennifer didn't even wear a hat or a scarf and her red hair blew about her. He took her to a hotel where they could sit outside under the trees.

Her face was crimson from the sunshine and her arms were burned and he could not help but think of Rosalind, how she browned evenly and was so slender and lovely and how much he missed her laughter and her conversation. Jennifer was too nervous to say much but over their steak and chips he caught her looking at him.

'Something the matter?'

'No.' She put down her knife and fork and then she said, 'I didn't think you were going to be like this.'

'What did you think I was going to be like?'

'Oh . . . I don't know. Ordinary maybe, bookish perhaps so that we would have something in common.'

'How do you know I'm not?'

She looked harder at him. 'You're like a film star,' she said.

'Oh God,' Freddie said, choking.

'Well, you are. You look like those pictures of English lords playing cricket. I thought you might have . . . endearing qualities like you couldn't ride a horse or . . . and then I saw you in London and my heart just gave.'

'I am very bad at most things.'

'Yes, but not those things. I understand you are an incredibly good driver and that you win races—'

'It's not like motor racing,' Freddie assured her, 'it's nothing like that.'

'Then what is it like?'

'Well, just little cars and skill and speed.'

'It sounds very clever. Tell me what you're bad at or I shall never be able to address another sentence to you.'

Freddie sat back in his chair and looked out at the river. They were in the garden of a hotel by the North Tyne and there were ducks.

'I was useless at school.'

'But you're good at sport?'

'Not team games, just hand-and-eye stuff.'

'You went to college?'

'No. You?'

'My father doesn't approve of women's education. He says there's no point. I wanted more than anything to go.'

'But lots of women do.'

'I know. He says an overeducated wife is not what men want. I was very good at school and I love books.'

'We have a wonderful library.'

'Will you show it to me?'

'I don't know much about it. I don't think anybody's been in there for the last fifty years,' Freddie said and made her laugh.

He took her out for tea. She looked dubiously at the cream cakes and said, 'I'm not supposed to eat things like that.'

'There's nobody here but us.'

He sat and watched her eating the cakes and he thought in a way she needed rescuing from her parents. He just didn't want to be the person to do it. When they got back and heard she had been out to tea her mother said, 'I hope you didn't eat too much,' and her father talked about her in the third person when she was there like she was a bitch he was considering having mated.

'There's plenty of meat on her,' he said. 'Men like a little of that, eh?'

And his mother thought that Rosalind was vulgar.

He took Jennifer into the library and that was when he began to like her. She was so excited and her face and eyes and whole expression glowed. It was the biggest room in the house and had at one time been used as the drawing room but it was so big and cost so much to heat that they had gradually given up using it. Four floor-to-ceiling windows graced the front of it which looked out over the formal terraced gardens and it had a huge cream-and-brown fireplace. The walls were entirely covered in bookcases but there were only a few books. Many valuable books had been sold to pay for things like mending the roof. A huge rug sat in the middle of the floor and there were one or two little tables and chairs.

'I like this room best of all,' she said, doing a little twirl beside the window where the sunlight fell in because it was south-facing and got all the light. 'Am I allowed to sit in here?'

'Why yes, of course.'

'I adore books. There's room for hundreds more, thousands.'

Freddie had the fire lit in there and that evening while the older people sat in the drawing room next door he and Jennifer sat on a big squashy sofa and watched the log fire and she had been sensible enough to wear something thick and she talked to him about books and he asked what he hoped were intelligent questions.

Later that day his father called him back into the study.

'What do you think of Jennifer?'

'She's very nice, if it weren't for her parents.'

'None of us can help that,' his father said and Freddie was surprised at the incisive remark.

His father looked patiently at him. 'Are you interested in her?'

'No.'

'You couldn't be persuaded to marry her?'

'Did you marry my mother for her money?' Freddie said.

'No,' his father sighed, 'but I married my equal. She didn't have any money and I didn't have much. That's one of the reasons we're in such a state now. I thought I wanted to spend my life with her.'

'But that evaporated when she presented you with four daughters.'

His father looked even more patiently at him. 'Shall we see how you do with your life? I want you to think seriously about Jennifer Erlhart.'

'She must be very rich for you to be so keen.'

'She is.'

There was a dance on the Saturday evening. Jennifer wore a dress which was gold and made her look even fatter than she was. They danced together twice without speaking and then he danced with several other people. He wondered what Rosalind was doing. All the evening her face tortured his brain. The musicians played, the champagne flowed. It didn't look as though there was no money. People laughed and talked and went outside into the gardens. It was like a summer's evening, warm enough though it came in dark soon and even then they sat outside because the light spilled from the windows all over the house.

He watched the light from the gardens and tried not to imagine what it would be like if he didn't marry Jennifer. He thought of bringing Rosalind here as his wife and how she would love it and how he would enjoy buying her wonderful dresses, a car, a horse and he thought of what it would be like to watch this place falling around him, of when he couldn't afford to keep the animals or mend the fences and walls, of how he would not be able to employ people. He thought of the roof dripping in and the tapestries and paintings having to be sold, of the furniture and the china and glassware which were kept in huge glass cases.

The next day his father had the accountants there and in detail they went over the debts. He had not thought things were as bad as they were though he knew that all through his life economies had had to be made and all the talk for years had been lack of money. He thought how tired his father looked and how the responsibility of the place had done that and he wished there was something he could do to make things better without marrying Jennifer.

Monday was the last day that the Erlharts were to be there and this time his father came to him out on the terrace in the early morning and he looked as though he had not slept. Pheasants walked the lawns in the dew and the trees were all in leaf. This time his father did not pretend. He looked at Freddie from tired brown eyes.

'She is everything she should be, I have checked. The money is sound, her background is good and she's a virgin. I want you to propose to her.'

'I can't.' Freddie almost choked. He had not thought his

68

father would be so blunt or that he would be expected to marry a girl he could never care for deeply.

'Oh, yes, you can.'

'I have someone else.'

'You can have someone else as well, if that's what you want.'

Freddie looked at him in panic. 'I don't want that. I want to marry the woman I love.'

His father nodded. 'Your mother told me all about her. It's not to be considered. Men of your standing don't marry girls like that. You couldn't possibly do it and you have seen the financial position. You have to marry well, there is no alternative.'

'You married Sybil.'

'Sybil comes from respected people.'

'She's the woman you love.'

'You will come to love Jennifer like that.'

'I never will! I love Rosalind West. I've never loved anybody like I love her.'

He was obliged to stop there because he choked.

'This land, this place is your responsibility. You will hold it for future generations.'

'By marrying a fat rich American.'

'Since it's necessary, yes. You will take her outside onto the terrace and you will propose to her. Do you understand me?'

Freddie didn't say anything.

'You have to marry her. You have to,' his father said. 'This place is dropping to pieces around us, can you not see it? This is your inheritance. You must do whatever you have to to protect it. If you want you can have this . . . whatever her name is for your mistress. I know that's an old-fashioned word but men like us have always had mistresses and there's no reason why you shouldn't. Have you considered that?'

'I want Rosalind West for my wife.'

'Don't be stupid,' his father said. 'You will ask Jennifer Erlhart to marry you. Your mother and I will never forgive you if you don't.'

Freddie didn't reply.

'Do you like being poor?' his father said. 'It's not as though we can sell. Somebody has to take this on and it's you. Well?'

'I don't love her.'

'You don't have to love her. She looks to me as though she'll bed all right and with luck you'll have sons. That's all you have to consider. She's suitable. You will ask her to marry you.'

There was dinner though Freddie didn't eat anything and afterwards, just as though she had known – no doubt she did – they went outside onto that same terrace and he followed her. It was the kind of evening which made you feel that you would never again want to go from this place and in a way, he thought, that would not be true. It had become a jailer, a debtor, it had become the whole world which he must hold aloft with his hands. He had not hated it before but he did now, the love was all destroyed on that day.

She wore a hideous blue dress in shiny material. It must, he thought stupidly, have cost a great deal of money. He couldn't breathe, he couldn't see. He stumbled over a non-existent step when he came outside and the air was so warm that there was a haze across the lawn, a coming down of white mist like a tent.

'You're leaving tomorrow?' he said.

'Yes.' She didn't look at him and he thought they bullied her into this, she doesn't want to marry me at all. 'We are . . . going back to London. I will be sorry to leave. You have such a beautiful house here.'

'You like it?'

'I love it. I couldn't believe it when I saw it.' She smiled. 'I thought lords lived in castles but you . . . you live in one of the most beautiful houses I have ever seen. I would give anything to live in a place like this.' She looked at him then, rather wildly, he thought.

'Jennifer—'

She rushed on. 'You can call me Jen if you like. My granny used to and I liked it so much. I shall miss you. You've been very kind to me even though I feel certain you wanted to be with your friends in London and . . . driving your cars.'

'Has your father said anything to you?'

She looked clearly at him. 'My father is a bully. He always has something to say. He wanted a son and if he couldn't have that he wanted a beautiful, slender, elegant daughter who would

70

say all the right things and be good at dancing and . . . all those other feminine things I can't manage.' She stopped and then she said quite suddenly, 'Don't do it.'

Freddie was astonished. He looked at her.

'Don't ask me to marry you. You don't want me.'

'What about you?'

'I shall have failed. He wants me to marry somebody with a house like this and a title and all the right connections and . . . He chose you. He thinks everything and everybody can be bought.'

'He may be right about that.'

'I've refused several men.'

'Have you? I didn't know that.'

'I couldn't marry any man I had no feeling for and I wouldn't like you to marry for such reasons either.'

'I have to,' Freddie admitted.

'I know. My father told me. He says he has you over a barrel. It doesn't sound nice. I have the feeling that this time I shall be sent away in disgrace. He dislikes me already. He will hate me if I can't marry someone of consequence but then . . . I could always go and live with my Aunt Freda in Connecticut. She's a very nice woman and has a circle of friends. It won't be very exciting of course because I shall be penniless but it can't be much worse than being rich and being wanted for that reason alone.'

'You don't think we could be friends?'

'I think it's probably very difficult to be friends when you're married.'

Beyond her Freddie could see the oak trees and he thought about the house and the buildings with the little windows, the clock tower and the green in the centre and the gardens across the road with the big lake where the ducks nested in the spring, the rhododendrons were twelve feet up and the trees were so high that if you tried to see the top of them you would fall over.

He thought of the walled garden which his mother had so much loved when she lived here where the lavender brushed against your legs in June and the thyme was silver and gold and gave off its heavy scent. He thought of the rooms he had played in when he was a child, of the way that the afternoon sun came in through the long floor-to-ceiling windows and he wiped Rosalind's face from his mind.

71

'Will you marry me, Jennifer?' he said.

'No,' she said and tried to run away.

He caught hold of her.

'No, don't do that to me,' she said.

'What do you mean?'

'No, don't do it, don't do it.'

Freddie took her into his arms and kissed her and her mouth came alive and she put her arms around his neck and responded, blindly and without guile, like somebody who had never been kissed before. When it was over she stood back as far as she could for somebody in an embrace and breathed quickly.

'Marry me,' Freddie said.

She was almost sobbing.

'You want to,' he accused her.

'No, I don't.'

'Yes, you do. You don't want to go home in disgrace or to Aunt Freda's. You want to stay here and marry me and get away from your bloody father. You can spend all day sitting over the library fire, reading, and I'll take you out to dinner and to dances and I won't tell you what to do and you will have everything you want because I'll make sure your father has to pay through the nose for the privilege. And best of all you'll be able to live here for the rest of your life. It's the most wonderful place in the world. In summer the night never comes down and in winter we have so much snow it's like a fairy tale. Stay here and marry me. Tell me you will. Tell me now. Marry me, Jennifer.'

He kissed her again, even harder than last time and she stopped trying to get away.

'Marry me.'

She took a deep breath.

'All right,' she said.

The light had gone from between the branches of the trees. Night had fallen very quickly, the sun had set. He had not noticed that long since the cream light spilled from the house onto the lawns and the sky had darkened. They went back inside and his parents and her parents and Sybil were there with champagne and congratulations.

It was like no other night had ever been. It was as though somebody else was being him and the person that he had been had become a small stone inside. Nobody could see him or hear the protests or realize that permanent damage had been done. Jennifer was happy, she was smiling and drinking champagne and her parents were smiling. Everybody was, even the new him. God, it was awful. The old him was hammering to be out, shouting until he was hoarse, but nobody took any notice.

Six

It was too warm for the gas fire. The weather had momentarily become sunshiny and bright. In a way it made things worse, knowing that Easter was fine in London and Freddie wasn't there. Rosalind wished it would rain. She had promised herself that she would do something constructive. All her friends had gone home for Easter and she had thought about it, that was how bad things were. She resolved to give Freddie up. She thought he had gone home. She couldn't be sure, he had not said anything definite, he had made vague noises when she had asked about the weekend.

She felt like one of her friends in the office who was going out with a married man. At weekends, at Easter, at Christmas, all the times when you would have liked to be with him he was not there. She thought that she knew he had not gone home with Jack but the idea wouldn't go away.

In the end she went round to Jack's house on Easter Sunday afternoon, just to clear her mind, to make sure, to escape the boredom. At first she thought he was out because she rang the bell and banged on the door and nothing happened. She was convincing herself that Jack and Freddie were in the north but a moment before she decided to go away, angry, Jack opened the door.

'I thought Freddie might be here,' she said.

'What the hell would he be doing here?' Jack said and went back inside, leaving the door open. She followed him. He went into the garden. It was rather overgrown but nicely so, she thought, not very untidy just interesting with grasses and shrubs in various shades of cream and green and it was a big garden with trees overhanging and little paths that appeared to go into mysterious nowhere so there was plenty of shade. It had a greenhouse at one end with nothing in it and a summer house near the wall at the back, again empty, and crazy-paving paths.

'Do you know where he is?' she said, sitting down on an old wooden seat under a willow tree.

'No idea.'

'Has he gone home?'

'Ros, I don't know where he is. I haven't seen him since the last time you were here together.'

'I'm going to give him up.'

'Good.'

'Why is it good?'

'He didn't like my car.'

'That isn't what you meant.'

Jack lay down on a rug on the grass beyond the wooden chairs and table which looked inviting, the day was surprisingly warm now that the sun had got out, and didn't answer. Rosalind got up and went to him and sat down beside him.

'You think I should?'

'Why ask me?'

'I have to ask somebody.'

Jack sat up and looked at her.

'How long's he been screwing you?'

'Jack!'

'Well?'

'That's not . . . that's not the point.'

'It bloody well is. I don't see anything on your left hand.'

'That's incredibly old fashioned.'

'Is it? And are those incredibly old-fashioned tears you're always crying over him?'

'It's – it's entirely up to me,' she said, rather annoyed at Jack's interference. 'You're archaic, do you know that? And – and you have double standards.'

'Double standards?'

'Yes. You think it's all right for men to go to bed with women they aren't going to marry but—'

'Did I say that? That isn't what I meant anyway and you

know it. Making your intentions clear from the beginning is different—'

'Yes, but who knows?'

'Didn't you know the first time you met him? I was there, remember.'

'You could see?'

'Can people see Blackpool illuminations in October?' Jack said.

'He felt the same way too. I know he did. So I assumed . . . only it isn't like that and I'm getting tired of waiting,' and then she said, ashamed, 'I'm going to try and stop seeing him soon.'

'But not now,' Jack observed as she searched for a handkerchief.

'He loves me, I know he does.'

'Then don't come to me crying.'

She wiped away the tears and lay down and watched the blue sky and she remembered something she had pushed away from her mind. She remembered Jack sliding down off the horse when she had shouted at him for riding her pony without permission. He had got her up against the side of the stable and kissed her.

He had tasted of apples, perhaps had even stolen them just before that from her father's garden and eaten them there in the paddock with the pony. And he had been incredibly rude and . . . She turned over towards him. He was watching her.

'I was fourteen,' he said apologetically.

'How did you know I was thinking about it?'

'You had the most gorgeous fat little backside, I couldn't help it. I fantasized for weeks. Sometimes even now . . . And it's gone. You can't think how disappointed I was when I saw you again.'

'I was a very overweight little girl.'

'Your breasts used to bounce up and down and your bottom did and . . . oh, God, those tight little trousers.'

'Jodhpurs,' she said, choking with laughter.

'You're so skinny now,' he said mournfully and then she realized he was making her laugh on purpose.

'I didn't mean to come and moan over you. Do you think he's gone home?'

'Probably. He always does at holidays.'

Jack lay back again and shut his eyes.

'I haven't met his parents,' Rosalind said.

'You haven't taken him to meet yours.'

'I wanted a ring on my finger first. I wanted to be able to show him off.' The tears were threatening again. She swallowed them but they came back until she had to let go of her breath in an effort to stem them. 'He's never going to marry me, I know he isn't, but I can't bring myself to believe it. I keep hanging on hoping something will happen and everything will be all right.'

Jack opened his eyes and sat up and she was sitting up too as though that would help stop the flow.

'Ros . . . ' he said and it sounded just like Freddie for once. She put her hands over her eyes and gave in.

Jack pulled her into his arms and she cried all over his shirt which had been so crisp and clean and white. He felt good. It took everything that she had not to lift her face so that he would kiss her. She knew that he would if she invited it but that he was in effect fighting her off.

Jack didn't have a woman, she knew he didn't and that it was deliberate. He could have had, he was successful and that meant everything here in this city and he was young and good looking and clever. There were men twenty years older than him who had not attained that respect. He had the ear of Sir Trevor and he was the only person. Sir Trevor believed in him, people spoke of him in soft voices and she knew that he had put everything at risk for this car, it was his obsession.

He had let nothing get in the way and that included women but she was close and he was hungry, she could feel that on him even though he did nothing except hold her carefully. He didn't even pull her nearer than she was. That was the kind of control which she had never met before. She was pretty and he wanted her. In such circumstances any other man would have put her down onto the rug and tried to make love to her.

It was not even that she didn't like him. When they had gone out to the pub at different times she had seen other women looking at him and she remembered how sweet his mouth had been. He wore expensive clothes and he was tall and dark and quiet and Rosalind knew that women could smell success and that it was the most powerful draw of all. He was competent and single-minded and ruthless, she knew that he was because even that close he didn't move his hands an inch the better to feel her against him.

Nothing would stand in his way, no complicated relationship would be more to him than his ambition. That little white car mattered to him more than sex, more than comfort or companionship. It was a lonely world, just himself and the car, and he had deliberately put himself there, beyond the limits of other people, he had bargained and risked everything.

If it failed, and she knew very well by now that the signs were that it would, he would be finished, people would laugh, some of them who were jealous would enjoy his defeat and nobody would ever take him seriously again. Yet she could not forget the taste of his mouth that sunny morning, the autumn day when she had shouted at him to get off the pony and he had looked defiantly at her and slid down.

He wouldn't know that it was the first kiss anybody had ever given her and it was so good that she had remembered. She didn't ever taste an apple now without thinking of his mouth and the feeling of him pressed against her and how he had slipped his hands down her back until they cupped her bottom. She had been indignant, thinking in her childish way how offensive that he had done it.

She smiled and stopped crying and drew back and looked at him.

'You're a saint,' she said.

'Aye, I am,' Jack said and he smiled.

Seven

Jack was at work early, long before Rosalind got there. She was very late, he thought after a while. That wasn't like her, she was on time almost to the minute. He couldn't understand it unless she was ill but she would ring and tell him. Maybe she was just too upset about Freddie to come into work.

There was to be a grand exhibition, with the press invited and all the important people. It was two months away and the car was not finished. He doubted now whether it ever would be.

He had got to the stage where he didn't care if it failed, where he was pleased to imagine himself back in the little village where he had been a child, where he thought he could enjoy normality, the relief of never having to be here again, of not waking in the morning after another night of not sleeping well and know that he did not have to face this problem again.

All he wanted was to go back there and not have to do this, not have to do impossible things every minute of his life. He didn't care any more. He wished that he could wake up like he had done when he was little and his mother would be singing some Charles Wesley hymn in the kitchen.

She always sang in the mornings and the smell of bacon would waft its way up the narrow stairs and he could hear his father's voice soft in the kitchen. He wanted the fells, he wanted the big space behind the garage where the buses lived, he wanted not to have to face this again.

There were to be final tests soon out in the Cotswolds. He had assembled a team and they would go there and hopefully the little car would perform well enough so that he could sleep and eat and talk to people without thinking any more. He couldn't even give it its name though it was well enough known by now. To name it was to display before the world a vulnerability which terrified him. He went into his office and closed the door and tried not to think about it.

Only moments later the door opened. Nobody knocked and Jack turned, for once his temper rising. It was Freddie. He didn't want visitors, he didn't want anybody spoiling his concentration and already it was gone. Where was Ros that she hadn't stopped him?

'Don't walk in here like that!' he barked but Freddie just shut the door and didn't retreat or say anything, almost as though he was not there or had not heard.

'I hear you're going to Bath,' he said after a very long pause. He didn't look at Jack, Jack wasn't sure why. 'May I come?'

It was on Jack's lips to tell him no he bloody couldn't, he could sod off but it was as though a great big wave had swamped the office. Jack could just about see it burst through the walls and past the door, the place was almost destroyed by it and yet nothing had happened.

'I just assumed that you would,' he said.

'But you didn't ask me.'

'I didn't think you needed to be asked. You beyond anybody wanted to drive the car, or at least the car you thought I was designing. You all right?'

Freddie looked at him as though there was a fog in front of his eyes.

'I want to drive it,' he said doggedly.

Jack relented. 'Hey, man,' he said, 'I built it for you.'

Freddie smiled. It took an effort, Jack thought, but he did. 'You sure you're all right?' he said.

It was half-past nine when Rosalind finally turned up. Jack went through. He was inclined to shout at her, the telephone had not stopped ringing in the last hour and he was damned if he was going to answer it but he didn't and was glad he hadn't, she was so pale.

'I'm sorry.'

'Don't you feel well?'

'I just . . . Bernice said Freddie had been in. I haven't seen him. I didn't realize he was back.'

'It was just to ask if he could come to Bath with us.'

'He needed to ask?'

'That's what I said. Shall I get you some coffee?'

'Thanks. I will stay late to make up—'

'Oh, be quiet. I don't care.' It wasn't true, they both knew it, but he didn't want to put her through any wringer at this stage, he needed her in Bath and he needed a lot of work doing towards that.

Rosalind didn't hear from Freddie that evening though she waited and waited for him to contact her. The following day she went to work and made certain she wasn't late. She tried hard to concentrate.

That evening when she got back Freddie was standing leaning against the side of the building with his head down. She stopped short, just as she turned the corner, looked long at him. She was so relieved for several seconds and then the feeling died as she looked at him.

Rain was pouring down and he seemed to be unaware of it as though he had been standing there for a long time. There was something different about him, she thought. He looked unhappy but in a concentrated kind of way like people did when they had just met with disaster.

She had to stop herself from running to him, shouting his name, being glad, as he leaned against the wall. She tried to harden her heart against him but he stood there with his hair in his eyes, his head down and his hands in his pockets and she couldn't. She wanted to ask him why he had gone, why he hadn't taken her with him, tell him how she had missed him, how pleased she was to see him but the words wouldn't come.

He had not waited at the house like this since they had first met, he always stood outside the office building if he wanted to see her and they had not made some arrangement. He looked up and his eyes were icy cold, like a frozen blue sea, and it was as though somebody gripped a hand tightly around Rosalind's heart.

'Is something wrong?' she said.

She put her key to the door while he hesitated and her heart did horrible things.

'Come in.'

'No.'

If he wouldn't even come inside it must be something awful.

The blossom was all out on the trees in London but here in this dark street there was nothing to show that it was spring beyond the sunshine during the day. The nights were still sharp and some of them were frosty and the cold night was stealing in past the shadows with rain. Rosalind's hands were beginning to shake what with the cold and his refusal and she could see that something had happened and that he did not want to be here.

'You must come inside,' she said, 'it's too cold to linger out here.'

He followed her in without another word. They went in and up the dark shadowed stairs which always seemed more gloomy in bad weather but she tried not to think about it, she always thought that she would not be there much longer, that sooner or later he would ask her to marry him and then everything would be all right.

She spent many hours thinking and planning how she would take him home and proudly introduce him to her parents and how he would take her up to his estate in North Tynedale and she would see her future home for the first time.

She hadn't thought much about who she would be but she had thought a great deal about wonderful things like how she would be the mistress there and how she would be so happy with him. It was meant to be, she knew it was. Nobody had loved anybody more than they had loved one another. It was fated, written in the stars, undeniable. She felt as though her life had only begun when she met him and as though it was complete because of him.

She had heard tales of his house with its huge rooms, big floor-to-ceiling windows, valuable paintings, antique furniture, acres of gardens, lakes, the quarry garden and she would make him happy there. He had not been happy there so far, she could tell, even though he never said anything. He was happy here with her and they had been happy together almost always and a little song began inside her.

She would not be bored or worried because he was there. He always brightened the days. Perhaps one of his parents was ill or he had problems at work but she felt certain it was something which could be sorted out.

The room felt damp and the gas fire made a horrid little hissing sound when it was lit and the room was very cold, the rain throwing itself in great swathes at the window. Beyond it the roofs were shiny and wet and looked so unfriendly that she was glad to be inside even here and she wanted to turn to him and tell him like people did in films that it was time for him to take her away from all this and he would laugh but it was true, she had had enough of this dreadful little flat.

She was tired of trying to keep up with his friends, tired of putting up with them. She was tired of London. She wanted to be away in Northumberland, for them to be married and happy and have children. It was their future, she knew it was. She wanted all that now, it was time. She had waited long enough.

'Did you have a bad time when you were at home? Shall I make you some tea and kiss it all better?' and she smiled encouragingly and would have gone to him but he shook his head.

'I've got something to tell you,' he said.

'I'll make the tea.'

'No,' he caught her by the arm as she went past him towards the tiny galley kitchen, 'just let me say it, please.' And then he didn't. She stood still for so long that she wanted to scream but she made herself be patient and wait while he didn't look at her or the room or anything.

She wanted to prompt him and then she wanted not to because she had the feeling that once he had said whatever it was he so obviously couldn't manage that nothing would ever be the same again.

'I'm getting married.'

She had been right. There was nothing in world after that but the ugly little room and them. She stared at him.

'I've . . . I've got to,' he said.

Rosalind could hardly speak but she managed.

'You've got somebody pregnant?'

He nearly smiled. 'No. No, of course I haven't.' He stood for such a long time with his head down. 'You're the only person I love in the whole world. I shouldn't say that now, it's useless and . . . unfair.'

He was beginning to cry. Rosalind was appalled. She knew very well that eleven years of boarding school meant you didn't cry, no matter how much pain you were in. And he wasn't lying about loving her, she knew he wasn't. He stood like a child in total despair so that she couldn't see the tears, one hand arched over his eyes.

'How can you be marrying somebody else?' someone asked. Someone else was asking questions and behaving normally. It could have nothing to do with her.

'For money.' He took the hand away and his eyelashes were all wet and when he could he went on, 'If things had been different . . . ' He stopped there, and then he said, 'I would have asked you to stay with me but I know you won't do that. I know I'm going to lose you. I can't ask you to do that.

'I know that you're so . . . respectable and that it's important to you to be married and have children and lead a normal life. I know you couldn't face your parents otherwise. I just pretended to myself that somehow it would be all right. I can't help what I am, I can't be something else for you.'

'Who is she?'

'She's an American. She's called Jennifer Erlhart.'

'Rich?'

'Oh yes, millions and millions.'

'Pretty?'

'Not in the least. She doesn't even want to marry me. I had to talk her into it. I don't have any choice. We are in a bad way financially. I'm sorry.'

Rosalind couldn't understand what was going on, it was just a nightmare, she would come round in her bed in a minute.

'But what about me?' she said. And when he didn't reply she said, 'You weren't ever going to ask me to marry you, were you?'

'No.'

'But you love me. You made love to me. What if there'd been a baby?'

'I was always careful,' he said, 'and there isn't, but . . . '

She stared at him. Even if they had had a child he wouldn't have married her. How on earth would she ever have told her parents? How would she have coped? To be discarded, to be second best. She shuddered over the very idea of being in a worse position than this.

'But how could you . . . how could you . . . '

'I don't know. All I know is that when I'm with you I never get bored and I never want to leave, I always want to be there with you. I've never felt like that about anybody else in my whole life. Nobody.'

She stared at him for so long that she felt dizzy.

'I should go,' he said.

'No! No, you can't. You can't do this.'

'I have. We're being married later in the year at the chapel at White Maddens and after that . . . '

'You can't marry her.' Rosalind could hear somebody shouting.

'I have no choice.'

'That isn't true. People always have a choice. We could run away.'

'I can't.'

'You mean you've made your choice. That's what you mean.'

'The place is falling down,' he said, looking at her. 'It's my responsibility.'

'It's a house! It's nothing but a bloody house! How can you possibly give me up for a house?' When he didn't answer she said, 'I don't believe you ever loved me—'

'I did. I do.'

'If you had you would have married me. That's what people do when they love each other, that's the whole point of it so that they can live together and marry and have children. What else is there? There's nothing. What on earth will I do with the rest of my life now?'

He tried to go and she tried to stop him. She cried and pulled at him and stood in front of the door and pleaded and begged. She could not afterwards bear to think that she had tried to coax him into marrying her. She was so ashamed of herself. But he went.

He put her aside, she thought as gently as he could, and after that she felt as if everything was over, that nothing in the world would ever matter any more and she would be left here in this dreadful little room and she would never see him again.

She felt as though she didn't want to live, it hurt so much, as though there was nothing left, as though there never would be anything more that would matter. She wondered how you got rid of yourself so that you didn't have to put up with this, whether you could throw yourself off a bridge and it would stop hurting but she had the feeling, from childhood visits to church, that you would be consigned to the eternal fire for doing such things so there wasn't even that left to you.

She hated everything, this flat, him, London, that she was not good enough, that he had chosen somebody else. She hated the woman he was going to marry. She wished she could murder her.

Jack couldn't settle, he couldn't stop thinking about the look in Freddie's eyes when he had called in at the office the day before and in the end he did something unprecedented, he went to Freddie's sister's house. He hadn't been there before and he didn't know why he was going there now, he had no invitation.

He had been at work and about to go home and do some more work but for some reason he didn't. He could not remove from his mind the sight of Freddie in his office the day before, the white face, the lack of words, the mood, the vagueness and how Freddie had not met his gaze.

There was no reply from the door but when he opened it it gave. There was no light in the house and no warmth. The rooms were big and cold. Who the hell would want to live in such a place? It wasn't a house, it was a bloody barn and must be worth a fortune, right here in the middle of London. He stood just inside the door and said, 'Freddie, you in?'

He felt for the light switch and when it came on it showed up the furniture, some of it amazing, gold tables with marble tops, big sideboard-type furniture with shiny bits inlaid in the wood, lots of uncomfortable-looking chairs with long backs, thin legs and satin seats. There were stone pillars in the hall which was marble-floored and a staircase went up one flight in gold and black wrought iron and then branched two ways with a wide sweep. The building echoed when he spoke.

'Freddie?'

He walked in further and it was all creaking floorboards past various oak doors, darkness, some of the rooms under holland covers, the thick curtains pulled across the windows making it look even worse, and the rooms had black and white marble fireplaces, hideous things, ornate. He went through into a big living room and here a single table lamp was lit, there were little round tables and chairs placed here and there and a grand piano further over.

Books lined the walls, there was the odd rug here and there and Freddie was sitting on the hearth rug as though the fire was lit which it was not. He was leaning back against the nearest armchair, regarding the white-marble fireplace with interest.

'Freddie?' Jack said again and then he knew that his instincts had been correct

'Now then,' Freddie said, in good northern style, but Jack was not deceived.

'Now. You all right?'

'Fine.'

'No money for the meter?' A joke. Where had that come from?

'What?'

'The fire.'

'Oh.'

Jack went over and got down and lit the gas fire. When he was satisfied that the fire would at some time in the next month lift the room to a decent temperature he went off and found the kitchen, put on lights in there. There was nobody about, no signs that anybody had been there. No washing up, no food. Freddie was obviously alone in this enormous house.

There was a great big long table in the centre of the room and dressers with lots of blue-and-white serving plates and some big old stove and copper pans hanging from the ceiling and various little rooms off the kitchen which he did not explore. He went around all the cupboards and in the end there was a bottle of whisky in one of them. He found crystal glasses in another.

He went back and sat down on the rug at the opposite side of the fireplace against another chair and he poured out the liquid and offered a glass to Freddie and when he had taken it Jack said, 'Somebody break your toy soldiers?'

'Not as bad as that.'

'What, then?'

'I'm getting married.'

Jack sighed and leaned back against the chair and sipped at the whisky. It was good stuff, single malt. Freddie didn't drink the whisky, he set the glass down and put a hand over his eyes like a plug in a sink. After a while he picked up the glass and downed the whisky in one.

'Want some more?' Jack offered.

'Yes.'

'It's not Ros, then?'

'No.'

Jack poured him some more.

'You told me.'

'I did. When?' Freddie finally looked at him and Jack saw the bleakness in his eyes and he wondered why he hadn't recognized it yesterday.

'When we were in Durham at Christmas but you went ahead and laid her anyway.'

'It was her choice.'

'Bollocks!' Jack said. 'She thought you would get married. She didn't believe all that upper-class stuff about houses and things. She thought you loved her.' He got up.

'I do love her.'

86

'You've got a funny way of showing it.'

'I can't help that.' Freddie's eyes were wet. 'Don't go on at me. For Christ's sake just don't.'

'How could you—'

'She'll get over it.'

'Do you know every time somebody says that to me about something I always want to bloody hit them. It's the most stupid expression in the English language. For God's sake, don't you care about her?'

'Of course I care about her.' Freddie sat there completely miserable but his eyes fired.

'Then why don't you just run away and get married?'

'I can't! Don't you understand anything? Are you really this stupid?'

'I'm stupid? You're giving up the woman you say you love for a bloody house and a moor!'

'It isn't. I can't let my family down like that. I can't do it. I can't put my personal happiness first.'

'So why didn't you let her alone in the first place?'

That brought silence.

'Did you think you could have both?' Jack said.

'I just . . . ' His voice was very slight, very quiet. 'I just wanted to have something for mine.'

'You've got half of fucking Northumberland! Isn't that enough?'

'That's not mine. You don't ever own the land, you just . . . you just look after it.'

'I never heard anything quite so ridiculous,' Jack said and it seemed to him that his voice echoed in all the emptiness of this God-awful monument to the upper classes. 'Who looks after Rosalind West?'

'As long as it's not you.'

'Oh, sod off,' Jack said.

'Have you never laid anybody you couldn't keep your hands off?'

'No.'

'No, you bloody wouldn't,' Freddie said and Jack was glad that he was at least that animated. 'I've never seen control like you have. The trouble is you think everybody should have it and I haven't.'

'Well,' Jack sat back and finished his whisky and poured

87

himself some more, 'maybe everybody shouldn't. Maybe it isn't a good thing.'

'It is a good thing, Jack, I've always admired it in you.'

'Nice to know you've always admired something about me,' Jack said and awarded himself points when Freddie smiled.

'When's the wedding?'

'I don't know. Later in the year, Christmas maybe.'

'It's a nice time to get married.'

'I want you to be my best man.'

'Me? No, you don't.'

'Yes, I do.'

'I'm not going to fit in there.'

'Please, Jack.' Freddie held out his glass for more whisky.

'Have you told Rosalind about the wedding?'

'Yes.'

'When did you do that?'

'Earlier on. I went and stood outside her flat until she came home.'

'I see,' Jack said.

'Do me a favour. Go and see her.'

'I thought you didn't want me to.'

'I'm worried.'

'Is she by herself?'

'She has nobody here except you.'

Jack was caught then. He didn't want to leave Freddie alone in such a state but then he didn't want not to go to Rosalind. God knew what she was like.

'Please go and see her.' Freddie took the whisky from him and filled up his glass.

'You will just sit there and get drunk?'

'I would rather you did.'

'I'll come back.'

'No, don't,' Freddie said, 'there's no need. And besides . . . I have to go home.'

'You won't drive in that state?'

'I'll get a taxi and then the train.'

Somehow, as Jack got to his feet, he understood.

'I'm so bloody sorry,' he said.

Freddie lifted glacial eyes.

'You always wanted her, didn't you?'

'Yes.'

'Now's your chance.'

'Could anything be more perfect?' Jack said. 'I want you to come to Bath. You will still come, won't you?'

'Of course I will. You built the number one for me. I'll always be eternally grateful to you for it.'

'You will shite,' Jack said. 'You've done nothing but bloody criticize all the way through,' and Freddie smiled again and he said, 'I'll be there.'

'I shall expect you to be. I can't do the tests properly without you. You won't forget?'

'No.'

Jack walked slowly out of the house. Freddie poured more whisky as he did so.

It was warmer outside. Jack drove the car across town to Rosalind's flat.

He didn't want to be involved but his conscience wouldn't let him go home. He banged on the door. His hands hurt with all the noise they were making. Eventually the woman who lived in the flat nearest the door heard him, recognized him and let him in. Jack took the stairs two at a time and when he reached the third floor he banged on the door of the flat, hard. He spent several minutes doing this and then shouting her name.

'Ros! Ros, it's Jack.'

Finally the door opened just a little way and she peered around it. She looked like an orphan, skinny, her face red and creased from crying, her hair all over the place and a pale despairing look about her.

'Can I come in?'

She searched his face as though she had already forgotten his presence and held open the door wider. She was not even wearing a sweater. The flat looked so stark and lonely. Night had settled outside with rain. She would have closed the door as she realized his intention but Jack got himself into the room.

'What are you doing here?' she said.

'Why don't you come home with me?'

'No, I . . . ' She tried to turn away and be normal.

'I know what happened. Come on.'

'How do you know?' She looked at him, frowning.

'I went to see him.'

'Why on earth did you do that?'

'I just thought something wasn't right.'

She laughed.

'Come on. Let's get out of here,' Jack said and he got her coat from behind the door, pushed her handbag at her and ushered her out of the flat. She didn't resist. She didn't seem to know where she was or what she was doing.

She stared from the car window.

'Is he all right?'

'He's devastated. Why wouldn't he be?'

'Did he tell you he's getting married to a rich American girl?'

'Yes, he told me.'

'Why couldn't I be a rich American girl?'

'You're better than that. You're a beautiful north-country girl.'

Jack drove his car into the garage. It was a 1949 Jaguar Mark V, cream, drophead, absolutely gorgeous, so that even he usually enjoyed driving it. Tonight he felt he couldn't enjoy anything. He helped her out of the car and into the house. She stood disconsolately in the hall and stared around her as though she had never been there before and he could not help but think how lovely she was, how even for work she dressed so well.

She was appropriately wearing black but her eye make-up had run and made black rivulets down her face and the pony-tail which had caught the rain between the house and the garage was sleek black. She looked like a nun, he thought, her face wide with hurt, her eyes huge and dismayed, as though she did not really believe what was happening. In spite of what she had told Jack he knew now that she had always really believed Freddie would marry her, she had to believe to go on because she cared for him so much.

'How could he do this to me?' she said. 'Why didn't he tell me we weren't going to be married? Why didn't I know? What stupid conceited girl thought she could marry some-body like him? He loves me, I know he does.'

Jack led her through and put a match to the sitting-room fire. It was a very modern fire, set in the wall, and it gave off a lot of heat. The logs burned reassuringly and he made tea and tried to get her to drink it and she couldn't. She sat way back on his white sofa and took off her shoes and pulled her legs up under her and a cushion to her stomach and she kept saying, 'Do you think he'll be all right?'

Jack didn't say much, he just sat there with her and tried to be reassuring and later in the middle of the night when he had found her some pyjamas – still in their plastic wrapping, where had they come from? – and put her into bed with a hot-water bottle and a glass of brandy he waited until she slept, he even went into the bedroom to make sure of her even breathing and then he got the car out and went over to Claudia's house, he was so worried about Freddie.

It was in darkness and the doors were locked. He hammered on the door and shouted several times but nobody answered. He tried to comfort himself that Freddie would have gone north but that made him think of Freddie driving when he was upset and drunk, even though he had said he would not, perhaps he had lost all judgement and done so and that was even worse. In the end there was nothing to do but go home.

She was still sleeping. He ventured into the room and checked. He sat over the fire until it was almost daybreak, he couldn't sleep. He wanted to tear north after Freddie and demand that he should come back, that he couldn't possibly marry some other girl but he did not want to leave Rosalind. There was nothing to be done, he thought, nothing at all.

Eight

The weather was foul in the Cotswolds. They stayed in Bath and some stupid bastard, Jack didn't remember who, had recommended the hotel. He hated Bath with a true hatred that only a northerner could have managed. It was so sodding polite, so bloody middle class, prissy, out of date, all so Jane Austen you could imagine her characters prancing up and down the streets near you in their stupid outfits.

Bath buns and tea all over the place, pianists, even bloody string quartets where people drank the water, white table-cloths, cakes, waitresses with black uniforms and white pinnies.

The hotel was meant to be one of the best that Bath could offer. God help everybody else, Jack thought. It had the kind of atmosphere which would have made a brave man shudder. He was convinced somebody had died in his room, the air felt so heavy. He flung open the windows and there was a lovely view of gardens behind, long lawns and a summer house at the far end and big wide spreading trees but it did not ease the feeling.

He had insisted on Rosalind being there. She had tried to refuse.

'I can't go where he is. Don't you understand anything?' she said.

They were in the office at the time. Jack made himself look at her. She was in a bad way and he was very worried about her. He thought she might have some kind of breakdown. He was afraid to leave her anywhere alone, he had the horrible feeling she might do something nasty. He played what he thought was the right card.

'You're my secretary. I need you there.'

'I can't.' She slammed out of his office into hers. Jack followed her, feigning anger.

'Try to be professional. This is what you get paid for and it's a damned sight more bloody important than your personal relationships.'

She glared at him. Jack held the look.

'How am I to face him?' she said.

'You've done nothing wrong. Why shouldn't you face him?'

'Because . . . ' Her lower lip wobbled. She caught her teeth into it to stop it. 'He was everything I wanted.'

'Really? Are you sure it wasn't just the illusion you wanted?'

'What do you mean?'

Jack tried not to think about her white face and the shadows under her eyes as though she'd been knocked about.

'You wanted a man who was happy to lay you, knowing that he could never marry you? Did he ever tell you that? He told me, ages ago.' Jack would have gone on with this but he was quite aware she couldn't stand it. If he couldn't make her

92

find some kind of anger against Freddie she would never get past it, and the bastard was just too worthless for her to spoil her life over him.

She would probably be of very little use in Bath but he had no intention of leaving her in London to brood.

'Come to Bath. You can be miserable there and useful.'

'You're such a comfort,' she said.

'I'm not here to be a comfort. I need your help, this is the most important thing we've ever done. I've spent years working towards it. I'm not having it scuppered because Freddie Harlington has chosen to marry some fat foreign bitch. Go home and pack,' he told her and then he walked through into his office and closed the door, hoping to God he hadn't said too much but just sufficient so that she would go with him. If she didn't he couldn't possibly either because he couldn't rest to concentrate without her, and how in the hell would he ever explain to Sir Trevor that he needed to be in London to keep an eye on his secretary?

Jack wasn't sure whether Freddie would be in Bath but he was and Jack was so relieved because he needed Freddie there to test the little car, he was the best driver they had. He had been ninety per cent sure that Freddie would come to Bath in spite of everything because he wanted the car so badly but all the way down there Jack argued with himself that maybe it would have been better if he had told Freddie he couldn't, that they would manage without him, that Rosalind would be better without him. Freddie might come just because she was there, like picking scabs off a wound, Jack thought, wincing.

They drove. For once Jack drove himself. He didn't think about the road or the car. He didn't think about the tests. She went with him and nobody spoke between London and Bath.

It was surprising how things took on perspective. The weather was dreadful, it didn't stop raining, and the food in the hotel was the worst he had ever encountered. He sent it back at every meal and gained himself a reputation for being difficult that first day. It was cold or overdone or badly cooked or just inedible. His mother would have had a fit if she had seen it.

The bed was uncomfortable so he didn't sleep, it was rock hard and so were the pillows. From dawn until dark the next day they tested the cars in the cold rain until everybody was shouting except Freddie and Rosalind.

Freddie was completely silent but after the first day Jack knew he changed. Freddie, for all his height, was built exactly right for the little car or was it that the car had been built for him? Strange. Somehow Jack knew that after meeting Freddie, driving with him, seeing his ability, he had tailored the car to suit so that it fitted perfectly.

Freddie drove the number one and it was poetry, music, it was a pure delight like a bird soaring for Jack, watching him learn how to drive it. It was a new way of driving and Freddie took to it with his fine instincts as though he had been made for it. He did handbrake turns like some men did ballet and high-speed cornering with grace. When the last of the light was gone he came to Jack and his eyes were shining.

'You bastard,' he said, 'it was brilliant. I want to take it to Norway in September and rally it.'

Freddie and Rosalind avoided looking at one another over dinner. Freddie ate because he was mentally still in the car and Rosalind didn't touch any food and looked to Jack like she was losing weight every day. The other members of the team drank champagne and congratulated one another.

The news of Freddie's engagement had been published in the newspapers. Everybody in London seemed to have seen it but nobody mentioned it.

That night was the first time that Jack let himself believe he had not made a mistake. There were still things wrong with the car but he could see how to deal with them and it was doing everything he had said it would do and he could see it as a separate thing away from him, the ideas almost complete, the car a being on its own and not his brainchild.

He was still worried, he still doubted, there was no guarantee that it would sell but if he could get the journalists to believe it was a breakthrough and encourage the rally drivers to take it on the publicity would make a great deal of difference.

After dinner he and Rosalind sat in his room with the windows slightly open even though the rain was cold because the room was so heavy. She typed up her notes at the table near the window and Jack sat on the bed and made more notes, many of which she claimed were indecipherable.

'What is this?' she said, getting up and going over. He looked hard at it.

'It says "steering".'

'It doesn't, Jack, it doesn't say anything of the kind. It wouldn't make sense if it did.'

Rosalind had been dreading Bath but armed with a notebook, a pen and the relief of work she stayed close to Jack. He had said that he needed her there and it was not a sop, he really did. He walked around frowning a great deal that first day.

She couldn't sleep, she couldn't rest. The night seemed endless and when the dawn came her eyes ached from lack of rest. She didn't eat anything either and then night came down again and she didn't know how she would stand it.

In the end, on the second night, at about one in the morning, she fled next door into Jack's room. They had connecting rooms for some reason but the key was on her side. She turned it and went in because she could hear nothing and her heart was pounding.

He was not asleep. The lights over the bed were burning. He was not even undressed. He was sitting on the bed as he had been when she had left him for the night and was writing furiously. He looked up. Rosalind put her hands over her front. She had not stopped for a dressing gown, she was afraid that if she hesitated she would not go to him, he would get the wrong idea or any idea, she would stay where she was and . . . She went in and closed the door.

'Still working?'

'Nearly finished.'

The nightdress had been bought for Freddie's benefit though not worn. She had not needed nightwear or any kind of clothes when he was there in bed with her and he had not encouraged her to be modest, she was only just now remembering such things. It was very short with tempting fastenings below its plunging neckline. She couldn't think why she had brought it with her, just that she wasn't thinking clearly about anything. She blushed now and brought her hands up in front of her.

'Here.' Jack got up and pulled a blanket off the bed and gave that to her. She wrapped it carefully around her.

'I wasn't trying to do a femme fatale thing,' she explained with a slight smile.

'I didn't notice,' he said flatly.

'Shall I go—'

'No, it's fine. Sit down. Sit. I just have to finish this.'

'How long will it take?'

'I don't know.'

She sat down. He didn't talk to her, he didn't stop working, he didn't even look up again and gradually with the blanket around her and the slight noise of his pen scratching on the paper she began to feel safe and warm and drowsy.

'Jack?'

'Mm?'

'Do you mind if I lie down?'

'Help yourself.'

The last thing she saw was Jack sitting writing and it was oddly comforting.

When Jack was quite sure she was fast asleep he stopped writing and looked down at her. She was huddled there, wrapped in the blanket he had given her, in the foetal position, like a little girl and Jack thought what kind of man could make her give herself to him when there was no hope of a decent relationship? It was so selfish on Freddie's part.

And he knew that men would say of such things, 'I couldn't help it,' but the thing was that that was the point. If you put yourself first like that, if you gave in to your worse self, then it produced this kind of thing. Had Freddie no integrity whatsoever? That was the trouble, really. He had been raised without it, given elevated ideas, his ego was so huge because of who he was that he could not stand the pain of doing the right thing and it was disgusting, it was not to be borne.

How could Freddie live with being the person who had done such a thing? And yet amongst the things that men had done it was not considered so very terrible. Maybe people were the better for breaking one another's hearts but he didn't think so.

Jack moved the papers off the bed and he got another blanket out of the wardrobe and put it over her. She stirred in her sleep.

'It's all right,' he said softly and she smiled as though she was having a good dream.

Jack put out the lights and opened the windows wide. It

was still raining. He liked the sound of it. In a way when he worked the rain was like music, somehow the rhythm of the rain and the rhythms in his head went together and he could work better that way. He liked having her there, even though she didn't want to be. At least he did not have to worry about her, alone in London. He vowed he would never let her out of his sight ever again.

In some ways, for Freddie, the first days with the car were the best, in the Cotswolds, like the beginning of a love affair, learning how to speak and when not to, the look and the feel and the wanting to be there and because Rosalind was present, even with things as bad as they were between them, it was better.

He would not forgive himself for what he had done but he felt as though if she were just there, if he could only see her, then he would survive. There was nothing left but the little car and himself and he thought it was funny but he had always thought Jack with his ideas and the car and everything else obsessed to madness and now it was as if they had changed places.

There were great marks under Rosalind's eyes and all the time she searched for Jack, like a child with a parent. When he went out of her sight she followed him and at night, Freddie thought with anguish, she slept in Jack's room, he had seen them coming out together in the early morning for breakfast and she kept close, sometimes even holding on to Jack's arm as though he too was about to run off and leave her. It made Freddie's heart ache to know and that he had no rights here.

What they did in Jack's room he tried not to think, though Jack did not look to him like a man who was having a good time in bed. Bedding a woman who was in love with another man was hardly his style and Freddie did not think that Rosalind looked at Jack as she had looked at him. Selfishly, he hoped not.

She looked at him no more and that was only bearable as long as he could drive the car. It was the only thing left which made him feel good.

They had been there for three days before he and Rosalind came face to face alone, too close not to speak. She met his eyes without flinching, he was the one who looked away but then he was the guilty one. He could not even ask her to forgive him. He would have gone, they were in the hall upstairs in the hotel, but she caught hold of his arm with her thin fingers and said, 'I wish you wouldn't drive so fast, it won't make things better.'

'It's the only thing that does. Besides, what does it matter now?'

'Don't say things like that. It does matter. You matter . . . to me.'

The pain was physical, it held him back against the wall. He didn't even remember how to breathe. There were voices from along the hall so when he opened his eyes she had gone down the stairs and no doubt into the throng of people in the bar. Jack would be there and she would hover beside him, not touching but close. Freddie went on up to his room and closed the door.

They were there a week. For the first three days Rosalind didn't notice much beyond the work and Freddie but after that the weather was bitterly cold and wet with a wind behind it and everything seemed to her to become increasingly difficult, not least of all Jack. He was so demanding.

They were friends and he was gentle with her but as the numbness of Freddie's leaving her began to wear off, when she saw him and felt pain she noticed everything else more somehow. She was sleeping in Jack's room every night – and the night before she had slept in his arms though he had slept inside one blanket and she in another, and that was too close – she began to resent everything.

There was no shelter while they did the testing and the rain and wind and cold did not stop him, nor did it stop him from insisting that what he wanted doing should be done. He worked at a frenetic pace. There was no time for coffee, there was no lunch. He dictated rapidly all day and she had to follow him around. He shouted. She had never heard Jack shout so much before. He shouted at her, he shouted at the mechanics, he shouted at Freddie and the other drivers.

He used language which she hadn't heard him use before and it sounded twice as bad in his thick dark northern accent which was even more northern when he was motivated like this and frustrated. In the horrible conditions he barked out orders all day, mostly from beneath cars or beside them. She had imagined that the drivers would be the ones to fume and curse and swear and complain when things went wrong but they didn't, they stood around making reasonable remarks in the pouring rain.

Jack didn't notice, he didn't know what he was saying as far as she could tell. He didn't know that it was raining, he was totally unaware of anything except what he was doing and what he could get other people to do, even against their own judgement or their own wills. Rosalind had never seen concentration like that. Her feet and fingers were numb and even when it grew dark, as the week went on, he seemed to think time was short and they used what lights they had or could rig up and at ten o'clock at night when she was almost in tears Jack was still peering into an engine by flashlight.

He argued with the mechanics, long after they didn't argue back and everybody was pale and quiet and tired and people kept going off and smoking and swearing in private when he was out of earshot but they were silent and obedient to his demands when he was there and it was endless to her. The fifth day was so bad that by teatime Rosalind went and cried behind a tree.

'What's going on?' said an icy voice behind her. 'I need you to write this down.'

'I'm cold and tired and hungry and I want to go home.'

'Not yet,' he said curtly.

'I'm not doing any more.'

'You can go and sit in the car for a few minutes.'

He meant his car. She turned around and glared at him.

'You've got all the bloody windows open! It's wetter in there than it is out here.'

'The conditions are going to change tomorrow. We can't stop now.'

'I can't do any more, Jack.'

He threw her a look that would have stopped a tiger. His eyes narrowed. 'Oh, yes, you will,' he said.

Rosalind had no idea either that she would remember this or that she was going to lose her temper. She hadn't lost it with Freddie, she hadn't lost it all this week even though things were so difficult and Jack was scary and unpredictable except when they slept.

She covered the short distance between them and hit him several times, firstly with the flat of her hand and when that hurt too much to go on with clenched fists and all the time she cried and the tears ran cold down her cheeks until she didn't know which was rain and which wasn't.

'I hate you. I bloody well hate you! You impossible bastard!'

Jack fended her off fairly well so that there wasn't much damage and then he pulled her in against him so that she couldn't hit him any more. He brought his mouth down on hers and it was such a relief, his arms solid against her back and the rain like a damp blanket all around. That was the first time she had wanted him badly and when she remembered what a betrayal it was to the memory of her love for Freddie and tried to get away he pulled her even closer and kissed her even harder and his will changed everything for good somehow.

She didn't feel alone any more. She got her arms up around his neck, put herself as close to him as she could and gave him her mouth just as she had with Freddie and never with anyone else and she thought if they had been anywhere but here she would have given herself to him gladly. It was the only place she wanted to be.

Finally she said, 'I'm sorry, I didn't mean to—'

'It'll be all right, really it will,' he said and he looked straight into her eyes and he seemed so calm.

He let her go. She tried to smile.

'I didn't mean to hit you. Are you hurt?'

'Course not.' He smiled at her.

'You taste of apples,' she said.

'I'm a Granny Smith.'

'You're an idiot.'

Then she remembered other people and dragged herself away from him though nobody was paying any attention, nobody was near enough to see. They were there four hours longer and she was incoherent with cold and weariness when they finally gave in.

'I want that typing up before we start again in the morning,' was all he said as they went back to the hotel.

Rosalind had a bath and a sandwich and began to read back her shorthand. It was almost one o'clock when she finished and knocked on the door of his room. She heard him call out for her to come in. He was sitting on the bed surrounded by papers, writing quickly, and didn't look up.

'Your notes.'

'Oh, thanks,' he said absently as though he had forgotten.

And then she realized. 'You don't really want them tonight, you just made me do them. All that work. I could have been doing something else.'

Jack didn't say anything.

She waited until he looked up and then she said, 'You think you're cleverer than everybody else, don't you?'

'I am,' he said.

'I don't think I want to sleep with you any more!' she said.

She slammed out and went back to her room and then she heard how childish, how petty she had sounded. He was having a hard time with the work but even so he had put up with her in his bedroom and in his bed and there had been nothing but affection except for that one kiss earlier. She went back in, without knocking, and she said, 'I'm sorry.'

'Hey, don't worry,' Jack said and he even smiled.

'I do think I should sleep by myself, though. It isn't fair.'

'That's fine.'

'You do understand. It isn't—'

'I said it was all right. Go and sleep. If you want anything I'm just here.'

'Can I leave the door open?'

'Yes, sure.'

And that was when she realized the incredible discipline which he had, the single-mindedness, was working now to her benefit. He was not the person who acted first and thought afterwards, it was all carefully decided and he saw ahead much further than other people did. She was so grateful. She smiled and nodded and said good night and then she went back to her own room and left the door between the bedrooms ajar so that the light spilled through and she got into bed and lay down and closed her eyes. She could still hear the sound of Jack writing, the slight scratching of the pen that he used.

That night she didn't think about Freddie or anything else. She was too tired. She slept soundly until her alarm went off and then she bathed and dressed and went downstairs and ate a huge breakfast.

Nine

The wedding had initially been set for November. Freddie couldn't understand why. What a month to be married in. He had the Norwegian Rally in September and after that the German Rally and that year the RAC Rally's date was moved to make the conditions more interesting so the wedding had to be put off. The RAC would start in Blackpool, run up to the Scottish highlands and down through Wales, to finish at the Crystal Palace race circuit in south London.

His parents and her parents were keen to have them married as swiftly as possible in case the bride, the groom or both changed their minds. The only thing Freddie was glad of was that she could stay with his parents and not have to put up with her father while he was away.

He didn't offer to take her with him and she didn't offer to go and the once he mentioned it she said that she thought she would just stay in Northumberland, she was getting used to it as home and she would be too afraid to go to any rally, that kind of thing frightened her and he said, that was fine, she could stay at home and read by the library fire.

His gift to her was not himself but White Maddens and her peace. She liked being there with his parents and she walked the black Labradors every day and she explored the area.

To his surprise once away from her father she was like a different person. She lost a lot of weight very quickly with walking the dogs and the sensible way that food was presented. Sybil had not kept to nine stone through eating cake and sitting around and she encouraged Jennifer to go out a great deal and taught her to play badminton and introduced her to various people in the neighbourhood. Freddie had never been grateful to his stepmother for anything before and was surprised at how much easier Sybil had made everything.

'We don't have to get married just yet,' Jennifer said.

'Yes, we do. I need the money in the bank and you need to be permanently rid of your father.'

She sighed.

'Is there something else?'

She looked down at her fingers and smiled then she looked at him. 'You didn't tell me there was another woman.'

'There isn't.'

'There was, though, wasn't there? I have heard a variety of stories from people all about how beautiful she is and how much you care for her.'

'I broke it off.'

'But you were in love?'

He was amazed. 'You didn't want me because you loved me, you wanted my title, my—'

'Yes, but I didn't know that you were in love. I didn't think it would be perfect but I did think we might stand a chance of some happiness,' she said.

'I'm not . . . I could never have married her.'

'Then how could you—'

'I don't know, I just took it day by day.'

Jennifer gazed out across the park in front of the house.

'If you want to call it off—' Freddie said.

'I don't but I want you to look at me and tell me that this is at least partly what you want or it will never work. If you can't bear the thought of marrying me tell me please and I will go away, in spite of my father. I will run away back to New Hampshire and buy a tiny cottage and spend the rest of my life reading.' She was smiling at him but only just.

'I want us to be married,' he said.

When she had gone to bed he liked her better than he had done before but that wasn't saying much, he liked many women just as much and there was a huge gulf between that and what he felt for Rosalind. He went outside and smoked a cigarette and thought about Bath and what it had been like driving the little car.

It was happiness. It wasn't perfection but it was only one rung down. It would never be perfect but it was the closest that he would ever get. Nothing else came anywhere near this. It was exciting, pleasurable, it was ecstasy. It was in the realm of things that God had not intended man to know, it was the giving away of secrets. Between life and death there was a closed door but here the door opened slightly and tiny shafts of light spilled through.

When he was driving that was what happened and the faster he drove and the quicker everything became the more his hands and feet and mind and body and spirit responded until it was all one, the fluidity astonished him. The car was better than any woman had been, joined to him, part of him, and he had a confidence and a sureness and the coldness came down on him like ice.

He was the best. He had always known that he was the best, he had just needed a car which matched his ability and Jack had built that car for him. He knew it was for him, it fitted him better than anything ever had, the gearstick was exactly right for his hand, the clutch and brake and accelerator were exactly spaced for his length of leg and for the movement which was required. The seats were true for the long, lean length of him and the back of the car clung like a woman in passion with its short fat tyres.

He envied Jack the knowledge and ability to have invented something which was like a perfectly tailored suit on him. The car belonged to him. No matter how many models were ever made of it, it would always belong to him and nobody in the whole world handled it like him.

Jack didn't envy him his ability, he worried, Freddie knew, and needed him there, worrying. He had realized when they were in the Cotswolds doing the testing that Jack's concerned face enabled him to drive the car. He felt like a magician with a bag of tricks, Santa with a present, the lucky dip at the show, they would all stand back, watching and he would get out at the end, laughing and Jack's colour would gradually return, the anxiety would be wiped from his face. Freddie could go over and slap him on the back and go off to the pub with him for a pint.

Later Jack would come to the rallies and Freddie acknowledged it for an act of bravery but Jack would come because he was not a coward. That autumn he flew to the different countries to be there, to watch the car.

Slightly the worse for brown ale in the north where they had a forest stage of the RAC and he had driven to the limits of his and the car's endurance Jack said, 'You'll kill yourself in that bloody car.'

'I might, yes. Does it matter?'

'Don't say things like that.'

But Freddie only laughed and was glad. 'You should be proud of it, it's the best car anybody ever built. This is our time, it won't ever come again and in years ahead when people look back they'll remember it and us.'

Freddie remembered that night especially, the north, the winter. The snow was thick in the forest and the ice was treacherous. They were staying at Jack's parents' house though in fact they were hardly there. He and his co-driver had come first in the stage. The trees were icing sugar coated with snow and the road was one big icicle and it was as if God had got him out there like some high-wire act at the circus and said, 'Go on, show them.'

Sam, his co-driver, was never scared but he was that night, in the snow, in the darkness. He went away and threw up afterwards, Freddie had seen his hands shake and his knees disobey him and then his stomach revolt but to Freddie it was all stars and possibilities. It had been gained and could not be lost. There had been nothing and there was something. He was further down the road, he had broken down barriers. He didn't even have to be told that it was the fastest the stage had ever been completed. There was restrained clapping, there was quietness. The sweet northern darkness looked down on him, the stars twinkling their appreciation of his magic.

'Well?' he said, making his way across the slippery surface to Jack.

'Jesus Christ,' Jack said and turned away.

'Was I good?'

'You were a whole bloody pantomime,' Jack said.

They went back to the little house on the edge of the moors beside the garage and hung out of the back window and toasted the moors with whisky.

'I love it best here,' Freddie said. 'I love it that it doesn't mind me, that I can't take it home or put a fence around it. Dear God, I love the fells.'

'You should give it up,' Jack said.

Freddie looked at him but Jack stared frontwards.

'What do you mean?'

'It isn't meant to be like that. You're going to die if you don't. You go too far, too close. I don't want to be left here feeling responsible because I built the bloody car. You have a lot, you have responsibilities and you're going to be married and have children.'

Freddie didn't answer straight away. He leaned further out into the sweet cold embrace of the night and the whisky sloshed about in his glass.

'You don't know what it's like,' he said, 'or maybe you do. Do you know when you sit down with a blank piece of paper and everybody else's ideas seem so ordinary and boring? And then you hear the sound of your own ideas coming to the front of your brain like the cavalry just as the Indians hit the wagon train? There's nothing in the world like it, nothing at all, not even the best fuck you ever had comes anywhere close. I can see God when I drive.'

'You're going to see him a bloody sight closer if you keep going on like this,' Jack said.

Ten

Freddie and Jennifer were married at Christmas. He hadn't asked Jack again to be his best man, especially the way that things were between them, with Rosalind in the middle, he asked an old friend he had gone to school with instead. It seemed appropriate but he missed Jack and kept looking for him.

Both sets of his parents were there and looked equally pleased and her parents didn't stop smiling. Jennifer and Freddie had barely seen one another, Freddie had been away all summer and almost the entire autumn. She had not asked him to come north, she had not told him she missed him.

She had tried to talk to him after hearing of his recklessness in the RAC. He had not won either but that had been the car's fault. It had let him down over and over again. Freddie heard Jack cursing even in his sleep.

The wintry conditions did not suit the little car, four of

which were entered. They all failed to finish because of clutches which slipped which in turn meant oil-seal failure. The snow created chaos and although the crews were supposed to take the briefest route between controls they could not because of the weather conditions so drivers had to fend for themselves and tried to achieve an impossible speed average.

People yelled and argued and nobody cared who won in the end, even Freddie.

He had not entered the Portuguese Rally in December because Jennifer had asked him to come home before the wedding. It was no hardship. The car had to be altered before the next rally, he hadn't needed to tell Jack that but had told him anyway. They met in Jack's office at the back of the works.

'You're not making it here,' Freddie said.

'I will.'

Jack didn't look at him. Freddie badly wanted to ask how Rosalind was. He knew that she was living with Jack.

'Is it selling?'

That summer there had been a big press reception when the car went on general sale and Freddie knew that it was not selling, that so far it was running at a huge loss, that it had so far won nothing except that one stage and that it was his skill which had won that stage. Jack had everything to prove.

'It will.'

'I've never seen self-belief like you have.'

Jack laughed. 'You mean you've never seen vanity like it.'

'We'll call it vanity when you fail.'

'I don't fail. It will win next time.'

The funny part about it was that Freddie believed him. He went back to the middle marches of Northumberland and got married.

He would have given a great deal not to have spent his wedding night beneath the roof of White Maddens. Somehow it felt to him that the house was watching everything he did, in a kind of smirking family sort of way, smug that he had done the right thing by it, secure in the knowledge that today's marriage meant that for years to come there would be enough money for the place to be lavishly kept.

He could even build more, as previous generations had been inspired to, if he chose. Freddie didn't give a damn about

107

building more, the bloody place was big enough and had taken enough of his time, energy and self-sacrifice. He would not spend a single day there or a single penny on it that he did not have to. Sometimes he felt so savage about it that he wished he could pull it down.

Jennifer, guided by his mother, whose taste was unerring, had chosen to wear a cream dress to her wedding, much more flattering to her colouring than white. It was an expensive item, he guessed, plain almost to severity, accentuating her best physical attributes and hiding the faults. She was, he admitted to himself, almost beautiful that day, as though they were in love, as if she was gaining everything she had ever wanted. Had she thought to fall in love? Evidently not, that she was ready to give her life to him and to this place.

He tried to keep his mind focused on the service and then on speaking to everyone at the reception, smiling, thanking people, saying all the right things.

His mother had enough decency not to tell him she was proud of him but he could discern relief in her eyes. The thing that upset him most was that his parents, both married to people they loved, did not seem to care that his happiness was sacrificed for money. They had, it was true, had a bad marriage but they had married because they chose one another which was why he was now required to marry this girl he did not care for.

They spent that first night at home and it was appropriate somehow. He had married her so that this place would go on as it should and even though he hated it because of that it seemed right that they should spend the night under the roof of the house which had cost him everything.

He could not that day put Rosalind from his mind as she had been in Bath, so skinny, with great dark circles under her eyes which were full of hurt and even then she had declared her love for him. He would not forget that she had said he mattered to her. He had betrayed her, left her, yet she had told him she loved him.

Freddie stood beside Jennifer Erlhart and felt nothing. He wanted Rosalind as he had wanted nothing before, he felt like an adulterer, but it was too late, he had made his choice, given her up for something which he did not understand.

That first night all he wanted was to run away but he knew

very well that he couldn't do that. This was not legally binding until the bride was bedded and he knew it. He could not afford to take any risks with such a large amount of money.

The guests went home or went to bed. His mother, who always found it difficult to be in the house she had loved so much with the man she had loved so much and now despised, had gone with her husband to a nearby hotel. Freddie and Jennifer went upstairs together. They had been allotted a set of rooms now that they were married, two bedrooms, a bathroom, a dressing room for each of them and a sitting room.

Once there he was glad of the peace though aware of the girl discomforted beside him. He gave her champagne and tried to talk to her, to put her at her ease.

'It'll be OK,' he said.

She looked at him. 'How did you know I was worried?'

'You're as white as the sheets.'

'I'm sorry. I know I'm ridiculous. I will try to be a good wife to you.'

He got up and poured more champagne.

There had been no other woman except Rosalind for so long, ever since they had met, and here it was impossible to forget what it was like to have a woman who loved you whom you loved. He and Jennifer hardly knew one another.

'We don't have to do this if you don't want to,' she said so she obviously hadn't understood the terms of the contract or how marriage like this worked.

It was the most important thing of all. No doubt if he had cared for her it would have been a lot better. Here beneath the roof of the house he had sold himself for, it was in its way as grim a business as the way the border reivers had gone on, it was all a rape, him, her, the house, everything.

He looked at her.

'Do you want to?'

'Yes, I think so. It just feels so formal, almost like an operation I have to go through.'

That made him laugh.

'You've done it before?' she said. 'With the girl you loved in London? How does she feel about you getting married?'

Freddie couldn't answer that. 'I could never have married her,' he said finally.

'Didn't she have enough money?'

His wife was already turning into a cynic, he thought. 'It's not just a question of that.'

'What, then?'

'She wasn't my social equal. My parents would have been appalled and never spoken to me again. We had no background in common. Nothing.'

'And we have?'

'Yes, I think we do.'

Jennifer got up and carried her champagne to the fire.

'I like being here,' she said, 'it feels right and I do like you though obviously I don't love you. You're very attractive. I wish I was more beautiful.'

'Who told you you weren't?'

'Don't be silly. I feel as though I was born here, or born to come here, and I want my children born here.'

'So do I.'

She did in fact make him a very good wife. She was easy to be with and they had a wonderful time spending lots and lots of money. He taught her to drive, she could only drive an automatic, and his father and Sybil saw to the boring repairs like the roof, while he and Jennifer bought furniture, paintings, lots of new clothes, good wine to replenish the cellar – his father said it was a necessity, Freddie was not going to argue with that. They went riding together and although he wasn't too keen about sitting over the library fire reading with her he was quite happy to distract her while she sat over the bedroom fire.

He took little pleasure from it beyond the obvious but he was determined that she should have no complaint to make though since she had nothing to compare it with that wasn't fair. The only trouble was that he missed Rosalind, her presence, her conversation, going out with her and going to bed with her. He tried to pretend it was the same but it wasn't.

One evening in the depths of winter when they were making love in bed she said to him, 'For God's sake stop it!' and when he did she rolled away to the other side of the bed and then she sat up, crying, and said, 'You don't want to do this. I wish you wouldn't,' and she got up and went into the bathroom.

Freddie stayed where he was for a minute or two but he could hear the sobs behind the bathroom door.

He went over.

'Jen, I'm sorry.' He hadn't realized until then that he liked her, that he was using a shortened version of her name which nobody else did, just as he did with Ros. 'Please come out.'

'No!'

'Please.'

'You don't care about me.'

'Of course I do.'

'No, you don't. You do this because you think you should, because you know you should and I'm so tired of pretending that this is something you wanted. It never was. You hate me.'

'I don't do anything of the kind. Come out, please.'

She did and that was when he realized that she had lost a lot of weight and she was not the better for it, she was never meant to be a skinny girl. He tried to take her into his arms but she avoided him.

'You don't have to mollify me. You didn't promise me anything beyond freedom from my wretched father and a place to live.'

'And a title and a country estate,' Freddie said with just a modicum of humour.

'Oh, don't try to be funny,' she said. She looked at him from drenched eyes and said, 'I didn't understand how very much you loved her. I really didn't or I wouldn't have married you. I didn't want to make you unhappy.'

'You aren't making me unhappy.'

'Then will you stop bedding me like I'm for reproduction only. It's very trying and you really aren't that good at it when you don't want to. I'm not pregnant and it seems to me that I'm not going to be pregnant just because you wish it.'

He had become his father, Freddie thought with a shudder of distaste.

'I'm not doing it just for—'

'Oh, shut up,' she said rudely. 'Go and sleep in the other room.'

He went. The other bedroom seemed very cold and unfriendly even though the fire was always lit in there too, the bed was aired and it was supposedly just as comfortable.

The trouble was he had got used to sleeping with her and didn't like it.

She didn't ask him back into her bedroom and he wasn't going to go back there until she did. Perhaps, he thought, she never would.

Eleven

That spring Jack's Uncle George died, his father's only brother, and he felt obliged to go home. Rosalind went with him to see her parents. They parted at the railway station, her father had come to pick her up and Andy, one of Nev's lads, had come in his dad's car to get Jack, his dad being busy making funeral arrangements.

They wound down the hill from the station and pulled out into the traffic and Andy looked sideways at him.

'Hear you're getting yourself a bit of a reputation,' he said.

Jack smiled. So the little car was famous. It was not making any money or winning any rallies but it was well known.

'Living in sin with Leonard West's daughter,' Andy said, changing gear.

'What?'

Andy grinned. 'It's all ower the village,' he said.

Jack had not realized he was coming home to a row, he had thought he was coming back as an adult, out of respect, but as soon as he reached the house he could see by his mother's face that George was not her main concern. It reminded him of the time he had come ninth in the class and she had looked at his report and said that would have been fine if that was the best he could do but it was far from the best and did him no credit.

On the first day he was at home his mother and father were distracted with the funeral but the next day when it was over, when George had been put into the ground and tea had been drunk at his Aunty Sadie's house just above the war memorial

112

on the Main Street and people had been too careful what they said to him, he went back home to the treatment that his parents seemed to think he deserved.

He half expected to be told to go to his room without any supper and was surprised to look back through the mirror above the front-room mantelpiece and see a grown man of thirty looking back at him. His father fidgeted by the fire and his mother stood behind the sofa as though she was going into battle and would use it as a shield and she said, 'I think you'd better explain yourself.'

Jack could see that the damage was already done, the silence from the rest of the family at the funeral had told him that much. He couldn't think of anything to say which would help.

'I didn't think you would do such a thing,' his mother said. 'I thought you had more respect for your family.'

'What thing?' Jack said.

'Do you need it saying?'

'Mary—' his father said and she stopped and looked at him and then at Jack.

'Living in sin,' she said.

'I'm not . . . living in sin.'

'They have another word for it in London, do they? A posh sophisticated word that makes it sound right.'

Jack thought of the work he had done during the past years which nobody had acknowledged and he thought of Rosalind. They had kissed once, in Gloucestershire when she was very upset about Freddie. Now they didn't touch. He had walked in on her in the bath one evening and she threw bubbles at him and he retreated with an apology.

They were very careful of one another but strangely respectful. They both knew that there was no point in anything more, Freddie stood between them now just as he had always and sex wouldn't mend it, it would only complicate things further and Jack couldn't do with any more complications just then and he didn't think she could but he liked having her there and she liked being there, he provided the very best of everything and there was nothing like luxury for making life easier.

Usually in the evenings he would come back at about nine o'clock and she would have a meal ready and they would drink a glass of wine and talk or they would leave work together at seven and go out and eat. He liked that best, he liked sitting in restaurants with her drinking wine and talking about work and eating good plain expensive food.

She had loved Freddie and Jack had learned to accept that she probably always would. People couldn't help these things. He couldn't help that he loved her and if she cared for him it was a caring born of desperation and lack of choice and his love for her was a man picking up crumbs.

'You didn't have to go to London to do that,' his mother said harshly. 'You could have lived in sin with Rosalind West in Durham.' He heard the wobble in her voice. 'When I think. All the lovely girls you could have had and what do you end up with, Leonard West's daughter. Do you think we let you stay on at school and become educated so that you could bed a—'

'Mary,' his father said again and more loudly.

'I'm ashamed, ashamed and disappointed, and you've made me say things I shouldn't.'

Jack tried to contain his anger but in order to do that he had to stay quiet and he didn't think he could for much longer.

'I am not sleeping with her,' he said.

'I don't want to know. I don't want the details of your debauchery. You were a decent lad. Why you couldn't have found a nice lass and married her I don't know—'

'We're living in the same house, that's not the same thing—'

'Don't tell lies,' his mother said. 'What on earth would you be doing that for?'

And if there was a reasonable reply to that Jack couldn't find it. His mother's face was dark red with frustration and shame.

'You can get yourself back to London,' she said, 'you needn't bring your mucky ways here,' and she stumbled out of the room.

Jack looked at his father. They had always been very close. He couldn't let his dad think he was doing something that he wasn't.

'We aren't—'

'It isn't that,' his father said.

'What is it, then?'

'It's what people think that your mother cares about. She's

114

ashamed of you. You must know that people are bound to talk. You took Rosalind in when Freddie Harlington got wed, didn't you?'

'How did you know that?'

'Your mother doesn't know it, that's the point. Do you want to tell her?'

'I don't think it'll help.'

'That's what I thought you would say. Try not to worry too much, Jack, there's a good lad.'

Jack left the house. He took his father's car. At the far end of the village was a solitary figure walking towards the fell. It was Rosalind. He stopped and picked her up and they drove a couple of miles along the fell road and he stopped the car.

'So, you didn't realize what a good time you were having,' Jack said when they talked about it.

'No, I didn't. I could have done a lot better than you, my mother says that so it must be true. You're common.'

'I know.'

He got out of the car and sat down on the bonnet and lit a cigarette and looked across at the fell which he had loved so much. She got out too and he lit a cigarette and gave it to her and even though she rarely smoked she took it and stood beside him.

'You could have played your trump card and told them that you had done a lot better than me.'

'You're an upstart, my dad says so.'

'I'm not even a successful upstart,' Jack said. 'I'm not going to last much longer there, the way things are going. How will I ever come back here?'

'Now that I'm used goods I'm not going to get anybody to marry me.'

'Slightly used – or would that be "slightingly". Only one owner.'

'We are the talk of the county among the would-be smart set,' she said, leaning in against him and pushing back his hair. 'I'm a fallen woman.'

'We could always go back to London and buck like bunnies.'

'You haven't even threatened me with rampant sex.'

'Didn't I say "rampant"?'

'Can't you do rampant, Jack?' she said wistfully. 'And here was me thinking that you had it in you,' and she finished her cigarette, threw it onto the road and put her foot on it.

Jack went reluctantly home to discover that his mother had already had enough of him.

'Don't come back here until you're prepared to put a wedding ring on that girl's finger,' she said. 'We didn't bring you up to behave like this. All the lads you went to school with are married and have given their parents grandchildren. We'll accept her though we don't have to. You could come and live here and help your father to run the garage,' and she walked out of the kitchen.

After a little pause his father said, 'She doesn't understand your work.'

'I don't understand it myself mostly.'

'Things bad, eh?'

Jack looked gratefully at him.

'If it goes down you can come back here. I'll be glad to have you and I'll sort your mother out, don't worry.'

Jack couldn't think of a world where he would not be allowed to design another car but if things got much worse he would lose his job and it would never happen again. It was the most terrifying thought of all.

His father drove him to the station and left him there and it was only a minute or so before Leonard West's Ford Prefect drew up. It sounded a bit off to Jack's ears. Mr West got out and came over. He was a big man, bigger than Jack who was six foot. Rosalind fairly ran across and she got in front of Jack, which was quite funny.

'Leave him alone,' she said, 'he hasn't done anything.'

Her father scowled but as he was over fifty Jack didn't think he would do much damage. Luckily the train came.

'I should sort you out,' Mr West threatened.

'It sounds like your car's missing,' Jack said and got on the train.

Safely seated as they pulled out of the station Rosalind began to giggle.

'It isn't funny,' he said.

'It's farcical,' but she stopped laughing before they reached the outskirts of the city and by the time they reached Darlington she was asleep. She slept all the way to King's Cross.

* * *

116

She didn't know what would have happened if he hadn't looked after her. Nobody else would have taken her into their home like he had when things were so very bad. She could not think how she would have lived in that awful flat with the damp, the sick green curtains and the way that the sounds of other people's radios came through the walls. There was always the smell of overdone Brussels sprouts somehow which was amusing at a distance but she had come to understand that it was the smell of near poverty.

She could have gone back to the Durham fells of course. She wished now that she had never left but she could not go home and leave Freddie and leave the life which she had wanted so very much to be a part of. Without him there was nothing in London but Jack had taken her to the cool white house with the high ceilings and long windows and it was a different level. He was rich by many people's standards. He drank good wine, he had an American fridge full of plain food, steak, salad, fruit, cheese.

He had given her a great big bedroom all to herself. She didn't really need to come out of there if she didn't want to. She had her own bathroom, and a kettle and biscuits and tea and coffee, and you could sit with your feet on the desk which sat beside the window and look out across the back gardens because other people's back gardens lay opposite and it was as good as the country, in fact it was better.

There was sometimes the drone of distant traffic and that was all. There were birds and lots of roses and there was the hugeness of the space which Jack with his infinite good taste had created. It was as peaceful as a convent.

The sex was on the same sort of level. He never asked even for a kiss. He gave her the luxury and the responsibility of being not quite alone. She had had time to sleep and think and his empty white house was so silent.

There was a great big untidy garden which in the spring was full of blue and yellow flowers and Jack had bird houses and bird tables and the one ordinary thing he did, she thought, was to go out each morning and feed the birds and they knew it. They had learned, the doves and the pigeons and the small birds, robins and chaffinches and others whose names she did not know. One day while she was sitting there a fox walked slowly across the garden.

The trees overhung on all sides so it was completely private and there were what seemed to her lovely old brick walls beyond. Best of all somehow they went to work together each day and she had never been as grateful for it as she was now. She and Jack were almost the same person there, they spent so much time together, sometimes she couldn't remember what he had asked her to do and what she did automatically somehow.

She never needed to ask questions and neither did he. She knew when he wanted to see people and when he didn't, when he was upset and would have shouted, when he wanted the door left open and when he didn't and just when she was becoming frustrated at his vast needs at work he would do something nice and put it all back on an even keel somehow.

He got her a lot more money for her salary for one thing. She had the feeling he had shouted about that to gain her so much. After that she didn't have to live with him, she could have bought her own place, except that by then she didn't want to, she liked being around him too much and she didn't think he had got the money for her for that reason except that she could have had her independence had she wanted it. She knew that independence was very important to Jack and therefore he valued it for other people. She would buy her own place but not yet. She needed to stay here just a little bit longer.

Twelve

The Monte Carlo Rally that year had thick snow but Jack well knew by then that the worse the conditions the more Freddie liked it. He and Sam won the rally and after that the little car began to sell during the spring and summer in huge quantities. It wasn't all because of the win, though no doubt that helped. Jack thought it was just that the timing was right.

He was more relieved than he could remember having been before about anything.

After that things got better and better. The little car began to win everywhere. It was of its time though Jack began to think it would always have a place. It was certainly doing well. He stopped worrying about it and began to work less. He went out with women and let himself have a good time. He began to go to the office only five days a week and to sleep long and well.

One day that summer, it was a Tuesday and warm, he went back early to the house – early for him, it was about six o'clock, and his eyes met a lovely sight. Rosalind was sunbathing in the garden. He remembered that she had gone home early to do exactly that. She was wearing a white bikini. It didn't matter, nobody could see into the garden, but it was a very small garment. He clattered about in the house a bit just in case she decided he was intruding on her solitude because she was very withdrawn about such things but she didn't move so he went outside.

He walked over the lawn. She was lying on a rug and she removed her sunglasses. 'I thought you were going to be late.'

He lay down beside her. 'I was fed up, wanted to come home and do something else.'

The bikini was lovely. It had little bows at either side which looked as though they came undone. Jack didn't look at her golden-brown body.

'Anything in particular?'

'No.'

She didn't put the sunglasses on again, she watched him and then she said, 'You make love to other women, don't you?'

Jack looked at her. 'What a thing to say to anybody.'

'You do, though, don't you?'

'No, I'm a monk.'

'They go to bed with you because of who you are.'

'Thanks.'

'That isn't what I meant.'

'Let me put it this way, Rosalind, I haven't broken anybody's heart or anybody's marriage.'

'Men always say things like that.'

'Oh God,' Jack said. 'Do we have to talk about it?'

'No, we don't have to.'

She was looking at him.

'What's up?' Jack said suspiciously.

'Nothing,' and then she put down the sunglasses and she reached up and kissed him long and slowly on the mouth.

Every day Jack reminded himself that she didn't love him. Every day he told himself that she loved Freddie. He had long since wished that she would leave, living with her was becoming hell. He couldn't remember now a time when he had not loved her and it made him do a great many things he was not proud of.

All he had left was that he had not tried to make love to her when she so obviously didn't care for him but the kiss and the sunshine and the bikini were too much. He didn't think anybody could have resisted and even though his mind yelled at him his body didn't take any notice.

It was very unfair of her. She couldn't possibly have done it on purpose he told himself because he was supposed to be in a meeting and anyway he never came back before half-past eight so she hadn't planned it but if it was nothing but impulse that made her reach up and kiss him that was even worse because it meant that she hadn't thought about him, didn't care even sufficiently not to do this to him without love. Sometimes they joked about it and that was all.

Jack had tried to get things right, had found good-time girls who liked champagne and men with money. He didn't think that he had hurt anybody but the truth was that they were all hurt and this would only make things worse.

He thought of Freddie driving much too fast for any form of safety and of the occasions he had known where Freddie had got drunk and bedded anybody who was willing and plenty of women were. He was famous now and rich and with his looks and background he could have anyone he wanted. Jack didn't ask him about his relationship with his wife but Freddie got drunk so often and bedded so many blondes that Jack didn't pretend to himself that the marriage was going well

As for Rosalind, as far as he knew there had been nobody and that was just as bad. He was reminded of it now, that between himself and Freddie there was no man to be compared to and she had loved him. Stupidly, none of these things made

120

any difference now. He untied the bows on the bikini and took off his light summer clothes.

She was so damned hungry he thought that the milkman would have done. She had little idea who he was, it was like an overdue maintenance on a car. It was nothing but a good screwing to her and he had been avoiding such circumstances for so long that he was angry with himself.

He should have gone to the meeting, he should have stayed at work, he should have gone out to the pub or to see friends, anything but this. He carried her inside and onto the sofa and after that he was lost in her.

Much later he went upstairs and stood under the shower for a long time, calling himself names. He found some clean clothes and left the house and for once he took the car, not the car he had designed, not a little family car with maximum room for people and luggage, the beautiful luxurious Jaguar with soft leather seats and the sort of power which all men wanted. He took it for the kind of drive which even Freddie would have been pleased with. He wanted never to come back.

And when he did, when the summer night was almost over and the dawn was well broken, she appeared like they were married and said in short tones, 'Where have you been?'

'A quick fuck in the garden doesn't give you rights like a wife, you know.'

She walloped him round the head for that which she was quite entitled to do, he thought. He went to bed and for only the second time in his life didn't turn in for work. He slept all day and then, after he had gone downstairs (she was back from work by then), he sat outside on the terrace and drank a couple of bottles of wine and watched the stars gradually make an appearance, like latecomers at the theatre. When it was quite dark she came into the garden.

'I'm moving out tomorrow. Bernice has said I can stay at her place.'

'Great,' he said, 'that's great. That's absolutely bloody wonderful.'

'You're drunk.'

'I hope so. It's taken me half the bloody night to get there. If you want screwing before you go the milk's usually here by four.'

She clouted him again but he didn't really feel it, he didn't want to feel anything, the alcohol had sorted that out. What he really wanted to do now was to hit her back and then get hold of her and . . . That was what men did when they had lost control of everything and he had. All the days and nights of being clever and thinking he had bettered himself and that they could go on being friends, he could go on pretending.

That was what Freddie did. One night after the Monte Carlo they had got drunk with two blonde girls and gone to bed with them and when the girls had fallen asleep they had gone outside with their glasses and they had drunk a toast, the old Jacobite toast, because Freddie said that his ancestors had been Jacobites and that his ancestor who had been beheaded had denied the king on the scaffold before he died, had pledged allegiance to James III for ever and ever in the name of the family and there in the bitter cold night which was as starry as bloody Hollywood at the Oscars they had lifted their glasses and Freddie had intoned the old toast to the King over the Water, to the Pretender, and they had fired the crystal glasses at the nearest wall, he could hear them now, shattering and smashing.

For the young pretenders and the old ones, for those who thought they could live their lives in exile and in loneliness and never long for the wild reaches of Northumberland, for those who ached for the high fells and the white streams and the places where their loved ones had lived for generation after generation, for those who died and never came back and for those who played out their lives doing what Jack's mother had called 'romancing', kidding themselves that they had got it right, making out that they had something worth having, that they would live for ever, that nobody would ever matter so very much that they would break their hearts and grieve and that the empty dawn would never arrive.

It was coming now, the bastard, its light was winking through the trees as though it was welcome. Let her go to Bernice's. Let her go to hell.

Thirteen

That autumn Jack's father died. His mother blamed Uncle George.

'They could never one of them do anything without the other,' she said.

His father had dropped down dead in the yard behind the garage, which was as fitting a place as Jack could imagine, but his father had been in his sixties so it did seem unfair.

'That's it, then,' his mother said, 'you'll have to come home and run the garage.'

They were sitting in the kitchen after everybody had gone. It was early evening. He didn't feel as if his father had died, he was in the office or seeing to the buses or somebody's car had gone wrong and he was taking a look at it outside. Beyond the windows the heather was in bloom on the fell.

He could remember when he was little, Bert from next door, who kept bees, putting the hives on the trailer and Jack going with him in the old van way up beyond Rookhope in Weardale, to a farm high up on the moorland so that the bees could gather the honey from the heather.

They had set off in a cool egg-yolk-coloured dawn so that they could put the hives in place beyond the farmhouse windows, low in the garden in the valley, before the bees were up and about. It was one of Jack's most treasured memories. It made him miss his dad more somehow, it made him want to run next door to Bert for reassurance.

'I can't do that, Mother, you know very well I can't.'

'Then who's to do it?' She lifted her chin and looked at him.

'Don't you really know what I'm doing or is it just stubbornness? I'm not going to leave London and come back here. What do you think I am?'

'I think you're a different person than when you were a lad, hard and unfeeling.'

'I designed the little car, I have a job, a future. Why don't you sell up and move?'

'Move? What am I supposed to do, come and live where you live? Oh, don't worry, I'm not going to bother you.'

'You could sell the garage and the house and the buses and buy another house.'

'Did she leave you?'

'What?'

'That Rosalind West.'

'It was never like that.'

'Huh.' His mother laughed shortly. 'You can't fool me. It was always like that, with you,' she said. 'It was one of the reasons I wanted you away from here. I never thought she would follow you to London. I remember you bringing her here when you were a lad.'

'Did I?'

'Can't you remember? A little slip of a lass she was. It was before we had the buses. Your father was away, it was wartime. Her mother pretending she didn't come from Billy Row and wasn't just like everybody else. Thought she was on to a good thing when she married him.'

'And wasn't she?'

His mother sighed. 'I suppose. At least he's still here and they have a great big garden. You weren't good enough for their Rosalind, eh?'

'Something like that.'

Rosalind wished she could go back to the time before she had tempted and lost Jack Neville. She missed him. She didn't realize until she got over being upset about it that she missed him as much though in a different way as she missed Freddie. There were plenty of men around but they weren't of any interest to her, she stayed at home, such as it was. She stayed with Bernice and her husband, Geoff, for the first week and there was no word from Jack even though she should have been back in the office helping him.

She wrote a note of resignation and went looking for a new flat and a new job. She heard that Jack had gone home, his father had died. She wrote him a brief note of condolence, the result being that Jack turned up at her new place, which was much like the old, one night about a week later. Rosalind had not been prepared for that and her face went hot when she let him in.

She tried not to think about what they had done to one another. Were all her relationships going to be so destructive?

'I just wondered if maybe you'd like to go out for a drink,' Jack said.

Rosalind knew that Jack's idea of going out for a drink was a wonderful restaurant, an excellent meal and probably more than one bottle of exquisite wine. Part of her wanted to say no but somehow she couldn't. She put on a coat, he hailed a cab and they went and she had been right, it was the kind of place she had grown used to, being around men who had money had its advantages. After two glasses of the sort of wine which made you think you might manage two more she said to him, 'I don't understand what went wrong.'

'It's simple.' Jack didn't look at her, but down into his wine glass which was already empty again. 'You love Freddie. It's my belief that you'll always love him. You took me because I was there and because you wanted somebody to hold you.'

It was the truth. Rosalind considered the salad she had not quite finished and ran her fork around the lettuce and tomatoes and lemon juice and olive oil and whatever else was in it. A plain salad, yet somehow you could never reproduce such things at home, even with the same ingredients.

'There has only ever been you and Freddie. Doesn't that tell you something?'

'Yes, that I'm near enough for you to pretend while I'm doing it to you.'

'Don't say things like that.'

'Does that mean you didn't?' He looked slightly hopeful

'I didn't think.'

'I noticed.'

'I felt safe.'

'I'm not sure safe ought to come into things like that. You aren't entitled to safe.'

'Then what am I entitled to?'

He didn't answer that. He said, 'Do you want something more to eat or just coffee?'

'I miss you.'

'Being friends with me?'

'I don't know. Maybe I'm just a gold-digger. I miss all this.

125

I miss your lovely house and the Jaguar and going to places like this and being in your company and . . . being at work with you, even.'

Jack laughed. 'Now that is desperate,' he said, and then into the silence he said, 'I haven't asked for anybody else to work with me. Would you come back?'

'Freddie is lost to me,' she said, 'but I always feel as though you're still there even if I don't see you.'

She went home with him, somehow that seemed inevitable and they went to bed and this time Freddie was so far away, it all seemed finished. It was such a relief to her, being there. Nothing had changed and it was such luxury after the flat. It was warm and cosy and the rugs were thick and the sheets were white, there was soft lighting and telephones in every room. The huge refrigerator hummed in the kitchen and was full of food. There were fresh flowers and the smell of polish and everything was neat and organized. Jack gave her good brandy in a big glass and coffee and in the morning they went to work together.

She could not bear the loneliness of leaving him. That evening they picked up her belongings and she moved back in with him. It was a good Christmas. Freddie had won everything in the little car though neither of them had seen him – they stayed in London, Jack's mother thankfully going away to family and didn't want him there and she had rather guiltily told her parents she had other plans.

They went to parties and had several days off. It didn't snow, the weather was mild. They drove to the coast on Boxing Day and ran along the beach. And for Christmas Jack did what she had for so long wanted Freddie to do. He gave her a diamond ring, a solitaire so perfect that she knew it had cost him a small fortune, and he asked her to marry him.

'Can I be your best man?'

It was a month later. Jack looked up. Freddie stood in the office doorway. Jack automatically scanned the outer office for sign of his fiancée but she was nowhere to be seen. Freddie looked tired. Jack didn't want to know how tired Freddie might be or see the unhappiness in his eyes so he soon went back to looking at the papers on his desk. Papers were such useful things, you could hide in them.

'We're going to a register office. We're not asking anybody.'
Freddie came in and sprawled in the nearest chair.
'Your mother will have a fit,' he said.
Jack didn't know what to say to that.
'You haven't told her,' Freddie guessed.
Jack went on with what he was doing.
'Do you want to go for a drink?'
'No, thanks.'
'Are we all meant to avoid one another for ever? Where is she?'
Jack went on writing.
'What the hell are you marrying her for?'
Jack stopped. 'Considering that she wants you?' he said.
Freddie was silenced.
'What did you expect her to do, go into a convent?' Jack said. 'Don't you think she wants marriage and children and a home? Do you remember how she lived? Do you want her to be lonely for the rest of her life?'
'I want her to marry somebody else, not you,' Freddie said.
'She likes me.'
'It isn't going to make her happy.' Freddie got up. 'It isn't going to make you happy.'
'It might if you stay out of the way.'
'Please, Jack, don't marry her.'
'Don't be soft.'
'She's never going to love you—'
'How the hell do you know?' Jack said as he got to his feet.
'Because that kind of thing doesn't happen twice to people. You can have anybody you want, you're clever, rich—'
'I want her.'
'It's impossible.'
'Of course it's possible.'
Freddie shook his head. 'I can't take the responsibility,' he said.
Jack thought of a dozen things to say and didn't say any of them and after he had discarded them all Freddie said, 'You love her. I didn't know that.' His voice was heavy. 'You wouldn't marry her otherwise, being a good northern boy. I should have known.' Freddie looked appealingly at him.

'Marry somebody else, Jack, somebody you don't love so badly. It's much easier.'

'For you, you mean?' Jack said.

'For all of us. Please don't do it.'

In the end they went north to be married. Jack's mother wanted them to be married at the chapel and Rosalind's mother wanted them to be married at the church even though, as Jack carefully did not point out, her parents didn't go to church. They were married at the parish church at the end of the lane in the summer when the hedges were pink with dog roses and the elderflowers were white like lace. Freddie and Jennifer were not invited.

It was not the happiest day of Jack's life, for a start June was like a monsoon, and the rain didn't stop for a week. All the photographs had to be taken inside. His mother and Rosalind's parents didn't like one another and made little effort to be friendly and both families had invited every relation they could think of. Rosalind's dress was several inches thick with mud and the day was dark. Jack was only grateful when they could leave and go back to London. Their wedding night was a case of falling into bed exhausted and being pleased to go to sleep.

He had imagined that the magic of a wedding would make things better and at first for a while it did. Rosalind gave up working. He wasn't quite sure how that came about, only that he had the impression that being with him all the time was a lot for anybody to put up with, but it was pleasant, she was there in the evenings, sitting in the garden with a drink ready when he came back. She made more and more adventurous food and they had help in the house so that she didn't have to do the housework. She seemed to have lots of friends and went shopping almost every day.

She tried hard but Jack became increasingly aware of the effort that she was putting into their marriage. If he suggested they should go out she always agreed though she had little to say to their friends in the evenings or on Sundays. If they went out alone she was quiet, if they stayed in she busied about the house, fussing over small things.

Jack soon came to realize that his love for her was not enough, that Freddie had been right, she didn't love him and never would and somehow her trying hard made it worse. She was the perfect wife. Not for her burned pastry and lumpy gravy and days when her hair didn't look good. The house was immaculate, the meals were colourful and tasted superb, the wine was at the correct temperature.

Jack was having a difficult time at work, it was beginning again, he had to start to design a new car and it was the hardest bit. It was four years since he had gone to Sir Trevor with the ideas for the last one and a great deal had happened since then.

London was changing, fashions and ideas were becoming the hold of young people. A group called the Beatles had had a hit record with a song called 'Love Me Do' and altered people's perception of music and the girls had long hair and short skirts and London had become a Mecca for everything that was new. He felt that it was time for him to design something completely different, in keeping with that mood, not something for families, something which would appeal to the younger market who had money in their pockets and were no longer living or dressing like their parents.

The world was changing too. There was a wall across the middle of Berlin. In a way, Jack thought, the politicians had made just as bad a job of the end of the Second World War and the beginning of the Cold War as they had in 1920 after the Great War. It was enough to make anybody shudder, trying to tell people how to live.

It was difficult to capture the mood of the times. Last time he had been alone and could work out his despair and shortcomings and doubts. Now he had to pretend to her that everything was fine because he couldn't explain the process that he was going through, not just to her but to anybody, it was not something he knew enough about to tell anyone else.

He took to staying late at the office during the autumn and winter because he had to present a front to Rosalind and that was almost impossible at this stage. Because he was not at home much she took to going out so that he would come back to an empty house.

That winter Freddie won the RAC and came to London to stay with his sister. He found himself wandering along the streets where he and Rosalind had spent their time in the local pubs and dance halls and he remembered how he would wait outside for her at half-past five until she finished work and how they used to go out and drink wine and how they had gone back to his house and made love.

He could not believe what had happened. The house in Northumberland, the place that he had sacrificed everything for, meant nothing to him now, he hated being there and avoided it as much as possible.

Jennifer was so withdrawn when he went home that he tried to go home more often and then he tried to talk to her but she wouldn't.

'How are we ever to have a child, going on like this?' he said eventually.

'I don't care any more.'

They were in the kitchen. She must have been the first person to be married to a man of his family who found her way into the kitchen. She had become a superb cook and going home would have been fun if everything had been as good as the food. Jennifer spent hours baking bread and making wonderful casseroles, picking herbs and overseeing the vegetable garden.

His father shot through the winter and the food was things like pheasant with cream, brandy and apples, roasted woodcock with pork fat, wild duck with sweet peppers and wine or his favourite partridges stuffed with ham, juniper berries and the liver of the bird. If the way to a man's heart had really been through his stomach Freddie would never have ventured from home.

'It was the whole point of the marriage.'

She looked sharply at him. She was so very attractive these days. Without the overpowering influence of her father and with only his father and Sybil for company she had blossomed to such an extent that he thought if he had never found Ros he could have fallen in love with her.

'You're despicable,' she said.

'Why?'

'My money was the main point of the marriage.'

'And children.'

'A son, you mean, not children.' She was chopping vegetables for soup, a white soup by the looks of it, the bottom part of leeks, potatoes and onions. As she stopped, knife in hand, he looked warily at her. It was a large knife. 'I don't understand how I could be so stupid as to do any of this.'

'You did it for the house. You're as bad as me. Come on, you love it. It's Christmas, Jen. Couldn't we have a truce?'

She pointed the knife at him.

'You know what you are? You're unreliable, unfaithful and you spend huge amounts of money on things which don't matter. You waste it.'

'So you won't go to bed with me because I'm unreliable, unfaithful and a wastrel. Even I'm starting to think you're right.'

'Very amusing.'

She put down the knife but she went on looking at him.

'You're right,' she said, 'I have grown to love this place and I love your father and Sybil and I'm very grateful that I no longer have to pretend about anything, that I have my own way and I can do what I like. I'm even grateful that I don't have to put up with a man in bed for whom I feel nothing but contempt.'

'Yes, well. I think I might go and walk the dogs before it gets dark,' Freddie said.

He remembered this now and he thought how ironic it was that he had married her and there was and presumably would be no child and there was nothing anybody could do about it. His father might harp on about the next generation but Jennifer had had her revenge on them all.

Freddie found himself going into a pub near to where he and Ros used to go and to his surprise there she was, with a group of other people, laughing and chatting.

She looked better now with Jack's money providing clothes, jewellery, make-up and an expensive hairstyle, short and angular which suited her, and she was fashionably dressed with a very short skirt but she had not changed.

She saw him after a while and he had been watching her for a long time before she noticed and she could not or did not hide the look in her eyes. He went across and she introduced him to the friends. He didn't hear what was said, though he must have taken part in the conversation, and not long afterwards she said that she must go so he said that he must go too and they walked out into the bitterly cold street.

'How's Jack?'

'Working hard.'

'I heard, designing something new. Hell to live with, eh?'

'I don't know, he doesn't come home except to sleep and then not much. It's impossible.'

'Why?'

'He doesn't hear what I say, he doesn't talk to me, he doesn't eat – he's lost weight – he lies awake for hours, he's short tempered and . . . '

'So you come out?'

'There's not a lot of point in being there, he barely notices whether I am or not.' Rosalind looked guilty. 'I shouldn't complain, he's very good to me. How's Jennifer?'

'Do you really have to get back?'

She didn't and he had known that she didn't.

They could have gone for another drink and another pub and Rosalind wished again and again that they had but at the time it was different. They went back to Claudia's house. It was obvious that Claudia was away and that Freddie was staying alone in the empty coolness. Rosalind did not forget those first moments when the closing of the outside door echoed through the house.

She did not want this. Jack had demonstrated love in this way, he was always the man that he was and she knew very well that the man that he was was also more gifted and more imaginative than other men. She loved Freddie but this was so that she could earn the past again, so that she could have that time when they had been together without anyone in the way, when Freddie had belonged to her.

He belonged to no one now, she knew that. His wife could not claim him and in the gossip columns and in the more salacious of the newspapers were accusations that he was in the habit of having sex with beautiful women.

It had been some comfort to Rosalind to realize that Jennifer Erlhart had never owned him, had never had him all to herself like she had. Those times had become like lost dreams and it was only when he took her into his arms now that she could recall them, have them in reality.

He had belonged to her as he had not belonged to other women, he had been solely hers and no money, no estate, no

132

family, no circumstances had had that hold on him and it was there still though faint, she could taste and feel it on him. And he was so desperate, she had not known anyone so desperate, it was as if he had not tasted another woman since they had last met, as though none of it had mattered. The triumph of winning, the women he had lain with, the victories and his marriage, it was all lost through the misery that she could feel on him.

He kissed her and clung and hid as she knew he would not have done with anyone else, that he would not have shown vulnerability or weakness. His unhappiness was like a deep wound. He told her how much he had missed her, how much he loved and would always love her.

In some ways, Rosalind thought later, it was a worse betrayal because she did not love Jack. It was worse because he knew that she didn't love him and yet he had rescued her time and again. Jack would probably not even be surprised that she had done this. She was the one who was surprised. She thought that she hated and had long hated Freddie for his leaving her and she had known that she would not come to terms with it.

This was proof. Here she was in the cold darkness of somebody's London house giving herself to him on a sofa. It would prove or explain nothing, this was not the past, this was no more than he had done with other women, why did it have to be with her? The rest of it was not love, why was this? But he didn't think like that, she could see.

Possibly with other women he was at least objective, careless, could help himself but he couldn't help this, had thirsted and hungered for it, was intent upon her body. Even if she had objected she doubted that he would have stopped. In his mind they had already done this a hundred times and it was no different. He wanted to be back there where they had been together, when things had seemed so much less complicated, he had just wanted things to be like that again, and she believed that they could be.

They went upstairs and there in the big bedroom he lit the fire and candles. The room was gold and white and in the candlelight his eyes shone as she had not seen them in so long. He shut the velvet curtains against the night and it made Rosalind think of how it might have been if they had been

133

married as they should have, big rooms with fireplaces, huge beds, expensive furniture. If the world had been as it should have been then they would have been together for the rest of their lives.

'I've thought of you so much, longed for you every day. I couldn't go on any more without you, you do know? You do know that, don't you?' He looked at her so that Rosalind could do nothing but nod. Had he ever, she wondered, lived in reality or had he always managed to keep it at bay and was that the only way he could survive?

She stayed there, holding him in her arms while the fire burned up noisily in the grate and the London traffic quietened to the odd car and the candles guttered.

'I must go.'

'No, you can't. You must stay here with me.'

'I have to go.'

He tried to stop her but Rosalind knew that she had to leave. She got him to call her a cab and then she left him, dressed, listened and watched downstairs and he dressed and went with her, listening and watching and holding her close to him and then the cab came. She ran down the steps and across the pavement and into the car. She didn't look back, she didn't cry, she closed the door and sat back in the darkness and went home.

It was very late, almost three o'clock, but the lights burned downstairs. She paid the driver and went reluctantly into the house and through into the sitting room where the fire was low but not dead in the grate and Jack was sitting in the lamplight with a brandy glass in his hand.

'You – you waited up,' she said.

'No, why would I?' His voice was low and dangerous.

'I can explain.'

He put down the brandy glass and his black eyes glittered like good coal. 'Why don't you just go to bed?'

She went. She didn't sleep, she kept waiting for him to come upstairs but he didn't and it was almost a late winter dawn when she finally closed her eyes and found the dark passage to oblivion. When she awoke he was there. That was unusual, mostly he went to work early, long before she got up, but this morning he hadn't.

He slept as though sleep was the only place to be. She got up at nine o'clock but it was midday before he came downstairs, dressed and ready to go to the works. He didn't say a word but after the outside door slammed she let go of her breath.

It was less than an hour before Freddie's silver Porsche skidded to a halt outside and she was amazed at his timing, at his daring, that he would even contemplate coming here. She wished that she had gone out, that she could not answer the door, but it wasn't locked, he could walk in if she didn't go.

She wanted to tell him that he shouldn't be here, that she wouldn't let him in, that he couldn't stay but the words wouldn't be said and anyway, he already knew all that. He took her into his arms as he walked in the door and after he had kissed her he picked her up and carried her up the stairs and she started to object. It didn't make any difference, he carried her into the bedroom, unerringly finding the right one, put her down on the bed and pulled her close.

The bed, she imagined, was not yet cold though Freddie wouldn't know that, from Jack sleeping there until late, but he well knew that this was where they slept together, there were so many things about the room which gave it away. She fought with him but it was only hours since they had made love, you couldn't fight where you remembered so much need, she discovered. Nobody said anything, it was a bitter victory in all the worst ways and she cried.

'I want you to come away with me,' he said.

This, when she had thought that lower could not be found. 'I can't do that.'

'Why not?'

He was looking so clearly at her, she thought. 'I can't leave Jack.'

Freddie laughed. 'Do you think you haven't done more than that already, do you think betrayal comes in cleaner forms?'

'He knows what I've done to him. His intelligence is his biggest problem.'

'And knowing what you've done he doesn't want rid of you?'

'No, I don't think he does.'

'I never thought Jack was the kind of man who would put

up with such things,' Freddie said. 'Come to Monte Carlo with me. I have enough money of my own now to keep us. We need never come back.'

'I can't,' she said again.

'He knows that you don't love him, does he expect you to stay?'

'No, I don't think he does,' she said.

'Then why?'

She shook her head and didn't answer.

'You love him,' Freddie accused her. 'You love him and yet you do this to him.'

'You're married and you . . . you've shown who you are. You left me.'

'I didn't feel as if I had any choice.'

'But now you have? What's the difference?'

'I tried to get things right and it didn't work but I had to try for my father's sake and for Jennifer's.'

'You've never said such a thing to me before. I didn't realize you cared for her.'

'It's difficult not to. She cares about me so much and she's kind and generous.'

'But you want to leave her?'

'I love you. I've never loved anyone like I love you. I feel as if we won't ever get another chance. Come away with me.'

Jack didn't realize that he couldn't work, it was only when his hands started to shake over the drawing that he acknowledged it. This was the most crucial stage of all, the beginning, so near the beginning that he was weeks away from the start line, he had no ideas, he couldn't see beyond the little car which had been successful and already they were crying out for something new, as though you could repeat or add to that, as though you were a high-wire circus act and could do it again every time the crowd called out.

He had learned to hate them. In his nightmares they screamed 'again, again', they saw nothing but the simplicity, they saw nothing but the product, they did not see the long nights, the abandoned meals, the doubt, the big terrifying space where he had assumed an idea would form. Over and over he turned towards the space, hoping to find something there.

136

He had been able to do that once, he had given it his total attention, he had let it be selfish, the very centre of his existence, and he knew as he had always known that he would not be able to create anything like that again. Now he had Rosalind and a home and he made space for her in his life, space where there was none, he had had to move the centre of creativity in order to make room for her and he was paying for that.

And she was going to make him pay for having married her while she didn't love him. She was going to leave him and he couldn't hold her, not with money, not with comfort, not with his body or his mind or his love. When you loved people, he had discovered, you didn't stop loving them. How convenient it would have been if you could, he would have stopped loving her long since if there had been an option.

Last night she had gone to Freddie.

He got up from the desk and walked across to the window. He had deliberately chosen an office without a view. In those days such things as concentration had mattered. He could smile about that now. The little car had in its own way been his lover, it had created the kind of excitement which he had never known before and the more time he gave the more the ideas flowed and as Freddie had said to him nothing mattered like that.

When you hit the centre of your own mind and the ideas were coming at you nothing from the outside had any existence or any importance and it was better than anything ever. Rosalind had muddied his life but not for long. He had known that it would not be for long and yet the fact that he had known her always had been one of the most important things about it.

There were so few things from his childhood which he had carried through. He could no longer live in the village where he had been born, not just from practicality's sake but because his brilliant high-flown mind had taught him to despise simple things and to be bored with simple people. He knew it for a fault but he could not better it.

Rosalind was something which had always been there and could always be there, except that she would not. He had gambled and lost. She didn't want him and he had wanted her for as long as he could remember. To him she was still higher, she was still out of reach, perhaps he had deliberately put her there, not wanted her at home waiting for him. What man of honour would wish a woman idle at his calling and yet he did wish her so, in the ivory tower of his house, in the cool rooms in the cool evening, with the long shadows in the garden, waiting there for him beyond the reach of other men.

He wished that he could go home and have his father there. He missed his dad. He felt that he could never again go into the Black Horse or the Golden Lion and dammit, part of that memory was caught up in Freddie. Freddie and his dad, that Christmas, it was, for God's sake, the best Christmas ever. He missed his dad and he missed Freddie and now Freddie had taken Rosalind, as Jack had always known he would, and there was no bottom to the misery, there was nothing to hang on to as you went down, there was no end to reach.

It was a long slow drop, like the fairground ride that you didn't get off. The only way off it, he thought, was death and that was not to be considered. There would come a time when it would slow down and then you would come back up, to your relief, but not too far, let's not get excited, but some way so that you thought you could see the light but it was not. There was no light to this.

He made himself stay late at the office, nudging the hurt in his mind with games. Had she left? Had she just gone out? Would she be there? Would there be dinner just as though everything was normal? Would she have gone out but come back later? And if she was out was it with Freddie? Would she come from Freddie's bed and into his, theirs?

It was after nine when he got home and the lights were burning in the house, too many for her not to be there and when he opened the front door there was the reassuring smell of food. He went straight upstairs and took off his jacket and threw it onto the bed and then he stopped. He had turned away from the bed and now he turned back to it. She had changed the sheets. It was only two days since she had done it but the bed was made up so neatly and the sheets were crisp and . . .

The house was full of silence and up here only the lights in this room and the landing were burning. He walked slowly back downstairs. She was sitting in front of the fire as she had done on so many evenings as though she was waiting for him, a glass of white wine in front of her, untouched.

'Are you leaving?' Jack said.

'I don't know. I will if you insist.'

There was whisky and a glass on a tray and ice. Jack helped himself and sat down. It was funny how your legs could ache from sitting all day. He felt as though he had walked fifteen miles.

Jack took a good mouthful of whisky and it slid so happily down his throat. If she was going to run away with Freddie, as she must if they were going to be together, then it would be another country, somewhere far away, somewhere they might have some peace and he would be left here in the cool white silence.

She didn't ask, when it was late, if he would go to bed with her, how could she? They didn't eat. He recognized the ingredients, it was something she often did, some wonderful combination of beef and onions and wine and orange and lemon peel. It was a winter dish, a comforting pleasure to come home to. There had been times when they had lit candles and the dining-room fire and sat there drinking red wine and talking. That had been real. Why she had made it today he didn't know. Had it been before Freddie made love to her in their bed or afterwards? That casserole sat hours in the oven.

Funny how comforting the idea of food had been, that she was at home making wonderful things to eat. He had grown used to it as he had grown used to her and to the meals of onion tart with cream, lettuce soup, pork rillettes, pork with prunes and cream, all those Elizabeth David recipes which they loved so much. Strange how it mattered. Now it was all gone.

'I think that you had better make arrangements to leave.'

She looked at him. They had been sitting there for a long time in silence.

Jack returned the look she was giving him but it wasn't an easy thing to do. Her eyes were like dark stars, so bright, so . . . She began to cry.

'I know you didn't ever love me,' Jack said.

She pushed a fist at the tears as though they did not belong to her.

'I liked you very well. I liked you better than anybody. Being with you is like coming home. Do you want me to go now?'

'Tomorrow will do. It's late.'

She went to bed. He felt so much better when she had gone, well enough to go into the kitchen and throw the casserole across the room and several other things after it, well enough to stay the tears with whisky. He even managed to go upstairs and check whether she was sleeping in their bed but she wasn't so he didn't either. She could take all the furniture with her, she could take everything if she wanted to.

Later, when the whisky bottle had taken all his judgement, Jack got into the Jaguar and drove it through the empty streets towards Claudia's house. There was a light in the hall and when he parked the car and went in off the street the door was open.

The entrance hall was huge and freezing from however many hours the door had been open and there was another light and another door open further along. Jack edged the door further back. A log fire burned, taking the edge off the cold as a campfire would, and Freddie sat sprawled in his usual fashion in a big armchair.

'I'd almost given you up,' he said. 'What's it to be, then, Jack, pistols at dawn?'

'In the morning you can come round and collect her. You can take anything you like but after that I don't want you in my house again.'

Freddie didn't say anything and his head got lower and lower.

'I didn't mean it to be like this,' he said.

'Don't give me all that shite. You have a wife, you'd already made your choices—'

'I couldn't do it.' Freddie lifted eyes of fire. 'Do you think I would do this lightly to you?'

'So it wasn't lightly. You took my wife in our marriage bed.'

'I wanted her to know . . . that I meant it this time, that I wouldn't leave her again ever. I sacrificed you for her. You were the best friend I ever had. I used to wish that I had known you sooner, so that now I would have the memories of that time.'

'You get the hell out of my life.' Afterwards Jack remembered that, the words echoing in Claudia's big horrible empty house with its stone pillars all over the place like she was living in bloody ancient Greece. 'You've ruined everything.'

Freddie got up.

'You knew she didn't love you. You insisted on marrying her. How did you expect her to resist all that money and all that talent and all that fame? She had nothing. Who could resist all those worthless superficial things which mean so much to people?'

'You could have given us a chance.'

'Of what? Were you happy? What are you doing at work, creating something brilliant? And what was she doing at home, sitting around waiting for you? That's not what women are for.'

'Don't you tell me anything about it, you've had plenty waiting around for you.'

'Never. I never did. I never put any woman in a box and expected her to sit around admiring me.'

'It wasn't like that.'

'Wasn't it? Can you imagine what it's like living with you? Having to stand back and be pleased all the time? Genius is a wretched thing at best and you're impossible. I've seen you, pretending to other people that you appreciate their minds when you're a dozen steps ahead all the time and bored stiff. Did she bore you or didn't you allow yourself to be around long enough?'

'I love her.'

'If you had given her a chance maybe she would have loved you. That sodding little car that you invented means more to you than anybody on earth. All you really care about is what's inside your own head. Your ideas matter more to you than people and that's the truth. It's a pity Ros wasn't a car, you could have kept her locked in the garage.'

Jack hit him. It was a most satisfying thing to do, he hadn't hit anybody in years. It took him back to Saturday nights and fighting on the village streets, rival gangs and broken bottles and admiring girls. Freddie was right, things had been different then. He had been part of it, at home, fitted in, he had not needed the kind of control which was essential to his life now. The loss of control didn't worry him and neither did the fight that followed.

He was glad to let go. He hated Freddie, he hated Rosalind, he hated the little car and his office and his neat white house and the way that his hands shook over the paper so that he couldn't draw. He hated the way that he had kept her waiting for him, he hated the way that he had put her down so many times and she had felt obliged to please him.

All those months she had dressed for him, agreed with him, kept the house free from clutter, put up with his moods, endured his body, not complained when he was late or unsociable. He got hold of Freddie and fairly knocked the hell out of him and it was wonderful. It was worth doing too because Freddie hadn't come through the public-school system without learning how to fight. They even knocked a few things over. He only hoped they were valuable, he hoped they were priceless and that when Claudia returned she would weep over her broken ornaments. People and their bloody ornaments.

In the end Freddie stayed down but it wasn't out of choice, he was hurt. Jack was pleased. He only hoped Freddie had broken both arms so that he couldn't compete at Monte Carlo, so that he couldn't produce the kind of magic that only he could conjure in the little car.

Somehow the two had become graceful like a piece of music or a poem. Freddie had been born to drive that car and when he did so Jack could see all the things which made up Freddie's life like they were written there, his name and his home and his obligations, the prison that it had become, the way that he had made himself not fight to get out. He had fought now and freed himself and they were to count the cost. Jack was half satisfied when Freddie didn't get up. He walked out and drove back and then he went to bed. He went to his own bed and got in between the clean sheets and went to sleep.

Fourteen

Freddie went home first. He didn't tell Rosalind that he was going and he didn't know quite why he wanted to go, just that he couldn't let Jennifer find out from anybody else that he was leaving her for another woman. It was cowardly enough to be doing it. He made an excuse and left Rosalind in Claudia's house. He didn't want to leave her, she was so upset over Jack that he wanted to shout at her that she should go back to bloody Jack if she liked him that much but he couldn't so in a way he was more than relieved to get out. He drove the silver Porsche north at a frantic speed. It was the only thing which cleared his mind now.

He reached White Maddens on a winter day so perfect that he got out of the car when he came around the bend and could see the house. There was snow on the roof and all across the lawns and it lay on the fields in green and white ridges like stripes. Everything was well-cared for now, the fences and walls were mended, the houses on the estate had been rebuilt, everything was neat, prosperous. He had Jennifer to thank for that. It made him feel even more guilty than he had felt before. If it had not been that he wanted to see White Maddens one last time he would have gone to Monte Carlo and that would have been it.

What they would do after that he could not think. Sir Trevor would not countenance him as a team member once the news got out that he had run away with Jack's wife. The scandal would be terrible. The newspapers would be big black headlines, he being who he was and an earl's son and Jack so well known because of the car and Jennifer a multimillionaire's daughter. He would not be able to drive again in a rally after Monte Carlo. He couldn't think what it would be like, not to compete, not to win. It was the greatest thrill of all. Perhaps later somebody else would take him on. They would need money to survive. He had wasted a great deal of what he had made. He had never been fair to Jennifer, never faithful to her, and in a way, he thought, she had not expected him to be. Her father, the bully, had given her such low expectations of men that she endured them rather than anything else. It made him think of his mother.

He stood back against the car, smoking a cigarette and watching the house. There were no signs of life, nothing altered, nothing moved, just the sunshine beginning to come out from behind a cloud and play its golden game upon the house and turn the stone yellow.

He would never be able to come back but then he had given this place so much, sometimes he thought more than it deserved. Finally he got back into the car and drove the rest of the way, and as he reached the house Jennifer came hurtling out, a black Labrador on either side, and down the steps at the front so that he was obliged, possibly for the first time ever, to bring the car to the front, where in the old days the carriages would go in a circle up to the house and then carry on in order to get back out, in the days of parties and music.

'Freddie! I didn't expect you.' She was laughing and she looked so pretty these days, with the right food and the small amount of happiness which she had accepted as her portion. She loved Sybil and his father, he knew she did and she did not resent or did not show that she resented his comings and goings. It made him so ashamed he could hardly speak. She kissed him and stood back slightly and he thought, why couldn't I have settled for this? For a lot of men it would have been enough. It was almost a rebellion against the house and his ancestry that he wanted to leave now. He didn't really want to leave, he just had this terrible compulsion to run and never to stop.

'I thought you were going on to Monte Carlo,' she said. 'I wanted to see you. I was so horrid to you at Christmas. I'm sorry. I've wanted to tell you again and again. How good of you to come when I was thinking about you. Your father will be pleased and are you staying the night?'

'No, I'm on my way to Monte Carlo.'

'Then what are you doing back here?'

'I just wanted to see you.'

'Come in.'

'No.' He didn't want to have to face his father or Sybil.

She looked at him and he could see the doubt, the beginnings of apprehension.

'Then come into the garden.'

They left the car and walked around the side of the house, past the outbuildings, the carriage houses, the stables, the pigsties, and around to the side and down the path which led to the gardens, the side of the house, the croquet lawn and on from there into the quarry garden. The quarry garden was more than he could face.

'Don't let's go any further,' he said, as they reached the gate between the walled gardens and the entrance to the garden.

Little pink flowers he didn't know the names of had let fall some of their petals there upon the path. Jennifer employed several gardeners. It was beautiful as it had not been for years.

'It's at its best now, don't you think?' she said, a little wildly and then she looked at him.

'I'm leaving.'

She went on looking at him, stubborn with herself, her New Hampshire backbone coming to save her. 'What, me?'

'Yes.'

'Because I haven't given you a child?'

He was about to deny it and then realized that it was true. Had they had a son or even possibly a daughter would he have gone? He didn't think he would. His instincts were working overtime, just like his father's always had.

'I'm going to Monte Carlo and then I'm going away with Rosalind.'

'I always thought you would,' she said.

'You know me too well,' he said, with a slight smile, 'or you know men too well.'

'I've brought this on myself,' she said.

'No, you haven't. It was me.'

'If I'd kept you in my bed, if I'd been nicer to you—'

'You aren't to blame. There was never any chance.'

She stood for a few moments and then she accepted it, he could see by her eyes. 'Are you going to leave me to tell your parents?' she said.

'Sybil isn't my parent.'

'Oh, God,' she said, 'even now you can't get over it, can you? Even though you're making the same stupid mistakes you can't get past what your father did to you. This is the perfect revenge, isn't it? Don't you know how hurt he'll be?'

'That's all to do with who he is in the world and I don't care about that.'

'You should because it's who you are. Come in and at least say goodbye to him.'

'No.'

Freddie began to walk away. He half thought she would run after him and beg him not to go as Rosalind had once but she didn't. He turned back and looked at her but she had already turned and walked the other way, into the quarry garden.

*   *   *

145

Jennifer walked. The high trees on top of the enormous stones dripped and in the dark corners there were little pockets of snow. The Labradors loved any kind of walk and were dashing here and there among the shrubs and bushes, sniffing for rabbits, looking for pheasants or anything of interest. She finally came out at the far side and there was the castle just over. She took several deep breaths so that she wouldn't cry and then she began to walk back, the other way, across the fields, the Labradors to heel because there were sheep.

Freddie's car had gone when she reached the house. She went around to the side and in the back way because the dogs had muddy paws. She fastened them into their kennel just outside until they were dry and went into the house.

Sybil had gone into Newcastle to do some shopping, Jennifer had driven her to the station earlier, but Will was at home. He had been busy that day, doing paperwork in the study and since it was by now almost four o'clock and nearly dark he had sat down before the study fire and gone to sleep. She could see him as she walked in, sitting in a wing chair before the big log fire. He opened his eyes when he saw her and put out one hand. She couldn't understand why Freddie didn't like his father. Compared to her own father he was easy.

'Jenny.'

He was the only person in the world who called her Jenny. At first, knowing how grateful he was to be saved from financial despair, she had thought he was only going to tolerate her but the truth was that they liked each other. Strangely he seemed to like her much more than any of his own children.

He read a great deal and so did she, they liked the same kind of wine, he loved the dogs and horses just like she did and most of all they both had a love for White Maddens which she didn't think anyone else had. Sybil liked it as a status symbol but Jennifer felt as though she had been born there, or born to be there. Only now it seemed she wasn't.

He saw her expression and sat up.

'Something wrong?'

She didn't know how to tell him. She sat down in the chair nearest him and regarded the fire steadily and then she said, 'Freddie was here.'

'I thought he'd gone to Monte Carlo.'

'He's just about to. He's going off with Rosalind . . . '
Jennifer couldn't remember the wretched Rosalind's name,
either her own, or Jack's.

Will stared at her.

'That's nonsense. He wouldn't do that.'

'He came to tell me that he was leaving me. That he isn't
coming back.'

For several seconds it seemed to her that his father didn't
understand and indeed he proved it by saying, 'Not coming
back here?'

His father could understand how Freddie might leave her
or his family, but White Maddens?

'That's right,' she said.

And that was the difference between the two men, she
thought. Will would never leave White Maddens, he couldn't
imagine his life without it, he certainly wouldn't have given
it up for a woman or for anybody else, she thought, or for
anything else. This place was his whole life.

Will got up and he was trembling. 'He can't do this to us,
he can't do it to you.'

'He has,' she said.

'Has he been gone long?'

'An hour or so.'

'You should have told me.'

'It wouldn't have made any difference.'

'You mean he wouldn't see me?' A hurt amusement lurked
in his dark eyes.

'Exactly,' she said, looking straight at him and at that
moment with the kind of timing which Jennifer thought would
make her love Sybil for ever Sybil came back from her shopping spree in Newcastle. She had found a taxi rather than
disturb them. It was so lovely to be home. She kissed them
both and had presents and Jennifer thought there would be
a right time to tell her that Freddie had gone but it wasn't
now. Not that she would care. She loved Will far too much
to care for the son who upset him so often, who had been
nothing but a disappointment. The only thing Sybil had ever
approved of was Freddie's marriage, and that, Jennifer
thought with the horrible light-headedness that is shock, was
over.

Fifteen

It was the first time that Jack had not gone to the Monte Carlo Rally, which was usually the first of the year, and, sitting in his office in London, he could not help but think of the previous two years when Freddie had won. This year he had little doubt that the same thing would happen again but he worked and tried to forget about the fun they had had, the joy and the relief when he had won. No doubt Rosalind was there with Freddie to celebrate his victory.

Jack stayed at work even though his inclination was to give up for the day and go home. The trouble was that there was no longer anything to go home to and for the first time he wondered how Jennifer felt. Jack knew that she had married for position and title but he knew now what it was like when your married partner was unfaithful to you. He was struggling to work and almost at the point of giving up when he was told that Sir Trevor wanted him.

Jack had long been regarded as Trevor's golden boy so he went without fear to the great man's office. There Trevor got up from behind his desk and his face was dark.

'I've got some bad news,' he said.

And Jack knew. All the times when something might have happened, when he and Freddie were friends and had such good memories, it was all right. Now when they had fought and quarrelled, when Freddie had taken Rosalind from him for good, there had been an accident. It was typical. Freddie, trying too hard and stupidly when he didn't have to any more, when he had given up everything for her sake, so he had everything to live for and was at the height of his fame, he would be able to keep and look after them both, why now?

'The race?'

'Yes. Sit down, Jack.'

'I'd rather stand, thanks. Is he badly hurt?'

Trevor looked at the floor and then back at him.

'He's dead.'

'Dead?' How did they know, what had happened, it couldn't be. Somehow though Jack had not known until this moment he had thought, he didn't know why, somehow he had assumed that the little white car would protect Freddie. How idiotic, how ridiculous. Cars were lethal weapons to men and those who designed them were monsters.

The most terrifying thing of all was that his whole world subsided in those seconds. There hadn't been much to hang on to after Freddie and Rosalind left. What there was slipped away.

Freddie's body was flown home and Jack travelled north for the funeral, being obliged to call in at his own home, where his mother had put the house and the garage on the market. She was going to Whitley Bay to live. All her family had originally come from there and she had cousins who had found her a nice little house on the seafront, she said.

Jack hadn't known up to then that he did not want her to sell up and leave. It was the only thing he could focus on.

'I'll buy it from you,' he said.

His mother looked uncomfortable. They were sitting across the kitchen table from one another. She had said very little to him about Freddie's death. His mother had been very fond of Freddie and it hurt Jack to understand that in fact she preferred Freddie to himself. It was amusing in a way that his mother, a good Methodist and socialist, should have succumbed to the charm of a drinking, womanizing aristocrat but then in a way he had succumbed too and somewhere in his muddled thinking one of the reasons he didn't want to give up the house and garage was because he and Freddie had spent so many happy times there.

Even now he half-expected Freddie to come bounding into the kitchen and cover his mother in kisses and hugs until she told him to 'get away with yourself', her cheeks flushed and her eyes bright and the laughter already issuing from her throat.

'What on earth would you want with this place?' she said. 'You never liked it. Besides, I've already shut the garage. I've sold the buses to that chap at West Auckland and the lads have all found other jobs. There's nothing for you here.'

149

'But you don't have a buyer?'

'Not yet but I will have.'

'You can name the price,' Jack said.

She looked at him and then away as though she was uncomfortable or embarrassed.

'I can't do that. I can't sell you your own home. I tell you what, why don't I just leave it for now—'

'You can't afford to do that.'

She looked patiently at him. 'You've been sending money home for years—'

'That was for you to spend.'

'Jack . . . your father kept us. We didn't need your money.' She got up and made some tea as though glad of the activity. 'I should sell it, make a clean break.'

'Please don't.'

She got up and filled the kettle and set it to boil and then she said to him, 'You can't have the past back, you know, lad, no matter how much you want to pick and choose your memories. You married the wrong woman, that was your problem. I knew from the start it wouldn't work. Where is she?'

'I don't know,' Jack said truthfully.

'Did she leave you for somebody else?'

And it was only then that he realized his mother didn't know that all the time Rosalind had loved Freddie best of all and because she didn't know and because he didn't want to spoil her memories with the truth he said, 'It just didn't work.'

'I always knew it wouldn't.'

'Will you come to the funeral with me?'

She said that she would. His mother was used to funerals, she had a black outfit which she kept especially, including a rather neat little hat. He thought she looked like a black bird but he was grateful she had said she would go. How strange to be used to funerals.

Jack had never seen the house which had cost Freddie so dearly and there had been no chance that he would like it. He deliberately concentrated on his driving and didn't look about him. He inclination was to burn the place to the ground, and nothing but his basic decency stopped him from wishing Freddie's damned father would be inside when it happened.

He was directed by a man at the gate to go around the house and across the road and the chapel was by the castle.

150

Where else would it be, Jack thought bitterly. Freddie and his bloody castle and his bloody house and his bloody chapel.

He parked the car alongside several others, got out and slammed the door. He ignored the way that his mother looked at him and he ignored his surroundings. He had never felt hatred for a piece of land until now. He hadn't thought he could hate any place in Northumberland when it was so beautiful, but he did.

His only hope now was either that Rosalind would not be there or that he would not have to acknowledge her but his mother didn't run her life like that and seemingly oblivious to everything that had happened, as they were going into the chapel she said, 'I can see Rosalind,' and she marched straight over and got into the pew beside her just as though they were a normal family so Jack had no choice but to follow. Her parents were there so it should not have been necessary and he knew that his mother didn't like hers but it was not even considered and he was proud of her for it.

Rosalind could not believe that her first sight of Freddie's home, the place which had caused so much trouble, would be at his funeral. She had come home to the Durham fells, her parents had both come to the station to meet her and although she had no doubt her mother was very ashamed of her for leaving her husband and running off with another man nobody said much at all.

Everything was normal in Durham. That was the stupid part. Here nobody had died. She kept reliving the car crash over and over again, the screaming of the tyres and the noise when the car hit the barrier. Miraculously, Freddie's partner, Sam, had come out alive and was recovering in hospital but Freddie was not there any more. It was strange. He did not come back to her, reassuring and laughing at her fears. She had to pack up his things in the hotel.

Freddie's father did not come himself but he sent somebody, a pale quiet young man who dealt with financial affairs as far as she could gather, to see to the legal and money matters such as flying Freddie's body back to Northumberland. Stupidly all she wished was that Jack was there, she needed him so much.

She kept reliving the few short weeks she and Freddie had

151

had together but she could not forget what they had done to Jack and all of it had been marred by the leaving of him. Freddie had not been happy either. They had lain in their hotel bedroom and pretended to one another but they had both known that this was wrong, that there was no way they could be together and have it be right.

Things were never as simple as that. Whatever had they been thinking about when they ran away? The trouble with running away was that you had to take yourself when in fact it was the self that you were trying to get away from. Certainly she wished she could get away from the awful person who would leave Jack Neville for a man who had abandoned her and then abandoned his wife and would probably as time got over abandon her to go back to that awful dreadful place which was, she admitted now with honesty, the real love of his life. It could not be anything else, he had given up his integrity for it and then his very existence.

She had the feeling that because of Freddie's lack of concentration, because of what they had done they had cost him his life, the misery of betraying Jack and somehow the impossibility of going on.

She flew home and was rewarded by the sight of her parents waiting for her. Her father, speechless, hurried her into the car. Her mother made fruitless conversation and soon she was back in the bungalow and it was snowing, just like it always did at this time of the year, she thought fondly. It was like coming back to the prison of her early twenties. In some stupid way it was as though she had never left, as though none of this had happened.

She stood by the sitting-room windows, watching the big square flakes come down. Her mother made endless cups of tea and fussed when she did not eat and she was suddenly aware of her parents as people – her father's car not working very well had chugged home, her mother's dismay that things had turned out so badly and that everybody would know and that everybody would talk. The bungalow was shabby and worn and they ate plainly.

They told her they would both go to the funeral with her and she was only pleased. She could not imagine ever being able to go by herself. She did not hear from Jack, she did not expect to. Was he in Durham? Was he shocked? Was he still so very hurt?

It had snowed in Northumberland too so her first sight of the house which had cost them so much was so beautiful that it made her cry. White Maddens was a study that day in honeyed stone, blue sky and sunshine, and its gardens were covered in intricate drifts of white. The ponds were iced. A pheasant walked about beside the car and a red squirrel ran up a nearby tree as they made their way slowly down the long narrow road.

There were fat sheep and white cattle in the fields and the buildings were well-cared for. She knew that Freddie's marriage to Jennifer Erlhart had poured money into this place. Ironic to think that the estate now had everything except an heir. He was coming back even so, she thought. Even now he could not escape and this time it was for good.

Neither of his parents acknowledged her so she needed her own parents on either side to shield her from the black looks she gained from people at the funeral. Jennifer looked very good in black, pale, thin, with her bright red hair the brighter against her dark clothes. Freddie had not told her that his wife was beautiful. Her parents were there too with her, her mother little and fat, her father huge, red-faced and angry looking.

Jack, standing at the end next to his mother, could see Freddie's wife and his parents at the front. Jennifer did not look up.

It occurred to Jack that the last place Freddie would have wanted to be buried was there but since all his family were buried there no question arose. Sir Trevor came to Jack afterwards and Jack introduced him to his mother but she was unimpressed, he could see. Lords were one thing, car manufacturers were garage men.

As they stood about, embarrassed and silent, Sir Trevor said to him, 'Maybe you should take a few days off.'

'I would rather not,' Jack said and thanked him.

Jack went to where Rosalind stood as people began to drift towards their cars and he said to her, 'How are you, Ros?' He hated saying it, he knew very well how she was, her white face and huge eyes told him everything and all he wanted was to pick her up and run away with her. She looked now better than she had ever looked in spite of everything, wearing a short black coat which made her look young and vulnerable. She wore no gloves, no hat. Her perfect bobbed hair framed her face. 'I'm so sorry.'

She looked at him. 'You're sorry?'

After that nobody said anything for a while and Jack took refuge in looking past her, beyond the chapel and across the field past where the ruined castle stood. It was so damned romantic, he thought. Would I have given up everything for these great gardens, this huge house and ten thousand acres? Maybe if I had always been brought up to think that it was my duty to do so I would have.

'Where are you staying?'

'With my parents.'

'We should talk later.'

She turned to him, tears streaming and she said, 'Why?'

'About divorce.'

'You want to divorce me?' The tears ran faster and she laughed. 'I didn't mean to say that. Of course you want rid of me.'

Jack tried again. 'There's the house in London and—'

'I don't want the house. I never liked it. It's like a – like a – like you, like one of your cars.' She finally looked at him and Jack wished she hadn't because he had the feeling that what she said now would be something he remembered and his memory was too good for his peace.

'We could sell it and—'

'I don't care what you do. I don't want your house and I don't want your money. I'll see a solicitor, I don't want to talk about it and I don't want to see you, not after what I did, I can't bear it and I'm sure you can't, and we can be divorced and after that we don't ever have to meet again,' and she hurried off down the path and into the road.

Jack's mother came to him.

'I think we should go into the house for a little while, don't you? They have asked and I would love a cup of tea.'

It was the last thing Jack would have suggested, he didn't know what to say to Jennifer or Freddie's parents, he had the feeling that they blamed him in part for what had happened but it would have been cowardly not to go so they went and at the first opportunity he walked all the way across the drawing-room floor to where Freddie's wife, having greeted

154

and been polite to everyone, was standing alone in front of one of the long, narrow windows which looked out over a thin covering of snow and the vast lawns.

They had never met before. She was not fashionably dressed, as though here in Northumberland it was another world from London. Her hair was long and rather unruly and in a way, Jack thought, it made her look beautiful as though, ironically, she belonged here now. It seemed incongruous and she turned to him in her wonderful way that Americans had and she smiled and she said, 'Jack,' and took his hand.

'What will you do now?' Jack said to her.

'My godmother has died and left me some money.' She glanced across without affection at her parents who were standing together, halfway across the room, drinking sherry and talking to some other people. 'I should never have come here. I had no independence, nothing of my own before now. I'm going to go and live in New Hampshire, buy a house beside a lake and do some painting.'

'It sounds nice,' Jack said.

'I think it's what I always really wanted to do but I was never allowed to. Now there's nothing anybody can do to stop me. Did your – did Rosalind stay?'

'No.'

'How decent of her. He always loved her, didn't he?'

Jack had not understood up to that point what people meant when they said that they wished the ground would swallow them up but he did then. He couldn't answer. Jennifer smiled.

'I was so naive, I thought he would learn to love me and we would have children and that we would somehow fulfil something important. How could we, starting off so badly and ending the same way? I did love it here but we both gave up too much for this place. I won't do it any more.'

Jack squeezed her arm. She kissed him.

'It was so kind of you to come. I know it was difficult for you too.'

The house was so silent after the mourners had gone. Did you still call them mourners? Robyn couldn't remember. She wanted to be away, she could remember all the times she had wanted to be away from this place and none of them came anywhere close to this feeling but at the same time she felt

155

deep sorrow for Freddie's father and that was new. She had hated him for so long, resented him for so many years but the look on his face at his son's funeral would haunt her for the remainder of her life.

She said to Alain, her husband, when he suggested they might go, 'I'd like to talk to Will alone. Do you mind?'

He shook his head.

She opened the study door quietly and moved in, stripping off her gloves and pulling the hat from her hair, a confection of a hat, tiny with a feather, something Freddie would have loved, it was so frivolous.

Will was standing by the fire. It was the prettiest fireplace in the whole house, Dutch, little blue and white tiles, depicting windmills and waterways and houses, frivolous and she had always liked it best. She said his name but he didn't turn.

'I made him do it, it's all my fault,' he said in muffled despairing tones.

'Oh no, no.' She had to stop herself from going to him and getting hold of him. He looked so lonely standing there and he had always had this power to engage her sympathies when most of the time he didn't deserve them. This time was different but she didn't go over. The faint tug of attraction was still there, she was surprised and rather cross with herself.

'I did. I pushed him into this marriage when he didn't want it.'

'What else were you supposed to do?'

'Anything rather than this.' Will seemed to remember who he was at that point and who she was and how badly they had betrayed one another and he looked apologetically at her. 'Whatever can I do now?'

'You have four other children, William, you even have a granddaughter, whom I gather you hardly ever see.'

He smiled slightly. 'She is in Australia,' he said. 'You only call me "William" when you're really angry with me.'

'I've been really angry with you for at least twenty years.'

'Exhausting, isn't it?' he said.

'Alain and I are leaving,' she said.

'You won't be back.'

'No, I shan't. It isn't that I blame you—'

'Oh, don't think about it,' he said and he looked at her and she remembered when they had first met, his beautiful dark eyes, his charm, his intelligence. He was pure north country, dark eyes and straight nose and black hair and sharp cheek-bones and he had been so romantic, she had thought, the boy who had everything.

Her parents had been so excited that she had managed to attract the attentions of such a man, he had looks, background, one of the biggest estates in the north, all the right connections and he was such a good dancer.

They had danced and she had thought she had a fairy-tale ending to look forward to. It was laughable really because in fact he was just as basic as his ancestors had been, the men who fought over the borders, murdered and plundered and did everything they could for survival.

She said goodbye to him and then Alain drove them slowly towards the main road and the village and she did not look back, she would never look back again.

Sybil paused in the doorway of the library some time later, thinking of how this room now looked as it should have looked all those years. Jennifer had bought hundreds of rare books, thousand of hard-backed leather-bound books, some of them in valuable sets, and the antique furniture and expensive carpet and the smell of polish combined to make it friendly and smaller somehow.

Very often Sybil had had to stop herself from making remarks over the alterations the American girl made – would she ever stop thinking of Jennifer like that? She was a lovely woman and she had made a huge mistake in marrying a man who was no good at all. Sybil had always been the mistress of this house and she had apparently been so even after Freddie and Jennifer's marriage but only apparently.

Will hadn't spoken to Sybil all day although she had seen him after the funeral, going around and talking to the people who had come back.

'Do you think he died on purpose?' Will said when he heard her. The sentence came out all in one breath as though he had difficulty getting the words beyond his lips.

'Of course not. Whatever made you think such a thing?'

He shook his head.

'His marriage to Jennifer was the best thing that could have happened,' Sybil said. 'It was the only way. He knew that.'

'Was it?' Her husband looked sharply at her. 'Now I'm left with this – this bloody place and no son.'

She didn't understand immediately. She understood that he meant he didn't know what he could do with the enormous burden of grief. She only afterwards knew that he meant he was left without an heir and that it had always been, as it must be, his first concern.

It was a week later that she found him sitting in the garden, having been to see his solicitor.

'Why?'

For once it was a fine day, at least in the sunshine, and it had been dry enough so that you could sit on a wooden bench outside.

'I'm trying to find a way round this problem, this house.'

'Can't you leave it to one of the girls, I've heard of other people doing that—'

He shook his head.

'Claudia's husband—'

'That shower. None of them is fit to have this place. There's something else as well. I don't want to put them through this again.'

'Then what are you going to do?'

'I don't know.'

Sybil didn't like to point out that none of his children, all of whom were married, had managed to produce a male child. It was like a curse. He had seen his granddaughter once. Would he have been more interested had the child been a boy? Of course he would. There was no question of it. How awful. What a system.

The trouble was that she was tired of living here and putting up with all of the problems and she knew that he had only been waiting until Freddie did what Will called 'getting this nonsense out of his head', 'this nonsense' being the rally driving, before Will and Sybil could move into a small house on the estate and spend quite a lot of time somewhere warmer.

Sybil had spent many hours thinking of the house she would buy abroad, they had plenty of money and once Freddie and Jennifer and hopefully a son were installed at White Maddens she and Will would be free. Now who could tell how long they would have to go on. It made her feel very weary.

Sixteen

After the funeral Jack returned to London but not before he had persuaded his mother to sell him the house and garage.

'I don't see what use it is to you,' she said, 'the drivers are gone.'

'I'd like to have it,' he said, so she let him.

He went back to work straight away and stayed there for as long as he could. To go home without Rosalind and with Freddie dead was almost impossible and within days he had grown to hate it so much that he could not face a single evening without alcohol. The office, the works became his only refuge.

Eventually even that failed him. Sir Trevor called him into the office one day some time after this. Jack was losing sight of the days, the weeks by then. Somehow the seasons had changed. When had that happened without him noticing? He gazed from Sir Trevor's office window and couldn't remember the date.

Trevor wasn't sitting down and that was a bad sign. He smiled in a sort of paternal way and hovered and then he said, 'I think you should take some time off, Jack. I think it's all been too much for you.'

As though it shouldn't have been. As though he should have been able to forget Freddie.

'The last thing I need is time off.'

Trevor said, 'You're in a bad way,' and looked at him so clearly that Jack looked away.

'It'll pass.'

'It's been eight months.'

That brought Jack's gaze back to him. It could not possibly have been so long. He gazed once more from the window and this time he saw. It was early autumn, the leaves on the trees

159

were beginning to turn and several piles of them lay in the gutter across the road. Once he had loved this time best of all. Now it seemed that he hated every season every day. He saw his reflection in the mirror on the opposite wall and was astonished. That scarecrow was him, so skinny, unkempt, the old suit, the three-day-old beard, the eyes narrow.

'You need time off.'

'I don't.' He panicked. What on earth would he do with all that time? He couldn't face a single day without the office. He couldn't manage the dawn, the late afternoons, the early evenings, the silence in his house which since Ros had left had got bigger and bigger until it was the size of the Grand Canyon. Sometimes he didn't go home at all. Sometimes he sat in bars and listened to music. Sometimes he even went to hotels, brown hotels with brown walls and . . .

'You aren't working. You haven't produced a single good idea since . . . '

Why couldn't the man say it? Since Freddie had died.

'I want you to go,' Trevor said.

'Go?'

'Yes. I think you should leave.'

'Leave? What do you mean?'

Trevor didn't look at him and Jack was reminded that you were only as good as your last idea. His ideas were all used up and Freddie had died because of them.

'You're finished, Jack, it's over,' Trevor said.

'But—'

'You drink. You sit in your office, the short time you're there every day, and you drink.'

'That's not true.'

'Yes, it is. You're finished. You've burned out. I've seen it happen to other designers. They give everything they've got and when it's gone they move on, at least the sensible ones do.'

'It's not the drink—' Jack said.

'I want you to clear your desk and leave the building and you won't be allowed back in.'

'You can't do that to me, Trevor. What the hell am I going to do?'

'I don't know but you're not coming back here. I don't like drink and I don't allow failure and you're failing here, badly. I thought in time you'd be strong enough to get over it and go on but you're a weaker person than I thought you were. There are only two ways to things like this, either you get them or they get you. You're burned out. I'll give you half an hour. If you haven't left by then I'll have you thrown out.'

Jack stood there for several seconds in the silence which followed and it seemed to him that Trevor's words repeated and repeated in the still air.

'Maybe you should drink, Trevor,' he said.

Trevor paused and then he said, more kindly, 'Go home, eh?'

'Sod you,' Jack said.

When he went back to his office the shock of being dismissed made him see more clearly than he had done in a long time. He was astonished that it was not as he had thought it. There were papers all over the place and he could not organize them into any cohesion even when he attempted to gather them to take them home. Hundreds and hundreds of papers, great piles of them on every available surface and on the floor, inches and inches of papers. His hands shook and to his astonishment the drawers of his desk were full of empty bottles, vodka, gin, sherry. The whole place smelled of drink. It was nothing like the clean surfaces which he had cared for so much, everything was covered, none of it made any sense, and as he turned over the various pages more and more of them, they were all cars which had never been built, all ideas which had not been followed through. He had repeated the same thing, every single day since Freddie had died.

He emptied the desk, he put all the bottles on the top for some reason and there were so many of them that they filled the area that had once been his love, his play. Jack stared at them and then with one movement he swept the whole lot onto the floor where they bounced and crashed and the dregs of the whisky and gin and brandy they had had in them flew across the carpet in big drops.

He didn't take anything with him when he left the building.

Seventeen

The winter nights were long in the north. Jack had forgotten. It was ten o'clock, and he had driven through the cold evening up the Great North Road. It wasn't called that any more but he always thought of it that way.

The past rose up to mock him, to tell him that there was nothing to be gained by going back, he wouldn't call it going home because it was not, going home could be nothing without the people you were meant to go home to and he could not go home to them any more. The trouble was that he could no longer stay away and for many days now it was the only place that he wished to be.

His brain would not be quiet and chronicled for him the faults of the car as he proceeded in full moonlight, the moon rising as though in a cinema directly for him, like cut glass in the autumn sky so that when the darkness fell and it was very late it lit the way up the road and there were few cars.

He went past the pub which had been a coaching house where a white lady was meant to appear beseeching travellers to stop and aid her but she was not there and as the night wore itself on even he wished that he had reached his destination and soon he got to Scotch Corner, the big hotel standing out under its lights.

Scotch Corner was always home even though he was still thirty miles away. It was the lighthouse of the north for weary travellers. It meant that you would sleep in your own bed, that your loved ones were waiting for you, the door was unlocked and the meal had been made ready.

He was afraid to arrive. What he liked best about journeys was the journey itself. Some people did not understand that. The point was to be on the road, watching the miles and the changing scenery. In some ways the motor car and fast trains had spoiled the whole idea of a journey because it was over too quickly, you could not indulge yourself with picnics and nights spent in new places, with the conversation of strangers and the delights of names which had never before been on your tongue.

Now it was how fast you could get there as though the time you spent on the road was wasted, unimportant. He had not understood at the time that things like progress and technology destroyed as much as they created, as though a balance had to be maintained, that it was indeed true, things did not change and the idea of change was fallacy because the more you progressed the more the past fell in behind you like a landslide.

He was afraid to go back, just as he had been afraid to stay in London, and as in London, when he had wished to be gone now he wished that he had stayed and it was tiring, this not knowing and never being sure. He wanted to stop the car and sleep but he couldn't because a greater part of him urged him on like a rider on a fleet horse.

He had been a child in the north and now he was past thirty and it was a long gap between childhood and who he had become. What he wanted to go back to was not what was there but what was gone, it was the past he wanted, the safeness of what had been.

He yawned and remembered how he had slept when he was a boy, the eight or nine hours and then woke refreshed, ready to take on the day and all its surprises such as an adult never could. Nothing in adult life was ever magical again, not like he had seen things. You could never be as absorbed by a book, as delighted by Christmas, as fascinated by what seemed now to be small things.

Food would not taste as good again, it was always summer there even when things had gone wrong, as long as you had one adult who was always on your side.

Crying and driving went so well together, it was an art form. Nobody saw you, you didn't have to stop what you were doing, you could even whinge a bit with nobody to hear you and the radio played out the most God-awful tunes which made you worse. Why did people have to write such songs, how did they know what you were feeling? He had heard it said that music was the highest art form and it was, even at its lowest, even at its stupidest, slushiest, it was still more effective than Shakespeare, nearer than Monet.

The road wound its way through County Durham. The road to Scotland, to Corbridge, the north, the border, the bonny road to end all roads, the sweetest journey ever, the promise of a view in every mile, the excitement of being almost into another country and such a country. God would have lived in Scotland if he could have chosen. Pure air, hills forever, streams that ran down from as far as you could see, whisky the same colour as your lover's eyes, stones as grey as the threat of rain.

There was something about the border country which you got nowhere else. When you asked for whisky the barman had forty different ones to offer and they conjured up such possibilities, the mainland, the islands, the highlands, the lowlands, the mist, the peat fire, the fishing and the lochs.

There was always a smoky fire in the pubs here in winter, possibly snow outside and if you were lucky the landlord's cats who would sit beside and take crisps from you and stare and if you were really lucky they would purr around your legs in their strange fashion and settle on the hearthrug to sleep in that instant way they had and he envied them. Would he ever sleep well again?

He was beyond Darlington now, driving swiftly towards West Auckland and then it was up the bank to Toft Hill and there at the very highest point he stopped because the moon lit the sky. Laid out before him were all the dreams of his life, the neat round shapes of the trees, the little square fields with the river at the bottom, the castle with its battlements stark against the night sky off to the right.

He had seen it in his mind's eye so often it was such a relief to know that it was still there, that in his dreams he had found reality, that there was still something left to hold on to. He sat there on the top road and gazed down over the dale and the little sleeping town before he plunged down the bank that was the last leg before home.

From there you had to climb some way but finally the small town came into view, the very outside of it, Bridge Street first with the council estate behind, then the war memorial, where if you went straight on you wound down into the glory of Weardale with its small grey farms and drystone walls but he turned right to go down the main street and a thousand recollections flashed across his mind, the memories of childhood, difficult painful images because of his dad not being there any more, which he quickly dismissed as he began to slow the car down to a halt before he reached the level crossing. The workingmen's club, the various shops, the pubs were all passed and then the slight hill.

He brought the car to a stop outside his parents' house, the garage next door, well back from the pavement, which was in darkness and the house had no lights. How had he expected them? He opened the glove compartment on the passenger side and found the keys and then he got out of the car.

The house was set back slightly with what it would have been an exaggeration to call a garden at the front and he put the key into the front door and when it was open he went inside. He had taken a flashlight because the electricity would be turned off. Quickly he ran the light around the walls and went up the narrow stairs and into the main bedroom which had been his parents' room. He thought of being a little boy and of getting into bed with them there in the early morning and he wanted the past back so very badly.

He drew apart the curtains, the moon shone in through the window. He took a half-bottle of whisky out of his pocket and went into the tiny bathroom at the back of the house and found a glass and rinsed it and then he went back and sat down on the double bed where his parents had slept for as long as he could remember. He sat there for a while, sipping at the whisky, and then he became aware that the house smelled stuffy as though nobody had been in it for a very long time, no windows had been opened.

He put down his glass and the bottle and got off the bed and he went across and opened the window. It took a bit of doing because it seemed to him that the window had been painted shut but in the end the sash operated and it slid up. It made creaking noises as it did so but when it was fully open he leaned out as he had when a child.

It looked over the back of the house towards the valley. There was a small garden which should have been overgrown but was not, due, he guessed, to Bert who lived next door and had been born a gardener. Bert couldn't have suffered to see the garden spoil. There were his mother's roses, carefully pruned and cared for. Just thinking of Bert and Betty made him smile. It was comforting to know that they were still there. They had been there throughout his childhood and it seemed to him now as though they always would be. Knowing that this was not true did not alter the way that his heart felt about it.

The night had grown completely dark but it wouldn't last much longer, three or four hours at most, it was beyond three o'clock now. That was comforting too, he found the darkness so hard to get through, the dawn was always a relief and to know that it would soon arrive and that he wouldn't stay awake through it made him feel better.

How immature, how stupid, his intelligent mind told him, to run for home but it was the only place he wanted to be. It was over, everything he had ever wanted, everything he had tried for. He wished and wished for his parents' presence, for the comfort of their experience and their knowledge and most of all for his father's understanding.

It was said that the very old returned to die. That was how he felt. He had come back here as though it was the finish to the circle of his life. There was nothing left but this. He went back to the bed and sat down, put the top on the whisky bottle, nursed his drink a little while longer, finished it and then lay down and closed his eyes. He felt as though the old house gathered him into its arms and for the first time in many months he fell into a peaceful sleep.

Eighteen

Whisky got Jack through the first night back in his parents' house though as usual when the light of day arrived his stomach revolted at the excess of alcohol and the lack of food. He was surprised to find himself at home for the first few moments and then rather disgusted. It had the coolness that came with empty houses. When he levered himself up from the bed once again it was because somebody was hammering on the back door.

The hammering did not stop and when Jack finally made

his way across the tiny landing, down the steep stairs and through the freezing narrow hall and into the kitchen and slid back the bolts and turned the key he found Bert standing there, looking concerned and almost apologetic.

'I saw the car,' was all he said.

Jack said nothing. Then it seemed Bert recalled his errand.

'Betty says you're to come round for your dinner.'

Jack tried to put him off, would normally have been short with such persistence but nothing was normal any more and he could not offend these people who had always been so kind to him, always the same age. In the end he went and it was only then that he realized it was Sunday because the smell coming from Betty's kitchen was the best smell in the world. It was Sunday dinner.

She didn't kiss and cuddle him, even though they hadn't met in so long. She said, 'There you are, lad. I knew it was you, one of those big cars you drive. Sit yourself down and have a beer with Bert. It's nearly ready.'

The table in the dining room was hideous with a thick central leg like a post and it matched the chairs and the sideboard and the corner cabinet which was filled with china but it looked to Jack like the world's most beautiful table. It was covered in a white lace cloth, glasses, cutlery, salt and pepper. Bert poured him his beer and when he tried to refuse Bert said, 'Aye, you were never much of a drinker,' as though it were a slight fault which Jack could make nothing better of and in spite of how Jack felt it made him smile. Bert topped up the beer with lemonade as though Jack had requested it and then Betty came in from the kitchen, just as his mother had done on so many Sundays, the pork all in one piece on a big oval plate, its crackling as dark as caramel, and various tureens with turnips bright in butter but dulled on top with pepper, potatoes, roasted and golden, Brussels sprouts, no doubt from their garden, a big sauce boat full of apple sauce and a gravy boat with onion gravy.

Jack's stomach had changed its mind about not being hungry and after two platefuls of dinner and a huge helping of rhubarb crumble and custard, two shandies and two cups of tea he was exhausted.

'Bert helps with the clearing up. You go and sit down,' Betty said.

167

Jack staggered off to their front room and by a fire you got only that large when you lived in a coalfield he fell asleep. The next thing he was aware of was that the evening had grown dark and wet beyond the windows and Betty had put tea and sandwiches on a little table by the fire. Jack's insides clamoured for whisky. He tried to make an excuse to leave but Betty said, 'You're not going next door, it's cold, damp and dusty. Your mother left nothing but the old bed, she said it was the worse for wear. No doubt she's right. You're staying here.'

Jack tried to argue again while Betty pressed him to eat sandwiches and cake and by the time he had eaten them Bert suggested they should walk up to the monument and go to the Black Horse for a couple of pints.

Jack had not realized how much he had missed the companionship of other people, the bright lights of a pub, the beer and the talk. They all knew him, they had been friends of his dad and some of them had been his own friends from childhood and schooldays which he had lost when he left to go to London. He did not miss Freddie for the first time and nobody mentioned him. Nobody asked any questions.

They did not stay late or drink too much and when they got back Betty directed him into her spare room, only asking if he had any clean clothes. Jack had to admit that he did not and she said he could borrow some from Bert for the morning, she would put them out. He did try to protest again but he had already realized that there was no point in arguing with Betty.

He awoke beneath the warmth of Betty's pink eiderdown, clean clothes already on the chair beside the bed. When he finally got downstairs Betty was in the kitchen. She poured him tea and proceeded to fry bacon and eggs. From the back window he could see Bert pottering around in the vegetable patch at the end of the long narrow garden.

Putting a plateful of bacon, eggs and fried bread in front of him, Betty sat down across the table, poured more tea and said, 'You can stay as long as you like.'

'No, thank you, I have to . . . ' He couldn't remember what. He didn't have to do anything, for the first time in his life.

'So, what are you going to do?'

It was the first direct question. Jack thought hard and couldn't come up with an answer.

'You can't live next door,' his hostess said. 'Why don't you stay with us for a few days while you decide?'

'I can't do that, Betty.'

'Why not?'

He didn't answer that either.

'Your mam and dad would never forgive me if I let you go back to London the state you're in.'

'I'm not—'

'Yes, you are. You can't even hold a knife and fork without your hands shaking. I don't want to hear any more about it. Eat your breakfast,' Betty said and she got up and went to the sink and began to wash the dishes noisily.

Nineteen

Jack's days took on a strange and languid pattern as though he was recovering from some strange illness. Without whisky, with nothing more than two or three pints inside him, and the window open to the fell beyond in the village, he slept long and well. He wore Bert's clothes which were rather too big for him but nobody cared. He ate three large meals a day. He read the *Northern Echo* after breakfast and since Bert was now retired they would work in the garden and on Bert's allotment which lay at the other side of the village towards the dale. He liked being there. Growing vegetables was so much easier than designing cars, he thought and made himself smile.

That spring, which came along in spite of the way people said it wouldn't, he helped Bert firstly to plant seedlings in the greenhouse and then to plant out the small cabbages and carrots and cauliflowers. He put muck into the leek trench, raked and hoed and weeded and he and Bert would spend time chatting to the other allotment-holders and sitting over a flask of tea in deck chairs beside the shed.

On Saturdays and Sundays they went to the pubs at dinner time, the rest of the week they didn't. In the afternoons Jack would go for a walk into Weardale or across the fell and come back for tea. When he ventured into his own house Betty followed him in, cleaning products in her hands.

'I'm thinking I might move back in here,' he said.

'Aye, I thought you were,' Betty said. 'While I'm sorting this lot out why don't you pop to the auction rooms at Durham and see if you can come by some decent furniture and I'll get Fred Hobson to take this bed away. Bert'll go with you.'

Jack bought a bed with matching wardrobe and dressing table and chest of drawers – all very old fashioned but he rather liked them – and a dining table and chairs and a settee, and when they got back, with promise of delivery the following day, Betty had done what she called 'turning the house out'.

Within two days Jack was comfortable in his own house though Betty still insisted on his going next door for his meals. After another week Jack strolled up the yard to the side of the house, unlocked the big gates and walked into the gloom of the huge garage. It was the first time he had done so since his father's death and it took every ounce of energy that he possessed but once he had done it he could see a sliver of sunlight from where the corrugated sheets on the roof didn't quite meet and he could hear his father's voice and the voices of the other men who had worked there and he saw the emptiness of the place not as something to be upset about but as something waiting to be filled. How strange.

Twenty

Rosalind had lived in London for too long, she thought, she had forgotten how harsh the northern winters were or she would not have gone there. London was wet in winter but the Durham fells were freezing. Nothing stopped the wind and the snow from throwing themselves across the bleak flat vastness. It was a study in black and white that March.

The bungalow had been pretty when her father built it of red brick with bay windows and steps down from the front door to the huge garden beyond.

The bedrooms were on the back and there was also a dining room, a big kitchen, a yard and the garages. It seemed so small after Jack's huge house in London. How odd that she still thought of it as Jack's house and not theirs.

She had had several letters from his solicitor. After opening the first she recognized the thick white envelopes. She had impressed upon her own solicitor that she wanted nothing. He had tried in vain to persuade her otherwise. She had no money and though she was considering how she could earn some her parents had said they were happy to have her there for the time being. She had the feeling that although they were horrified she had left Jack and gone off with Freddie they blamed Jack because the marriage did not work.

They pretended to her that everything was all right as though they were afraid to admit that she might have problems.

'You are entitled to a hefty share of Jack's wealth,' her father said. 'He must be a very rich man by now.'

'I left him,' she said.

Her father blustered for a few minutes. They were sitting by the window which looked out over the gardens. There was snow across the lawn and in the fir trees.

'There must have been a good reason for that,' he said.

'There was. I was in love with another man. Surely you know this. You must know that I loved Freddie Harlington. I always loved him. Jack did nothing—'

'He didn't make you happy.'

'How could he, knowing how I felt? I don't want anything from him. Don't you see how badly I treated him?'

'You were his wife. You are entitled—'

'I don't want anything.'

'Then what are you going to do?'

'I don't know yet. I just want a little time to think about it,' she said.

The trouble was that as the weeks went by there was another problem. She was pregnant. By April she was sure of it, went to the doctor, had the pregnancy confirmed and then sat her parents down in the kitchen by the Aga and told them.

'Now you must go to your solicitor and tell that man you must have money for his child,' her mother said.

'It isn't his child.'

Her mother went pale.

'Are you sure about that?'

'Quite sure, yes. I can hardly ask Jack to pay for another man's baby after what I did to him.'

'Then the Harlington family must pay.'

'No. They must never know and if either of you mentions the matter to anyone I shall deny it and say that it's Jack's child.'

Not really given to praying, Rosalind did several times during the summer, as the pregnancy began to show, that the baby would be a girl. She had the feeling that if it was not there would be all kinds of problems. She had never felt so alone. She missed Freddie but the trouble was that she missed being able to run to Jack as she had always done, she realized now, when things had gone wrong. Freddie had been in and out of her life so often that she could pretend for short stretches of time that he was away whereas she knew very well that Jack was in London and it took all the strength she had not to go to him.

She felt that people in the village were talking about her and it was not hard to imagine what they were saying and she got to the point where it was very difficult to go out because of the gossip which she imagined. People stared, sometimes did not speak and even when she had no doubt they were being natural with her she always imagined more than what happened.

In the late summer the baby was born and it was a boy. Rosalind was more dismayed than she had thought she would be for the first few days but then, with her mother's help, and when she had had a decent amount of sleep for several nights, she could not help being glad that there was something left of Freddie and how important the baby had already become to her.

Jack had forgotten what the garage was like, the smells of oil and cold fells and the noises, and as he stood inside with the echoing sounds of the north wind around him all the sweet memories of his childhood came rolling back and they seemed

172

to surround him almost as though his father was there, as though the drivers were shouting up the yard in good-humoured fashion at one another, the buses standing in a neat line with his father's name on the side; it all came to life so much that Jack was filled with confusion and it was only when he heard a noise behind him that he turned, suddenly angry that anyone should intrude upon his emotions.

It was Betty. This was somehow not the place he had expected to see her and he could see by the look on her face that she had something to say.

'You've been trying to talk to me for days, haven't you?' he offered.

Betty hesitated. 'I didn't think you were in a fit state to hear anything hard.'

'You could be right.' Jack walked away from her, across the dark floor where a thousand memories opened like the lids off boxes, but he knew that it was a delaying tactic, that he was avoiding her, as he had been avoiding the hesitation of other people, the hard looks of the men in the pubs, the way that people shut up talking when they saw him. 'But you think I am now.'

'I think you need to hear it and from me before somebody else tells you. Every day I've thought somebody would and you would come back and start drinking again—'

She stopped there as Jack turned around in surprise.

'I'm not daft,' she said.

'You've been so kind to me.'

'Somebody had to be. You think folk here don't know or don't care what you've done but the thing is it's just that it's outside their ken. You were always a loner, not fitting in, and it's difficult for other people, they don't know what to say in case you think they're daft and they don't understand what you do because it's too clever. People don't want their children to be clever, they want them to be settled and for there to be plenty to talk about and for them to be around.'

'I've never been any of those things.'

'How could you, being the man you are?'

Jack walked around the dark depths of the building as though he might gather strength from it and Betty went on standing just inside the door with her arms folded and her face set with he thought whatever it was she was going to tell him.

173

'Rosalind is living with her parents and . . . there's a little lad.'

Had Betty known that it would be the hardest blow of all?

'I didn't want to tell you,' she said, 'but since it's a fact you have to know.'

'How long has she been here?'

'Ever since the funeral. I think she had nowhere else to go.'

He wanted to shout, 'She could have come to me,' but he didn't because it wasn't true.

When Betty had gone he continued walking around the building, wondering whether things might have been any better, wondering what to do now and how long he would hold out against the impulse to get into his car and drive like hell to the Wests' bungalow. He lasted almost an hour, which he thought was good.

They lived at the far side of the village, considered the polite end by those who knew and cared for such things, the streets where people had tiny little gardens at the front of their terraced houses though only yards and back streets behind, the streets where the men who had owned the little pits around the village lived in the end houses and they would have a bigger garden and a front door down the side of the gable with stained glass. Beyond that was the Mechanics' Institute and then a short road where Leonard West had built his bungalow.

Jack parked above and walked down the short path to the back door and he banged on the door until it was answered. Mrs West stood there and she stared.

'I'd like to see Rosalind,' Jack said.

Mrs West let him in without a word. The back door led straight into the kitchen and on the hearth there set to rise were bowls of dough, two of them, the tops high and brown, and the smell of yeast filled the kitchen and the smell of baking bread.

Mrs West took him through there and through the house out to the sitting room which had a bay window and over-looked the lawns and there Rosalind was seated on a big sofa and she had the child in her arms. She no longer looked prosperous or fashionable, she had about her a look of defeat. Her hair had been allowed to grow with a fringe which partly hid

174

her eyes and her face was white and tired. She wore blue jeans and a T-shirt and he was filled with longing for her and as always the desire to whisk her away to somewhere that he could take care of her.

'Ros,' was all Jack said.

'Why,' she said, 'it was good of you to come.'

Mrs West muttered something about tea and hurried out. Rosalind asked Jack to sit down. He eyed the baby.

'Did you call him Freddie?'

'He's called Ned.'

'Nice. And Freddie's surname?'

She hesitated just long enough for Jack to notice and then she looked straight at him. 'No. He has your surname.'

'I see.'

'I don't expect you do.'

'Well, you have my surname, such as it is, you could hardly call him West, could you?'

'He's called Edward Neville. I did hope you wouldn't mind, though I would understand it if you did. It's more than convenience.'

'Why is it?'

She took a deep breath and looked at him properly for the first time.

'Because Freddie's father is trying to claim him.'

Twenty-One

She had not expected the summons, she had not expected to hear from Freddie's family at all, and when she had received a haughty letter from the earl's secretary more or less commanding her to appear with the baby at his home on a certain day at a certain time she had ignored it.

However, when the second letter came she hardly dared open it and needed her father there. It was written more politely, it asked her to state a time and a day when she would come.

She had ignored that too. Her father was a stubborn man when he chose. She was even more glad when he was stubborn for her sake and she was proved right with her instincts. Giving the baby Jack's name would protect him.

In the end Freddie's father came to see her and after some hesitation she allowed him to come in and she could not suppress the feeling of triumph, the elation of power. Never had a man looked more out of place than Will Harlington did in their sitting room. He was too rich, too expensively dressed, slender and good looking in a way that middle-aged men were never meant to be and his Bentley took up the whole of their drive and she hated the way that it made her father's car look so old and so dilapidated. Ros hated him that he was so important, that he thought he was so important. She hated everything he stood for.

And then she thought savagely, my father never made me marry anybody I didn't care about, he didn't make me feel as though my responsibility to my name and a piece of land was more important than my life. She blamed this man for his son's death, even though she knew that was slightly unfair.

'May I hold him?'

'He doesn't like strangers,' she said, the small child close and sleeping in her arms. He was getting quite heavy but she had no intention of letting Freddie's father anywhere near. She knew it was illogical but she had the feeling he would run outside and away with the child.

'Let me explain the circumstances to you. My grandfather was an only son. I was an only son. Freddie was . . . do you see the pattern? As far as I am aware there is nobody to inherit the title and if left now it will die out. He is the heir to a vast and proud inheritance and a title which is hundreds of years old. We have thousands of acres and a huge house and various other . . . lands and properties. We even have money since the Erlharts.'

Rosalind decided this was less than tactful.

'You hold it all in your hands in this child,' he said.

Rosalind had put in a great many hard days because Freddie's family would not accept her. She believed that if they had been married he would still be alive. She had not been good enough and she had had no money. Well, now they had the money but she held all the cards so she merely smiled politely at him, pushing down the way that she wanted to scream and shout and tell him it was because of him that Freddie had died and she said, 'This is Jack Neville's child.'

'Are you quite sure?'

'Certain.'

'I have thought about this a great deal and I think you would lie to me over it. If this is my son's child for God's sake have a little pity and tell me that it's so, it is very important and means everything to me. I cannot hold that place together for ever and I cannot hold it together if there is nobody to come after me. I've given my whole life to it. If he is the heir to such a proud inheritance and the title please tell me.'

'He's not Freddie's.'

It was almost worth it to see the look on Will Harlington's face. Revenge, she thought, was just as sweet as people said it was but she kept the triumph out of her face until he had gone.

Jack stared at her. 'You told him the baby was mine?'

'Shouldn't I have?' She looked fiercely at him. 'Do you think I'm depriving him of his "rightful inheritance"?' She put such scorn into the words. 'I'm not asking you for anything—'

'Except my name for your child?'

'It's my name!'

Afterwards he remembered with some pride that she had proclaimed herself a Neville and that too was an inheritance to any northerner. The Nevilles had a long history in Durham, just as long if not more so than the Harlingtons in Northumberland, Jack thought.

'I don't want anything else from you.'

'Except a divorce, perhaps? I haven't heard anything from you. You wouldn't be changing your mind, by any chance?'

'No, I wouldn't.' She hesitated. 'Do you think I did the wrong thing, telling Freddie's father the baby wasn't his?' She looked appealingly at him.

'No, I don't think it was wrong and even if I did you wouldn't give him up for such a reason when it cost Freddie his life.'

'It wasn't directly—'

'All right, so it was indirectly,' Jack said, shortly, 'he drove like somebody with a death wish. You know he did. Harlington

177

sold his son for a piece of Northumberland moor and there's
no getting round that. In the old days perhaps things were
different but for God's sake people shouldn't have to live like
that and die like that. There's no justification for it at all and
we both know it.'

She let go of her breath, he heard and saw and she even
smiled a little.

'So what are you going to do?' Jack said.

'You're not the only man left in the world,' she said.

That too, he remembered. The trouble was that in a way he
was. He was the only man beside Freddie that she had ever
cared for. Perhaps she could care for somebody else. He
doubted it. It was all very well for people to go around spilling
their emotional guts all over the place but it wasn't love and
it was all very well for people to go sleeping around but it
wasn't love. She had loved Freddie and perhaps, in a very
small way, with the little corner of her heart and mind she
had loved him too.

There was nothing to do but go home. When he got there
a car was pulled up in front of the garage.

'I've broken down, mate,' the man said, getting out, 'and
somebody told me that this used to be a garage. Can you
help?'

It was upon Jack's lips to say he couldn't, that everything
was finished, that the buses were gone and the drivers were
scattered and that it was over but the car on the pavement
beside the garage called to him because it was one of his. He
could have laughed at the irony of it. It was a super version
of the little car that he had designed and loved, sweated over
and lost everything for, and it sat there, squat and quiet, and
it was almost like a child come home.

'I've got to get back,' the young man said, 'my wife's pregnant, the baby's expected any day now and I don't like to
leave her for too long. Can you do anything?'

Jack lifted the bonnet. He could have seen the engine with
his eyes closed, knew exactly what the problem was, fixed it
within seconds. It was nothing much. Engines, cars, they were
a closed world to some people. The young man stared, offered
to pay. Jack refused. 'It was nothing,' he said.

As the man drove off he watched the little car, the idea

178

which had cost him so very dearly. It was like a child leaving home. You didn't want it to, this thing you had created, you wanted to keep it safe and close and warm but you couldn't because you had created it so that it would go out and do things you couldn't, see worlds you had no knowledge of, be there when you were gone and it would be, he knew and all the love and resentment he felt was mixed up together, like a tearing.

Perhaps it would always be there in some way, in some form or version, the car which had enabled millions of people to decide where they would go and what they would do, it had altered their lives, it had given them independence and huge choices. Somehow, as he watched it, it ceased to be as important as he had thought. He had not felt like this when he had finished it but then it was always hanging around in one form or another like an unwanted relative. Now as it chugged its way up the hill, out towards the fell it was like seeing somebody off to Australia. You might see them again but it would never be as close as it had been.

He should have known. The following day he was messing about in the office – there were hundreds of files and papers which nobody had seen fit to sort out and since the law said that papers from a business must be kept for several years he was trying to think what to do with them – when there was a noise on the outside door and a man popped his head round.

'I was talking to our Johnny yesterday and he said thoo fixed that little car of his and I was wondering if thoo could do owt with mine?'

Jack cursed inwardly. This was exactly what he didn't want, people interrupting. An inward voice, one he hadn't heard for a while, said scornfully, 'Interrupting what?' so he went out and took a look at the car. This time it was a bigger car and a bigger problem. He lifted the bonnet and then put it down again and got the man to bring the car around the back because there was a bitter wind coming down the main street and it was beginning to snow.

He walked around to the back and opened the great big doors which had been built to accommodate the buses and he waved the man inside and then he switched on the lights and it was remarkable how efficient they were.

The man drove the car in and Jack set to work and as he did so the old familiar feeling of contentment and excitement and the I'm-where-I-should-be feeling came over him, as it had done when he had new ideas, when he designed. He hadn't felt that since long before Freddie died, possibly since before he had been married.

'Shall I come back?' a voice enquired.

Jack lifted his face out of the engine and stared. He hadn't noticed the passage of time.

'Just get in and try it,' he suggested and when the man did Jack could hear the engine turn over, sweet and full.

The man thanked him, tried to pay. Jack shook his head.

'I can't let you do it for nowt,' the man insisted, 'what will I do when I want to come back?'

So Jack let him pay a little and when the car had driven away and he was listening carefully all the time in case it faltered, but it didn't, he looked at the money in his hand and thought, Oh no, now he will expect to be able to come back. It was too late. He was angry with himself, about to shut the office and go into the house but he didn't. He went back inside to where the fire was low and built it up and he sat down and began sorting out some more papers.

The following week he had a letter from Rosalind's solicitor and he had been avoiding sorting this out, he didn't realize until then, avoiding letting the divorce go ahead. How long had it been? Pretending nothing was happening. So he ended up going to his father's solicitor who had been dealing with this since Jack had come north and had his offices a few miles away in Weardale. There Jack heard the disquieting words, 'She ran away with another man. That should make it easy.'

'He's dead.'

'Oh. And the child?'

Now there was the difficulty, Jack thought. If he told this man that the child was Freddie's then the world would know officially that it was and although he didn't think Freddie's father could have any claim on the child he had no intention of giving anybody the chance.

'He's mine.'

'So she ran off when she was pregnant with your child?'

That made it sound even worse.

'I don't think she knew.'

'It's not a very sound base for divorce, though, is it?'

'Can't we do it the other way round, can't we say it was my fault? It was my fault.'

'You had an affair?'

'No.' But he had. It was not women in his case, it was the little car and he knew now that all the way through their marriage he had given his time, his energy, his full commitment to the work, knowing that she loved Freddie, knowing perhaps that it would not last, that it was not real or had he run away in the first place, only taking her in because he loved her, knowing that she would never return the feelings and that the whole thing was only temporary?

'The law might say that it was a . . . a momentary lapse.'

Jack wanted to laugh. She had loved Freddie all her life since the day that she had met him, he felt sure.

'The marriage was a momentary lapse,' he said.

'On both your parts?'

Jack eyed him.

'Divorce ought to be something both people want,' the solicitor said. 'It seems to me that there may be a cause for conciliation.'

'There isn't.'

'Are you quite sure?'

'She doesn't want me,' Jack said. 'She never wanted me.'

It was not quite true, he thought afterwards when he made his way down the dales, past the little grey-stone walls and the small square fields across the winding road which made its way through the narrow valley. There had been good times and she had wanted him but he thought it had more to do with the elegant lifestyle he had achieved than anything honest.

That made him smile when he got back to the garage and his neat little terraced house. Such elegance, he thought. He had Mrs Whittington from up the street to see to his house now. He had insisted that Betty could not keep on running and cleaning two houses and he even had his meals at home now. Mrs Whittington did the washing and the cooking and although her cooking was not the same as Betty's it was as good in its way though he missed the companionship.

Betty and Bert were still being careful with him, he thought. Bert called for him most evenings to go to the pub but more often now Jack would be in the garage when he called because the local people, having been without a garage for so long, had found out he was mending cars and very soon he had a whole yard full of other people's vehicles and had discovered to his instant regret and horror that he had to buy parts, keep books and records, make sure he was open all day.

'It's eight o'clock, man, Jack, are you not done?' Bert complained amiably, one spring evening when Jack had congratulated himself that the nights were getting lighter and he didn't need to put the lights on in the big garage until well after tea.

'I've just got to finish this.'

'That's what you said last night and I stood about for half an hour. Howay, man, let's out of here.'

Jack took a rag to his oily fingers and then had to go inside and wash and find a clean shirt so Bert was right, it was at least half an hour before they got going. As they did so a familiar figure came towards them out of the looming darkness and Jack's heart did a funny little twist because he had known her by the way that she walked. It was Rosalind.

He wanted to greet her with enthusiasm, to tell her all the things that had gone on since last he had seen her at her parents' house, he wanted to pull her into his arms and tell her how much he loved her, he wanted to tell Bert he couldn't go to the pub, that he had to be with her. He wanted to grab her and run upstairs with her and take her to bed and during the seconds before she reached him he ran through his mind as a precaution the way that she had left him and how she had Freddie's child and then all the old horrors came upon him and his body clamoured for whisky.

'Jack.'

It was all she said but he could remember her saying his name a hundred different ways, the breathy way she said it when they were making love, the reproving way she said it when he was late home, the apologetic way when she had told him that the baby was not his. It made him feel so wretched he could hardly look at her. Was he never to get used to being without her and why in hell couldn't she leave him alone to recover what he could of his life? Did she not know that he would have given up the company of anybody else on earth for five minutes of her time? He greeted her casually and was proud of himself.

'Ros. How are you?'

'I'm so glad I caught you,' she said, 'the car won't start.'

Not 'I've changed my mind, I love you', not 'Would you like to come over for coffee some time', not 'I've missed you' or even 'How are you' and Jack thought that for the rest of his life people would be saying to him 'the car won't start' and of course that was what they should say.

'I'll catch you up,' he said to Bert and followed her and there just around the corner was her father's old car.

'Didn't he ever think about buying a new one?' Jack suggested.

'He can't afford it,' she said.

That had not occurred to him. They had always had money though it was true that the little pits in the area were worked up and he could not remember her father ever going to work much over the past fifteen years.

Without comment Jack looked at the little car, lifted the bonnet but it was too dark to see anything. He managed to get it going without the benefit of being able to see but it was not going to last five minutes, he could hear it.

'Get in. We'll drive round and take it into the garage.'

She did and they went and Jack opened the big doors and flooded the garage with light and then he lifted the bonnet again.

'It'll take time. Why don't I drive you home and you can come and pick it up in a day or two?'

'A day or two? I need it.'

'You can borrow mine.'

'I don't want to . . . ' she said and then stopped.

They drove the short distance out of the village to her parents' home and then they got out and he handed her the keys.

'I'll walk back.'

'I don't want anything from you.'

Jack looked at her. 'Try not to hate me quite so much.'

'It isn't you I hate.'

He didn't stay to listen to any more, he couldn't bear it. He walked away and then had to persuade himself not to go into the little house which seemed like a refuge and attack the whisky bottle and then he remembered that he didn't have any whisky, he had poured the last of it down the sink, and he walked up to the Black Horse and there Bert was, propping up the bar with a dozen other men, and the relief was enormous.

'You all right?' Bert said in a quiet moment when they had played darts and talked and were walking back down the street towards home.

Jack assured him.

'It's not your bairn, eh?' Bert said and Jack realized then that he hadn't confided in anybody.

'No.'

'We thought it mustn't be. I said to Betty that you wouldn't let any lass of yours live like that.'

'What?'

Bert looked down.

'Her mam and dad, they've got nowt. I know a lot of people around here are the same but the Wests, they were important people at one time. Leonard's dad he was well respected and Leonard too and now they're trying to keep up a front and there's nowt left to keep it up with.'

'Surely Rosalind could get a job.'

'With a car that won't go?'

'Somebody round here would . . . ' His voice died away as Bert shook his head.

'Folk are funny. She walked out and left her husband and it's always been rumoured that the baby wasn't yours.'

'I have claimed it as mine.'

'Maybe that's worse to some people. A marriage is marriage, at least it should be. You are her husband and well off, everybody knows it, and there they are . . . '

Bert was right, Jack reflected, the following day when he looked at the car. It was in a bad way. She came to the garage later.

'My father isn't happy about me running around in your car,' she said. 'He says it looks bad.'

'You think we can look good?' Jack said.

'He says I shouldn't have asked you to see to the car. We can't afford it.'

'It isn't going to make any difference. It's not fit for anything but the scrapyard. Why don't you come and help in the office and I'll pay you?'

She looked startled.

'Your mam'll look after the bairn, won't she?'

'You really need the help?'

'You haven't seen, have you?' He led the way inside. 'I've been going to sort it out ever since I got here.'

Inside there were two rooms with overflowing filing cabinets and desks. Although he had tried to sort it each time he went in there he seemed to make it worse somehow.

'What a mess,' she said.

'I was never any good with paperwork.'

'Are you sure you want me here?' she said and that was laughable. 'People will talk.'

'They are already.'

'I don't think my father will like it.'

'Won't your father be obliged to like you making money?'

She agreed and she went back, in his car, to tell her parents that she was starting work straight away and the way that her eyes lightened made Jack glad he had suggested it for their sakes but when she had gone he was hard put not to do a little dance around the bus yard just because she would be there and he thought to himself, You're never going to get over this.

You're never going to get past her. When you love somebody like that the only end to it is death and even then, even then, he thought, maybe she'll go on loving Freddie in that way that she has loved nobody else, maybe there is never any end to it and maybe there never should be.

He was right. It was torture having her there. One day during the second week he stood outside the garage doors in the pouring rain for so long that she came out of the office.

'What on earth are you doing?'

'Thinking.'

'About what?'

That was part of the trouble too, he knew it. He had nothing to think about any more. Where his creative mind had been there was a kind of big grey wall and nothing was interesting. The novelty of having the garage, mending the cars, seeing to the everyday problems had worn off.

It was second-hand ideas, dealing with engines and designs that other men had built, and while that was interesting for a while it was the replacing, mending and knowing exactly what

185

had gone wrong and finding it the same over and over again that was beginning to be so boring that he could have yelled.

And she was there. The offices were starting to look so clean and orderly that it made him feel he didn't belong and should escape somewhere. He kept going off by car just to sit up on the moors and watch the spring arrive because at least it kept him out of her way.

He had never thought he would hate her being there, never thought he would not want her around, but it was awful. She worked in the office, she brought cups of tea out to him and after he had delayed her going back in as long as he could she would go in.

He didn't blame her. The spring was late in arriving as it so often was in the north and the cold was almost cruel in the garage but worse still was the way that at six o'clock she would climb into her car – he had built her a new one out of something old and it was sporty and reliable – and go back to her child and her parents and the bungalow and do what?

He didn't know because they didn't discuss it and every day the wanting and needing of her got worse and worse until Betty started asking him if he was all right and asking him around for meals to keep him from the temptation of the whisky bottle. Every night he reminded himself that he mustn't drink because Rosalind would soon know if there was something different, something the matter. Worse was to come.

As he and Bert walked up the street one May evening towards the Black Horse, Bert said abruptly, as though he had been holding back the information for fear of offence and was only now speaking because he was afraid of not saying anything, 'I hear your lass has a man friend.'

Your lass. Wasn't that nice? And how ironic, since she never had been.

'Sorry?' Jack looked at him.

'Your Rosalind. She's got a feller.'

'She's not mine. We're divorced.' It wasn't quite true. They were almost divorced and he got letters from his solicitor about stupid things from hers and he had already said that she was to have a great deal of what he owned but she wasn't having that either, too proud, both too stupid, so much owing and there was no decision, no court date.

'She's entitled, if she wants,' Jack said.

'Oh aye?' Bert looked at him.

'Course she is.'

There was a short awkward silence into which Bert eventually said, 'You always had a shine for her, didn't you?'

'Aye.'

'Even now? Even with another man's bairn and after all that's happened?'

'Can't help it,' Jack said.

'I know. I sometimes lie awake at night and think what it would be like if Betty had married Stan Green. She nearly did, you know. And sometimes I wonder what it would be like if summat happened to her.'

People were so lucky, some of them, Jack thought. That was the main thing he couldn't work out in life. Some people were so lucky.

The worst thing of all was he couldn't talk to her the next day. Even though he had reasoned with himself. It was none of his business, whatever she did, but somehow the words stuck in his throat so that in the end she came out to the garage.

'Is something the matter?'

'No.'

Jack was thankfully lying under a Ford Consul at the time. He didn't have to look at her.

'You haven't spoken all morning and you didn't drink your tea.'

'I'm just busy.'

'Come out from under there, Jack. I want to talk to you.'

'Later.'

'Now.'

When he did so she said, 'Not here. It's too cold. Can't you get any heating for in here?' and she stotted back over the wet yard, it was still bloody raining, in her neat little heels and he watched her go and he thought, I love her so much, all the neat shape of her and her stockings and the daft shoes and the way that her hair falls and the line of her shoulders.

He followed her more slowly and when he got into the office, the fire was on and she was making tea and he thought, Is this the nearest we're ever going to get to domesticity? He

187

wished he could photograph it, print it, put it on the wall and remember it.

'I got another letter from your solicitor,' she said, back turned as she poured boiling water onto the tea in the big brown pot which had been there for as long as Jack could think.

'So?'

'So.' She put the lid on the teapot and turned, trembling. 'You don't have to be so nice to me.'

'What else am I supposed to be to you?'

She hesitated, didn't meet his eyes. 'Jack, look—'

'I know,' he said. 'It doesn't make any difference.'

'You know what?' She looked clearly at him then.

'I know you've got somebody else. You'd think I'd be used to it, wouldn't you?'

'Somebody else?'

'Yes.'

She looked even harder at him. 'So that's why you're not talking to me.'

'No, it isn't.'

'Jack, you're as transparent as glass. I haven't got anybody else.'

The cloud lifted. He wanted to run round the office, screaming in delight. Stupid, stupid.

'I thought . . . '

'You think I have time for romance? I have you and your office to contend with until six and then the baby and my parents. When do I have time for another man?'

'People find time for things like that.'

'Well, I haven't. I know what people are saying.'

'So who is he?'

'Philip Wainwright. His wife just died. We went out for a drink.'

Philip Wainwright? Was a widower? They had gone to school together. He had been a bright boy, had gone to Bede College in Durham and was now a teacher, at least Jack thought he was. And he was a widower. Jack had the feeling widowers were the most dangerous men on earth. They couldn't stay on their own. They were pathetic, they needed a wife.

'You like him?'

'He's somebody to go out with.'

Somebody to go out with? Jack stared at her.'You need somebody to go out with?'

'Of course I do. I can't stay in that damned bungalow for the rest of my life. And another thing, and this is the point, you don't have to give me all that money. I don't want it. I never wanted your money. I'm not entitled to it.'

'We were married.'

'We were never married, not really.'

Oh God, there it was. The stuff you could put up in lights.

'I never really loved you,' she said.

After that it was a bit like at Freddie's funeral when they had lowered the coffin into the grave. You knew it couldn't get any further down, it was the bottom of your life. The trouble was you ended up mucking about down there because it was easier, safer. She obviously didn't think so and was ready to try again with Philip sodding Wainwright.

'I sold the house in London—'

'You didn't!' she said.

'So I can afford to pay you well.'

'You didn't have to sell it.'

'What did you think I was going to do there, remember what a wonderful time we had?'

'There's no need to be bitter,' she said and it made him laugh.

'I have to get back to the garage. Mr Turnbull's coming for his car in half an hour.'

'Is that what you've come to?' she said.

Jack looked at her.

'Aye, that's exactly what I've come to,' he said. 'I've got no marriage, I've got no family, I've got no job and I can't work any more at the only thing I love. What do you suggest I do?' and he walked out and slammed the door. It didn't do the door any good, it was too old for slamming and all he heard was a hollow sound. Nobody's heart broke. In a way everything had been broken on the day of Freddie's funeral. It was not going to mend now.

Twenty-Two

Philip Wainwright was the kind of man her parents had always wanted her to marry. Her mother had invited Philip and his parents for a meal and Rosalind was feeling so guilty about all that her parents had done for her and they were so enthusiastic about him that when he had suggested going for a drink the following weekend she hadn't liked to refuse.

He was nothing like Freddie had been, was her first thought. He was safe. He loved teaching and talked a lot about that. He also talked about his wife. They went out to dinner the following weekend and she tried to tell him what she had felt for Freddie. It was a subject she couldn't discuss with anybody else and by the anxious look on his face she wished she hadn't mentioned it. He asked about the baby and then about Jack and that was the first time she had realized that people round about thought Jack had treated her badly and that she had run away from him when she was pregnant.

'Surely everybody knows that I left him for someone else?' she said, gazing across the little table into Philip's brown eyes. He crumbled the bread bun on his side plate and she thought despairingly about the food. Here in the north and no doubt many other parts of the country a culinary delight was prawn cocktail, a mixed grill and Black Forest gateau.

The food was awful in so many places, not least this little pub a few miles out of Durham where people ate chicken or scampi with chips out of a basket for some reason. She thought with nostalgia of all the wonderful meals she and Jack had eaten in London. What did he do now, she wondered.

The only place you got good meals here was in people's houses but she had a sudden longing for the beautiful home which Jack had sold and she thought, He had loved that house. The trouble was, when people were dead, houses didn't matter. Jack had turned into a man who had no direction. Freddie had killed Jack's talent as surely as he had killed himself and she was part of the cause of it all.

Jack was thin and wary and silent and sometimes he stood outside in the pouring rain and didn't even notice. She wished so badly to be back in London when Jack had been that impossible genius of a man and Freddie had been alive. It was all so dull here.

Suddenly she couldn't bear any of it, having this dreadful meal with this very nice man who had never been outside Durham except for a holiday in Spain. He was talking to her about Jack, about how everybody knew that Jack had treated her badly and that was why she left him.

'He had a serious temper on him at school,' Philip was saying. 'He was always fighting and he always thought he was better than everybody else.'

'But he was,' she said.

Philip looked sceptically at her. 'If you like him so much and you have his kid why aren't you living with him?'

She couldn't tell him that it was from a sense of misguided loyalty. She couldn't expect Jack to care for and bring up Freddie's child when she had treated him so badly. He had already done too much to help. Working with him was bad enough. He barely spoke any more. He didn't laugh at all. She had to take his tea out of the back door and across the yard to the garage. The only conversation was when people came to deliver and pick up their cars or when the manufacturer's vans came with spare parts.

The following day somebody telephoned and she couldn't find Jack in the garage so she went to the house. It was the first time she had been there in years and, shouting his name from the back door and getting no response, she went inside.

She was astonished. It was furnished with cheap second-hand stuff, the very opposite of the way that Jack had lived in London. He came clattering down the stairs.

'I was just looking for a paper.'

'Mr Wilkinson's on the phone for you. Did you . . . ' Unable to help herself she stood there, in the hall, faltering and made her way through firstly into the sitting room where there was a very shabby brown-and-orange three-piece suite which made her stop herself from wincing. 'Did you . . . did you buy all this stuff?'

191

'Why, did you think my mother had taste this bad?' he said, with a touch of humour.

'I can't imagine you sitting in here in the evenings.' There were no books, no clue that it belonged to him.

'I don't. I go to the pub with Bert.'

'What, every night?'

'Yes.'

'What do you do there?'

'Drink beer, play darts, dominoes sometimes.'

She wandered up the hall into the dining room and there was a dining table and four chairs and they were so hideous that she came straight back out again.

'I don't know how you can bear this, considering the life you used to lead,' she said before she could stop herself.

'You'd be surprised,' he said and walked out of the house.

When she got back into the office he was talking on the telephone in the other room, which was officially his office so she couldn't tell him that she hadn't meant to be so tactless.

That night she went out with Philip Wainwright again and he took her dancing. She loved dancing. She and Freddie had spent months dancing before they slept together and if she closed her eyes she could imagine herself back with him. It was the only time she did. The music and his arms and the past was all she seemed to have left.

That night when he took her home he asked her to marry him.

'We've only just met,' she said.

'I know.' He stared at the steering wheel of his car. 'But I hate being alone. Susan has been dead for almost a year and it feels like forever. I know you don't love me but your situation is difficult and your divorce is almost through. We could start again. I have a lovely stone house. My parents bought it for us. They're quite well off, you know.' She did know. Her parents would not have known them had they not been. She thought her mother must be able to tell a man's income just by looking at him.

'Where is it?'

'Just about six miles away. Would you like to go there?'

'No, no, I mustn't. I can't leave my mother all day and all night with Ned. He screams.'

192

'I don't know much about babies. I'd be willing to take him, of course.'

'That's very kind of you,' she said and then, avoiding his mouth as he tried to kiss her so that his lips met her cheek, she got out of the car and walked slowly down the path towards the house.

Her father was standing outside, for some reason. Perhaps he liked the night. It was a sweet warm June evening. She turned and waved Philip away as he turned the car around and then she said to her father, as he threw down what was left of his cigarette and put his foot on it, 'Philip asked me to marry him.'

'Well, that's very nice. And are you going to?'

'I should, shouldn't I?'

He didn't answer for enough time for her to try to see his face in the shadows and she thought how much she loved him.

'I don't think you're finished with your first marriage yet, are you?'

'It's almost over.'

'Philip is a good man. Your mother would be pleased.'

'And you?'

'Do you know why I married your mother? It was something to do with the fact that I could put my hands around her waist and they met. Isn't that a silly reason? She was a poor girl from Billy Row and I was a pit-owner's son and her parents thought she'd done well. They weren't to know the pits were nearly worked out.'

'I don't think she's regretted it.'

'Perhaps not.'

'Have you?'

'No, I can't stop being surprised that she actually said yes, even after all these years. She never liked Jack.'

'He's chapel, at least his mother is.'

'That's right,' her father said with a smile.

'And you?'

'I don't believe in divorce,' he said and went into the house.

When she followed him she was surprised to hear the silence. Ned was not crying. Her mother came out of the sitting room, smiling.

'He went to sleep,' she said.

Twenty-Three

It was a week before Betty came into the office. Rosalind was surprised. She liked Betty but she had the feeling that Betty was in a permanent huff because she had walked out and left Jack and in Betty's eyes Jack could do no wrong and it was such a silly old-fashioned idea that it annoyed her even though she knew in this instance that Betty was more or less right, except for the bit about Jack being the soul of goodness. It made her want to laugh in derision. Jack was almost as much to blame as anybody else.

Betty never mentioned it and sometimes she would call in and leave cake. It was really for Jack but Rosalind always got the benefit and Betty made wonderful cakes, chocolate with coffee icing, coffee with chocolate icing, orange cake so light it made you think you could eat the whole lot and ginger biscuits which were crisp on the outside and sticky within so when Betty came in that morning Rosalind looked up from her work expecting to see a plate covered by a tea towel in Betty's hands.

'I wanted to say something to you, lass,' she said finally and then stopped because obviously she didn't want to say it but was making herself. 'I don't want to interfere—'

'Then don't.'

'There's no need to be like that.'

Rosalind had had a sleepless night. The baby had a snuffly cold and couldn't breathe so didn't sleep and she was not tired but irritable.

'I'm sorry, Betty. Had a bad night.'

Betty looked sympathetically at her. 'The bairn playing you up?'

'He wasn't well and it's always at three in the morning somehow.'

'A nice problem, though?' Betty said with a hint of envy

194

and it had not occurred to Rosalind before that Betty lacked children though perhaps if she had known her better it would not have come as a surprise. And then she understood. Jack was Betty's substitute for a son. Oh dear. What was it?

'I hear you're getting married,' she said.

Rosalind threw down her pen in exasperation. Did everybody in this village know everything?

'Who on earth told you that?'

'I heard it in the Store when I was buying the weekly shop. He doesn't know, though, does he?'

She meant Jack.

'Betty—'

'It's none of my business but don't you think you should tell him before somebody else does? I know you think you don't owe him anything and I'm sure you had good reason for going off and leaving him. He was never easy, even as a little lad. I don't think I know of a woman who left a man without a very good reason.'

Betty stopped there and Rosalind wished she hadn't felt that she had to explain but she did because she couldn't have Betty thinking the worse of him, even now.

'You're right,' she said, 'he's impossible to live with. He lives in another world most of the time, inside his head, and there's no room for anybody there—'

'I don't think he's there any more,' Betty said.

'But it wasn't that.'

'It was the other lad, the one who used to come and stay? Aye, he was bonny, bonny and clever and funny and posh. Every woman wants a man like that. Jack's mother was taken with him and she was never taken with anybody. He lit the place when he stayed.'

She was right. Freddie had lit the room he was in, made people laugh, made people glad to be there, made them excited about things, gave them the impression something good was always just about to happen.

'He wouldn't marry me. I wasn't good enough for him,' she said. 'And I married Jack . . . and then I betrayed him.'

'Everybody makes mistakes.'

'It wasn't a mistake, Betty,' Rosalind said. 'It was like magic being with Freddie. I would have given up anything in the world for him.'

195

'And you have his little lad?'

Rosalind looked at her.

'It was just a guess,' Betty said. 'I wouldn't ever tell anybody. I know everybody thinks it's Jack's bairn but it occurred to me that if it was you would be living under the same roof.'

'Why should he bring up another man's child?'

'But Philip Wainwright would?'

'I haven't said I'll marry him. I've only just met him. It's him, he misses his wife. He . . . '

'You're so bonny you could have anybody,' Betty said. 'Even my Bert blushes when he talks about you. Every man in the village fancies you. You don't have to wed the first man that asks you.'

'You don't think I was lucky, then, considering all the things I've done?'

'Lucky?' Betty raised her eyes in derision. 'There's no reason why you should marry anybody, put up with any man. You're perfectly capable of making your own way in this world.'

Betty, Rosalind could not help thinking with an inward touch of humour, had a lot in common with another Betty who was urging women's rights in the States, ideas which were filtering through, many of which had been held in high regard by some women all along.

Rosalind was suddenly aware of Jack in the doorway. He stood for just a few seconds but she did not delude herself that he had not heard what Betty had said. Betty saw him too and left hastily, saying that she had something on the stove. Jack didn't linger. He went into his office and closed the door, something he never did.

Rosalind tried to work and failed and he did not come out of the office for a long time and when he did he didn't speak. She couldn't work. Long before she should have been going home she went out to the garage and said, 'I think I might go home if that's all right with you.'

'That's fine. See you tomorrow.'

When she had gone Jack worked. Bert came at eight but Jack said he was too busy to go to the pub and though Bert tried to persuade him he said he had to get on. Shortly afterwards Betty came in.

'You haven't had anything to eat.'

'I'll have something later.'

'It is later. Come away in.'

'I will in a minute.'

He said nothing more. Betty left. He worked until midnight and then he switched off the lights and locked the garage and the office and went into the house and there he searched the cupboards for a bottle of whisky but he had been too clever for himself. There was nothing and everywhere was closed because he had deliberately made himself stay in the garage until it was too late. It had taken all his energy. All he wanted to do now was sleep.

He went to bed and lay there, looking up at the ceiling, and then for no reason he got out of bed and switched on the lights and went downstairs searching for a pen and a piece of paper and he sat down at the dining-room table and began to sketch. He didn't notice how the time passed until the light had begun to open out in the sky and then he stretched and got up and went through into the kitchen and boiled the kettle.

He went out into the back garden and saw the dawn in and it was so beautiful, he couldn't understand how he hadn't seen it before now. He made some tea and then he went upstairs and drank his tea in bed and then he went to sleep and he slept more soundly than he had done in years.

When he awoke again it was mid-afternoon and somebody was hammering on the door. He pulled on the nearest clothes and went downstairs, opened the door to reveal Rosalind on the doorstep.

'Whatever have you been doing?' she said. 'Are you all right?'

'Fine.' Jack pushed the hair out of his eyes and blinked at the light. 'I was asleep.'

'I've had Bert and Betty round here, wondering what on earth you were doing.'

Jack laughed. 'They do fuss,' he said. 'Come in, I'll make you some tea.'

As they went past the dining-room door Rosalind paused and he went back slightly and then he followed her into the room. She stood gazing at the sea of paper which he had produced overnight.

'You're working again,' she said.

'Looks like it.'

'Oh, Jack, I'm so glad.'

'It might not be anything. It must just be a one-off. I worked all night.'

'May I see?'

'I don't think any of it's decipherable,' he said, picking up the various papers and staring at them and then handing them to her.

'But it is,' she said. 'It's perfectly understandable. Look at it.'

'It doesn't look like much.'

'Yes, it does. Look here,' and she pointed and then she smiled. 'No wonder you were tired. Are you feeling all right?'

'Grand. Come into the kitchen.'

They went through and he made some tea and they sat down at the kitchen table.

'We should get somebody in to help in the garage and then you could—' she said but he interrupted.

'No,' he said, 'it isn't going to be like that. It might just be a flash in the pan and I'm not going that road, even if it isn't. I don't want the pressure of that anymore, I'm not doing it again. I'm done with London and all that stuff. They threw me out. I know I deserved it but I'm not going through it again, it isn't worth it.'

'You can't help who you are.'

'I can help what I do with it and I'm not doing it again like that. This time, if it works out it'll be different and under my terms and if it doesn't I'll just go on with the garage. I was thinking actually that I might get some petrol pumps and that I might even start up a bus company.'

'I think you should do all those things,' she said.

'Would you come and look at buses with me?'

'I don't know anything about buses.'

'Neither do I. I need the moral support. I could ring the coachworks and see if we could go over and talk about what we might need and you could get adverts into the newspapers for me to find drivers.'

'Your mother would be pleased.'

'She might even come home,' Jack said and pulled a face and Rosalind laughed.

* * *

They spent several days talking and making plans and Jack was almost happy. He told himself that he didn't care if she married Philip Wainwright, he would have his work, he would be able to go on by himself. He might even be glad in time that she would have a successful relationship. It would be a very long time, though.

On the Friday of that week he had a letter from his solicitor saying that the papers had not been signed for the divorce and he did not seem able to get any sense from Rosalind's solicitor. Jack took the letter into the office just after it came mid-morning and flourished it in front of her.

'Is there a problem?'

She stared at the paper and her face went almost as white. She didn't say anything.

'I thought you wanted to marry whatshisname.'

'Philip. I don't remember saying so. I hardly know the man.'

'I've split everything in half. You seemed to think it was fair—'

'It was never fair,' she said, getting up.

Jack sighed. 'I wish you would tell me these things.'

'I did. I kept on telling you. Your money was never the issue.'

'Oh, come on, it always was.'

She stared at him.

'You liked the money,' Jack said. 'You liked the lifestyle it brought.'

'That was before . . . I couldn't live with myself now taking your money, having betrayed you in the most basic way possible.'

'It wasn't anything like that,' Jack said, 'I knew how things were, I always knew and I never thought it would last.'

'Didn't you?'

'No. I try to live in the present with one eye on the way things were and we had a lot of good times and I'm grateful and we did things with our lives that we wanted to do. It's as much as you can ask, don't you think?'

She didn't answer.

'So, are you going to let this divorce go through?'

'No. Yes. I don't know.'

'What about Philip Wainwright?'

'I don't care about him.' She was shouting. 'I never did. It was everybody else. My mother . . . '

199

'Wants you to marry somebody respectable?' he said, biting his lower lip so that he wouldn't laugh.

'I would like to please her just once.'

'I think it might be asking too much.'

'He's boring,' Rosalind said, not looking at Jack. 'He bores on about teaching and . . . and he eats Black Forest gateau.'

'He doesn't really, does he?'

'It is not funny.'

'You don't have to stay married to me just because you can't find anybody else—'

'I can find lots of people,' she declared, glaring at him.

'I'm sure you can but you may not want to, at least not at present, and the money will make you independent so that you can spend as much time as you like deciding what you want to do. You may never want to marry again.

'You might like a house for you and Ned and not have to live with your parents and you might want to help them out. After all, they looked after you for the first twenty years of your life and they have been pretty good about all this. Take the money and let the process go through. There's no point in hanging on, is there?'

'Isn't there?' Jack looked away then and was glad he had when she added, 'Are you wanting to get married again?'

'No.'

'Once was enough?'

'I can't do that again. I can't – I can't work through it.'

'That's very selfish.'

'I know but it's how I feel. I need some peace of mind to work. I know I do and if I have it in time I might turn out something good again.'

'So you want me to go away and leave you alone?'

'Of course I don't. I can't run the place without you and besides, we've got drivers to interview and – and lots of other things.'

'Do you know what I think will happen, Jack? I think you'll do just what you did last time and invent something very special and it will all happen over again and you will leave and this won't matter any more.'

'Maybe. But I need it now. You have your child.'

* * *

That sentence went over and over in Rosalind's head when she got back to the bungalow that night and she thought, He's right, I do need to help my parents and I do need a place of my own. I don't want to go on living with them, they're getting old, they have different ideas and I think my mother is very tired of looking after Ned and why shouldn't she be, she's already done this once.

When she went to work the following morning Jack was in the garage and she said to him, 'I'll take the money.'

'All right. I'll tell the solicitor that you'll sign the papers and then it shouldn't take long.'

'It always takes a long time,' Rosalind said and she went back to the office.

She looked around. It was so orderly, she had made it so. Every time Jack came in he made a mess and he did the same in the office next door. It drove her mad.

She had just begun work when her father's car stopped outside the window and she hurried to him as he got out of the driver's side door. He was pale.

'It's Ned, he's fallen and hurt himself. I took him straight to the hospital. Your mother's there with him.'

She ran into the garage and told Jack.

'I'll come with you.'

'No, there's no need. My mother is there and my father will drive me.'

'I'd like to be there.'

'All right.' She let go of her breath. Jack peeled off his overalls and within moments they were running back down the yard.

Twenty-Four

Hospital corridors had to rate as some of the worst places you could ever be. Time was different there, fear absorbed the hours. Mrs West cried. She had fallen with the baby, it was all her fault, she had tripped and he had banged his head and she would never forgive herself. Everybody made comforting noises.

Jack and Leonard, feeling at one possibly for the first time ever, Jack thought, went outside, glad of the excuse to breathe fresh air and smoke and stand there together. Jack thought he couldn't have stood it if the older man hadn't been there somehow. He had not been glad before that Leonard was so big but now he was, a giant of a man, six foot four, and his bulk was oddly reassuring.

'It will be all right,' he told Jack and that was the first time that Jack thought, given a few decent days or an evening or two at the pub with him and he could really like him. 'This sort of thing happens to babies. They look so badly when really they aren't.'

'You think so?' Jack said gratefully. 'Then why doesn't he wake up?'

'He will.'

Jack threw his cigarette on the cold wet ground and put his foot on it.

'I suppose you think I'm overreacting and he's not even mine.'

'Parents always overreact,' Leonard said, 'it's part of it.'

'I'm not his parent, though.'

'You could be.'

'Philip Wainwright's nearer to that than I am.'

'God, he's boring,' Leonard said and Jack felt quite warm towards him and grinned.

They went back inside and strangely, miraculously somehow, Leonard was right. The baby had woken up and was apparently fine. Mrs West cried and in an act of what Jack thought was sensitivity, Rosalind let her mother carry the baby out of the hospital towards the car. She stood there, watching as her parents left, the child cradled in her mother's arms. Then she turned to him and smiled.

'Thank you.'

'I didn't do anything. I just stood outside and your father told me it would be all right and I believed him.'

'He's good at things like that. We should go. I just wanted to give them the chance to . . . '

'I know.'

He drove her back to her parents' house.

'Give yourself a day or two,' he told her. 'You needn't come to work. I'm . . . I'm thinking of going to London.'

She looked at him. 'Taking your ideas to Sir Trevor?'

'Something like that.'

'You said you weren't going to do that again.'

'I've changed my mind.'

She looked clearly at him. 'I'm going to marry Philip Wainwright.'

'Something told me you were,' Jack said.

London was just the same, that was the shock, and Sir Trevor, rather than keep him waiting or refuse to see him, came out of his office and shook him by the hand and insisted on taking him out for lunch.

'So glad to see you again,' he said, 'I knew it was only a matter of time before you came up with something else.'

'I'm not sure what you'll think of it,' Jack said, trying to eat what looked like a huge amount of food on his plate. He had refused wine. He felt as though Trevor needed reassuring about that. They drank water.

Later they went back to the office and Trevor studied the designs and they spent all afternoon talking about them and what they would do next and Trevor said he would have to consult his fellow directors but he was glad Jack had come to him and if Jack would stay in London for a day or two he would have a decision for him by Wednesday.

Jack stayed. He went to see Nigel and Anna, who had moved into central London and now had two children. He had dinner with them and was glad to be there and they invited other people who had known him and he felt at home once more and glad to be away from the north, from the garage, from all the problems which were being solved in his absence.

He tried not to think about Rosalind or the baby which was not his or Philip Wainwright who would get to bring up Freddie's child but it was difficult because all the people he had known when he was young were married and most of them had children and it was as though everybody had gone on without him. He felt so left out, so short-changed, like an alien being, like the unluckiest man on earth, out of time.

London was vibrant, exciting. The shops were full of boutiques, the girls were wearing the shortest skirts ever, Carnaby Street was full of tourists. It all changed so fast, he thought, that maybe you needed to be here in order to go forward with your ideas.

After two days Sir Trevor called him back into the office. He got up as Jack was ushered in and Jack could tell by his face, open and pleased, that he had good news.

'The genius is back,' Trevor said, taking Jack's hand and pressing his shoulder. 'I knew you could do it. Your ideas are splendid, Jack, just as good as they ever were. Welcome home. We're all very happy to have you here. I'm going to give you a better office than you had last time, everything is going to be wonderful.'

She missed him. It was all right for the first two days while she was still angry with him for having gone to London like that and leaving her and during those few days she wanted to telephone Philip Wainwright and tell him she would marry him straight away because Jack had gone off to London and anyhow he was a bastard and he wouldn't come back and during those two days she signed the papers for her divorce which she had put off doing for so long.

She hadn't wanted to be divorced, felt as though she would lose Jack for good and then it didn't seem so important. All that mattered to him was his work. It was all that had ever mattered to him for any length of time. Why should anything change now?

After two days it was obvious that Ned was well again and because she did not want her mother to think that she did not trust her she left the house and went to the office, just for something to do. She opened the post and filed everything and tidied up and then she pushed open the huge garage doors.

There was nothing inside. It was typical of Jack. He never left anything unfinished. Except his relationships, she thought. Her footsteps echoed and that was when she missed him.

She walked slowly back across the yard in the rain and went back inside and into Jack's office and there on the desk was one sketch he had forgotten, something presumably he should have taken with him. It was detailed, unlike anything she had seen before, and so typical of him, exciting with flourishes. It was obvious that he cared very much for what he was doing.

She could not go back. She didn't want to go and live in London, it reminded her too much of the best days of her life when she had first met Freddie and by all accounts London was a different place now, things had moved on. Either you moved with them or . . . or what? She wasn't sure, but neither, she decided, could she stay here like this. Her parents had been good to her but—

The door opened and Philip Wainwright looked apologetically at her.

'Your mother said you were here. Sorry to hear about the baby. Is he all right?'

'The doctor says he'll be fine. We got a bit of a fright.'

'You would.' Philip looked around him. 'A comedown for Jack Neville, this, eh?'

'What do you mean?'

'Well, playing the big man, people thinking how clever he was and now he's back here.'

'As a matter of fact Jack's gone to London.'

'Really? Why?'

'He had an idea.'

'Above his station?' Philip smiled.

'You don't like him, do you?'

'I don't like what he did to you.'

'He didn't do anything to me. I wish he would come back.'

'He probably will, any minute. Is that what you want, somebody who failed?'

She stared at Philip. He was jealous of Jack. How strange.

'Jack didn't fail. He invented and built the most important motor car of the age.'

Philip laughed. 'A slight exaggeration, surely. Teams of people do such things.'

'I'm sure he would say so too but he did.'

Philip looked down at the almost cleared desk and then he said, 'You're not going to divorce him, are you?'

'Of course I am.'

'You love him.'

'No, I don't.'

Philip looked scornfully at her. 'Then why do you defend him so readily?'

'I don't.'

'Yes, you do. Every time I mention his name disparagingly you leap up.'

'We were married.'

'Yes, "were". Or is it?'

'I've just signed the divorce papers. I doubt Jack will be coming back. He doesn't belong here. He belongs in London and he will know it by now.'

'I'm glad to hear it. So. Will you marry me?'

Jack was overjoyed at Sir Trevor's decision. He would have his old job back, no, better than that, they were going to pay him more and he could have a bigger office and he would have a new design team. They looked so much younger than the team he had had before. London could be his and he could continue the love affair which he had had with it. It held the same promises that it always had. And he was back.

He rejoiced. He and Nigel went drinking. Nigel introduced him to a lot of new people, fashionable and intelligent and interesting, and Jack began to think that everything would be all right. He even went and looked at houses. He could afford something big and in the best area and people were so respectful and eager to please him. He looked out of his new office with the huge window and he saw the London rain and the possibilities and he was eager to get started.

And then all of a sudden, in that stupid time of the morning when everything was hideous, when his dreams had been running-away dreams and not catching-up dreams and lost dreams, he came to in bed at Nigel's house and didn't want any of it. He told himself that he was too excited, that things had happened too fast that week but it was not true, he had to acknowledge, when he went downstairs because he couldn't bear to be upstairs.

He was there only a few minutes before Nigel followed him into the sitting room.

'Sorry,' Jack said, 'I didn't mean to disturb you.'

'I wasn't asleep.'

'Were you worrying about the new designs?'

'Hell, no, I don't worry about things you do,' Nigel said, smiling. 'I'm going to miss you, Jack.'

'What do you mean?'

Nigel looked at him.

'You're not staying,' he said.

Jack hadn't realized it until then. Nigel was right. He didn't want to be here any more. London was fine when you were twenty but unless you had a very good reason to be there you wouldn't want to be. You needed family there or a job you couldn't move from and in his case neither of these things was true. Sir Trevor wouldn't want him to go but you could design a car in Durham just as well as you could design one in London. And he had.

'You thought up those new ideas when you were in the north. You don't need to be here. And you have reasons to be there, don't you?'

'No,' Jack said at first and then he knew that that was not so, he did have reasons to be there. He was happy there. How stupid, he hadn't realized that he liked the house and the garage and having Bert and Betty next door. He liked the view of the fell from his bedroom window and in a way he liked the awful furniture. He liked the way that everybody knew you and their beautiful accents and how they were unimpressed with him because they knew him no matter what he achieved, no matter what he did. It was finally home, the Durham fells, and he had a longing to go back such as he had never felt before.

That night, for some reason, he telephoned his mother in Whitley Bay and he said, 'I'm coming back and I'm going to start up the buses and we're going to have petrol pumps and . . . and I've designed a new car which Sir Trevor likes and he's going to put it into production.'

There was a little pause and then she said, 'Your dad was so proud of you, Jack, and so am I. When you reach home give me a ring and I'll maybe come and visit. I'm not stopping, mind. I like it by the sea too much.' Before she rang off she said, 'How's Rosalind . . . and the bairn?'

'They're fine.'

'Give her my best,' his mother said. 'You will be seeing her?'

'Aye, I'll be seeing her,' Jack said.

Sir Trevor wasn't happy about him leaving. 'What would anybody want, living almost in Scotland?' he said, which made Jack smile.

Having made the decision to go he then hesitated and couldn't somehow. He lingered there in the office which could have been his, and wondered how he would manage when he got to the stage that he wanted help from other people – when he needed drivers, he admitted to himself. How would he do the testing in Durham?

It's two and a half hours, he told himself, that's all. I can be in either place as I choose. I don't have to buy a house in London but I might.

He didn't buy a house but he did rent a flat, a big place with plenty of light for those times when he had to be there.

Sir Trevor seemed pleased with that and said he would keep the office for him anyhow and put his name on the door in big letters but Jack was happier when he was on the way back home. He was determined to have this the way that he wanted.

It was almost midnight when he reached the door of his house and he was exhausted but pleased. He only wished it hadn't been too late for him to go over and see Rosalind and the baby.

Betty had been picking up the post but had not been in that day because a huge cream envelope lay on the floor and when he opened it it was the divorce papers from Rosalind. She had signed them. Jack went straight to bed. He didn't sleep but at least he was in bed. He couldn't drink. He couldn't drive over and demand to see her. He couldn't bang on the back door of Betty and Bert's house and spill all his troubles on to them. They must be so sick of him, he thought. He wished then that he had stayed in London. He resolved to go back the very next day.

The following morning was Sunday and he had fallen into a deep sleep by then and was only vaguely aware of where he was when he awoke. He had slept with the window shut, the room was stifling. He got up and threw back the curtains and sunshine spilled into the room. He pushed open the sash window and gazed at the view. The bell heather was purple across the moor. He could see the haze of it in the distance beyond the fields up on the tops. He stood there for some time and then he bathed and dressed and then he went down-stairs. Somebody was banging on the back door.

It was Betty.

'When did you get back?'

'Late last night.'

The scent of roses was heady out there.

'I'm not staying,' Jack said.

'No, I didn't think you would be.'

She followed him inside.

'It went well, then?'

'Yes.' Jack didn't look at her. 'I'm just . . . going to put a few things together and then . . . '

'You will come round for your dinner.'

'Thanks.'

Betty got to the door and then as if she had changed her mind she stopped and she stood there with her back turned for what felt like a considerable time and then she turned and looked at him.

'I hear your Rosalind's getting wed,' she said.

'Yes. She told me.'

'That was why you went.'

'No. I was going to go anyway.'

'It's a sad thing, is a divorce. I'm not saying I'm not in favour of it. I've seen too many marriages where people stopped together for years on end being miserable but when there are bairns—'

'He's not mine,' Jack said before he could stop himself.

'Is that right?' She gazed at him for a long time before she said, 'What do you think is more important to a kid, a man who died before he was born or a man who brought him up? And you could have other bairns, did you think of that?'

'Of course I thought of it.'

'Well?'

'Freddie will always be there. She'll always love him best.'

'Philip Wainwright's prepared to take second place.'

Jack didn't answer that.

'You know what your trouble is, my lad? You were an only child. You always have to be the only one. You have to be first. It must be a very uncomfortable way to live. He's dead, the poor lad, and do you think he wants his bairn brought up by Philip Wainwright?'

'Maybe.'

'Rubbish,' Betty said. 'You were his friend. You were good to him—'

'I wasn't.'

'You let him have the lass you wanted—'

'I didn't let him. He took her and she always preferred him.'

'Well, she's in no position to prefer him now. I'm not saying Philip Wainwright isn't a nice lad, he's probably a lot nicer than you, but she'll be fed up with him in six months and then where will she be and where will you be? She'll be stuck here and you'll be in bloody London, that's where,' Betty said and she walked out.

Twenty-Five

Rosalind had finally managed to please her mother. She got a great deal of satisfaction from telling her that she had agreed to marry Philip.

'I only wished you'd had more sense than to marry that Jack Neville in the first place,' her mother said, shifting the baby from one arm to the other as though he was heavy.

'Shall I take him?'

'No, I'm fine. He's got stability has Philip and he has that gorgeous house his parents left him and I hear it's full of his dead wife's china.'

Her father, to give him credit, didn't laugh even when her mother had gone into the kitchen, Ned tucked in against her. Rosalind was not deceived.

'You don't want me to marry Philip, do you?'

'I think he's a fine man,' Leonard said.

'Better than Jack?'

'Much better than Jack.'

'But you like Jack?'

'I do, as a matter of fact. You can't help who you like. I'm sure you'll be very happy with Philip and your mother will be ecstatic, to say nothing of the china, which I'm told is Wedgwood. What more could a woman ask?'

Rosalind went over and kissed him. The truth was, she thought, that her father didn't mind who she married, as long as somebody could afford to keep her and Ned which he was increasingly unable to do. She hadn't told him yet that when the divorce went through she would be a comparatively rich woman and able to keep them all, she didn't have to marry anybody, the words echoed. There was a rumour going around that her father was about to lose his house, he was so much in debt. He needed rid of her. The other thing was that Philip Wainwright had a big enough house for all of them. And it was not all about money, she knew that her father was a proud man, whether he would accept anything from her she didn't know. She had a feeling he would see it as failure on his part. But if she could persuade them to live with Philip – would Philip want that?

He took her out to eat the following evening but when she suggested that her parents might live with them he frowned. She didn't blame him. There couldn't be many men about who would want to take on his parents-in-law and another man's child. It was a great deal to ask.

'Why would we want to have them to live with us?' he asked, tucking into a mixed grill.

'They have no money.'

He stopped eating, put down his knife and fork. 'Correct me if I'm wrong, Rosalind, but your about to be ex-husband is a millionaire, is he not?'

'He's nothing of the kind.'

Philip looked disbelievingly at her. 'Has he deceived you?'

'I refused his money.'

'I don't believe I'm hearing this. You refused to take a share of Jack Neville's money? He's rolling in it.'

'I know he is. That's not the point.'

'Money is always the point,' Philip said. 'You're divorcing him—'

'It was my fault.'

'You were his wife. You – you gave yourself to him—'

'I never did. That was the trouble.'

'You never slept with him?' Philip's eyes widened.

'Of course I slept with him,' she said. 'It was one of the few areas of our marriage that was all right.'

Philip winced.

'He was always accusing me of thinking he was Freddie . . . and in some ways I did and in some ways he always is because of all the memories, all the good times when they were both around. He misses Freddie almost as much as I do. I know he does.'

'I'll bet he doesn't miss the way you walked out and left him and got yourself pregnant to a man you weren't married to.'

'That's why I couldn't take his money.'

'I would have thought, if your parents are as badly in debt as people say, you would have taken his hand off.'

'You do know, then?'

'Everybody knows.'

'But you wouldn't help?'

'I can't afford to help. I'm not Jack Neville.'

'I can go out and work. My mother will look after Ned and my father is very good with him.'

'I want to have you to myself. Is that so much to ask?' He smiled across the table at her and finished eating his meal.

She didn't understand why she had not told him how much money was involved and that Jack had given her half and that she would be free but she was beginning to have the awful feeling that the money was more important to Philip than anything else.

He drove her back and when they came down the main street she saw that the lights were on in Jack's house. She hadn't realized he was back. After Philip dropped her off she debated whether to go over but it was late and Jack was probably at the pub with Bert by now. Maybe he was back if the lights were on.

She didn't go into the house. She waved goodbye to Philip and then she got the car out and drove to Jack's house, sitting outside for a few moments, not sure whether to go home. It was almost midnight. Most people, having to get up for work, had gone to bed, their windows were black.

In the end she got out and knocked on the door and moments later a surprised-looking Jack answered the door.

'Ros.' He looked weary, she thought.

'When did you get back?'

'A couple of days ago. Come in.'

'It's late.'

'It's all right.'

She went inside, into the hideous sitting room.

'What did Sir Trevor think of your ideas?'

'He liked them.'

'I knew he would. I'm so glad. When are you moving to London?'

Jack hesitated. 'Soon. My mother will be disappointed. I think she thought I was here for good. I had ideas—'

'She wouldn't want you held back.'

'No, she wouldn't want that,' he said.

'So you'll be closing down the garage. You won't be . . . buying the buses and petrol pumps and setting things up and . . . you won't need me.'

'That's right,' Jack said. 'You won't need a job after you marry Philip.'

'Because of your money.'

'It's not my money. Your mother must be really pleased you're marrying somebody respectable at last.'

Ros laughed. 'She is. I had better go. Thanks for sorting everything out. I still feel guilty about it all, I mean I feel guilty financially.' It was not what she meant at all, she thought and they both knew it. She moved towards the door, very embarrassed and not knowing what to say, just wanting to get out.

Jack saw her to the front door.

'Goodnight, then,' she said, 'I don't suppose I'll see you if you're going straight back to London.'

'I suppose not,' Jack said.

She leaned over and kissed him on the cheek. From there it was no distance at all to his mouth and once she had acknowledged this truth there was no way she could not have kissed him on the lips and when she did she couldn't stop. Philip had been so respectful, so careful. He had barely touched her. Jack hardly touched her now. He returned the sweet kiss and she could feel his fingertips at her waist and that was all.

She drew back. She didn't want him to be able to accuse her of being nothing but hungry as he had once before. She even said goodbye. She had a hand on the door. And then he got hold of her and as she turned in protest he pulled her into his arms. There was nothing respectful or careful about what happened after that and she could not believe that she had not walked out, that she had not gone home.

They didn't even get as far as the sitting room before he pulled her clothes off her. Rosalind did wonder slightly whether anybody had ever used the hall for such a purpose before but she had forgotten how good he felt that close. She couldn't leave him. This time Jack did not lose his temper and shout at her and she did not walk out on him.

They made love in the sitting room too, Rosalind was rather pleased that the dreadful sofa and rug in front of the fire had such treatment, and then they went upstairs to bed and she

213

was happy there in his arms for the first time since Freddie had died, no long before that. She had not been happy with Freddie. She had the courage to admit it to herself now. She had not been happy since she had left Jack.

The summer night was short and hot and all the windows were open and they lay in bed with a white sheet on them and she kissed him.

'We should have done this before,' she said.

'That's what divorce does for you,' Jack said.

'I should go. My parents will wonder. They think I'm with Philip.'

'Will they think you're coming back, then?'

'Of course they will. I can't stay out all night.'

'You don't – you don't go to bed with him, then?'

'Not that it's any of your business,' she said, 'but no, I haven't. I was trying to do the right thing.' She smiled. 'I don't seem to be able to, do I? But I want to live here, Jack. I think it was where I was meant to be all along. London just reminds me of how awful everything was and you and Freddie fighting and me behaving so appallingly to you.'

'You didn't.'

'Oh yes, I did.'

'You weren't the only one who behaved appallingly,' he said, looking down.

'That's just who you are, you can't help it. You belong there, you and your . . . your genius.'

Jack laughed. 'You make it sound like a nasty disease.'

'I sometimes wonder,' she said, 'what it would have been like if you had been like your dad and we had got married and never gone to London at all.'

'You would never have lowered yourself. Your mother wouldn't have allowed it. You would never settle for second best.'

'It wasn't like that,' she said.

'It was exactly like that,' Jack said. 'You're doing it again, settling for a man you don't really care about. If Freddie was still alive you'd be with him.'

'No, I wouldn't. He would have gone back to his wife. I've thought about it more and more.'

Jack looked at her in surprise. 'You believe that?'

'Oh yes. He needed an heir, you see, a legitimate one. He

would have bred from his wife like his father bred from his mother, like she was of no more significance than a farm animal. Disgusting. And look what it did to him. It destroys people. No old age, no contentment, no watching the child grow you had from the woman you really loved.'

Into the silence that followed Jack said, 'Would you have come back to me?'

'I hope not. It would have been so very unfair to you, just like this has been. I always run to you. I didn't mean to sleep with you. I'm sorry.'

'Oh, don't be,' Jack said.

She kissed him and smiled.

'I ought to go.'

'It's almost morning.' He indicated the light which was just beginning to break beyond the window.

She got out of bed and then she knew that she had something to say to him, something she had never said before and barely acknowledged to herself. She looked at him lying there, watching her with affection, and she looked straight at him and she said, 'The affair with him was over before I left you. It took me time to realize it but it was and it was never more than that, it was never going to be something that lasted a lifetime. It was never the same. I want you to know that. Now, I have to go.'

She dressed and left. She drove back to her parents' house. Her father was sitting in the kitchen. It always smelled faintly of bread and warmth even though the Aga was not on because of the weather. He didn't look concerned. He smiled at her.

And suddenly she did hope very much that he wouldn't have to give up this house because he had worked so hard to keep it all those years and to keep herself and her mother and now he was older and he had lines around his eyes and she remembered him from when she was a little girl and he would throw her up to the ceiling and catch her when she came down and how much he had loved her and how much she had and always would love him. There would be a way to convince him to take the money which she had.

'Your mother thinks you're asleep in bed,' he said, 'and for once so is Ned. Did you have a good time?'

'Oh yes,' she said and she leaned over and kissed him.

*   *   *

215

When Jack awoke it was the middle of the day and he was alone. At first he told himself that everything was going to be fine and then he remembered he was too old to believe that. He got up and pulled on the clothes he had taken off the night before – they were all over the place downstairs and reminded him of the sweet madness of having her there and then he stumbled outside.

It was summer. When had that happened? It was warm. The bees were buzzing in Betty and Bert's garden and all the flowers were in bloom and they were so pretty, pink and red and purple and lilac and Bert was out there, digging away in the vegetable patch and Jack could smell the midday meal coming from where Betty had the windows open in the kitchen and oh joy, it was the tiny little beef pies that she made, with carrots and new potatoes with beef tea poured over them.

As he stood there she came outside like a miracle and said, 'Are you coming in for your dinner, then?' just as though he always did.

Jack tried to protest but the truth was that he wanted more than anything in the world at that moment to sit at Bert and Betty's table and partake of their food and their geniality.

'Is it right, then,' she said, after they had eaten, 'you're going back to London?'

'No,' Jack said, 'I'm not going anywhere.'

'But I thought . . . ' Betty said and stopped herself. And then she went off to get the summer pudding and a big jug of thick cream from the pantry shelf.

Rosalind put Jack from her mind. She told herself it had been nothing important, just an impulse, and she must move on. She had determined to do some shopping for her wedding the following day and got up and briskly told her mother as they ate tea and toast at eight o'clock.

'How was your evening with Philip?' her mother said.

'Oh, fine.'

Her mother looked at her. 'It must have been better than that, Rosalind. It was very late indeed when you got home.'

'Yes. We talked. It was . . . '

Her mother looked more severely at her and sighed. 'I suppose it's the way nowadays. You are getting married. I want to say to you that . . . if you wish to stay over at Philip's house your father and I . . . it's your life.'

Rosalind attempted to lie but was suddenly desperate to confide in her mother. 'It wasn't Philip,' she said.

Her mother sighed again and with more foresight than Rosalind would ever have thought she had she said, 'Well, I did think that perhaps he wasn't right for you.'

'Did you?'

Her mother looked levelly at her. 'I remember when you were fourteen, coming into the house, full of indignation, telling me that Jack Neville had kissed you. You looked so pleased with yourself somehow. Why don't you try to put this right, just for once?'

'I can't,' Rosalind said, starting to cry. 'He's going back to London.'

After he left Betty and Bert's house that afternoon Jack wandered into the office and called Doxbridge Motors. Sir Trevor was genial. He was everything he should have been, Jack thought, smiling to himself and listening and then he said, 'It's very good of you, Trevor, to go to all this trouble but I don't think I want to sign a contract with you. I've decided to start up my own business.'

Sir Trevor spluttered and protested and even threatened but Jack wasn't about to change his mind.

'You can't build a business that big in the wilderness,' Trevor said.

'Oh yes, I can,' Jack said and it made him want to laugh. When the newspapers did travel articles they called this area 'the last wilderness in England'. He was rather proud of it – no, he decided, he was very proud of it.

'You've lost your mind,' Trevor said. 'You lost it when Freddie Harlington died. I'm glad you've decided not to come back here. I can find other young men to do your job.'

'You do that, Trevor,' Jack said, 'and thanks for believing in me in the first place. I would never have got anywhere without your inspiration and backing.'

'Oh, go and bugger yourself, Jack,' Trevor said and it made Jack laugh even as Trevor put the phone down.

Jack hung up and was about to get into the car and go to see Rosalind when the little car he had made for her came over the hill, down past the council houses on one side and the bank on the other, down past Dick's shop where they had bought their sweets on the way back from school when they were little, past the Cattle Mart Inn and the pub on the other side and the entrance to the steel foundry and the Salvation Army and over the railway crossings and then she stopped.

She got out of the car, not looking at him as Jack stood there on the forecourt of the garage.

'I'm not going,' he said.

Then she looked at him through her fringe. 'Why not?' she said. 'I thought you were set on it.'

'Because I want to stay here with you. Can I?'

Her mouth trembled. He could see it.

'How did you know I had decided not to marry Philip Wainwright?'

'What, after you'd slept with me?' he said and she came over and thumped him and said it had nothing whatsoever to do with that and he said, well, what had it to do with then and she said, 'It was just about time somehow.'

Jack buried his face in her hair and in her neck and she held him close and he thought maybe she was right, everything had a time, like it said in the Bible, a time for every purpose under heaven, so maybe they would have their time now, somewhere among all this space and mess and all the glory of these beautiful fells they would have a life together, if it wasn't too much to ask.

It was summer in Durham. The pheasants were plodding up the edges of the fields. The lambs were skipping about the grass. The old farmers stood in the lanes, gossiping. The stone houses baked in the sunshine and up on the tops the sky went on for ever beyond the fells. If there was any chance at all it was now and Jack put an arm around her and he said, 'Do you know we could have petrol pumps right here?'

She laughed. She said, 'That is the most romantic thing anybody has ever said to me.'

'Will you come and choose the buses with me?' he said.

She said, 'Jack, I would love to,' and they walked back into the garage together, into the office. She got down to pick up the post and the summer sunlight flooded in amongst the old filing cabinets and the scarred desks. It was a beautiful summer's afternoon in Durham and you don't get too many of those.